Praise for *FreeK Camp*

Thanks to my years writing at Hanna-Barbera and Warner Bros. Animation, I find it hard to avoid seeing story flaws or author "cheats" when I read, even for pleasure. Steve Burt is the real deal—his stories are clean, his imagination is awesome, his writing is flawless, and I sail through his stuff turning pages as fast as I can to see what's coming next. My biggest problem with Steve's writing is that there's not enough of it—and even a book like this one for teens kept me interested and engaged. Thank goodness *FreeK Camp* looks like it's going to be a series!

— LAREN BRIGHT, AWARD WINNING ANIMATION WRITER

Your best book yet. Other kids my age will really enjoy this one. It's scary and suspenseful, but it still has some funny parts. I didn't want to put it down.

— STEVEN SAWAN, AGE 12, DOVER-SHERBORN MIDDLE SCHOOL (IN MA),
WHO READ THE MANUSCRIPT BEFORE PUBLICATION

It must be magic. Somehow Steve Burt manages to hook both teen readers and adult readers with the same story—and he delivers for both.

— JIM DONGWECK, AUTHOR, MOONBEAM CHILDREN'S BOOK AWARD-WINNER

FreeK Camp takes readers on a wonderfully scary trip into the wilds and wonder of a Maine summer camp—but not a typical one. Captivating, fascinating, heroic and weird characters weave their way through this tale to the delight of readers. Another great read by a terrific storyteller.

— RICHARD WAINWRIGHT, CHILDREN'S BOOK AUTHOR AND WINNER OF THE
BENJAMIN FRANKLIN AWARD

FreeK Camp reminds us about the importance of unique gifts in our society—an important message for all adolescents struggling to fit in. Teachers will discover in Burt's artistry a "mentor text" for use in character analysis for young readers and character development for young writers.

— JOYCE HITT GORDON, NATIONALLY KNOWN LITERACY SPECIALIST, LONG BEACH, CA

Praise for *Stories to Chill the Heart* Series

Steve Burt's stories are set in a recognizable world, but they never go in the obvious direction, preferring instead to take off down dark alleys and twisting roads which leave the reader shivering and looking nervously into dark corners when the book is closed.

> — BARBARA RODEN, EDITOR, *ALL HALLOWS: THE MAGAZINE OF THE GHOST STORY SOCIETY*

These are stories kids want to read and talk about! They're asking for his books and want to know when we can have him back. The most successful author visit we've ever had.

> — FRAN JOHNSON, MEDIA SPECIALIST, NEWFOUND MEMORIAL MIDDLE SCHOOL, BRISTOL, NH

When I teach high school seniors story-writing, I always include Steve Burt's books. Teens know the real thing when they read it. The next best thing to camping in the woods.

> — MARYLIN WARNER, PIKE'S PEAK BRANCH, NATIONAL LEAGUE OF AMERICAN PEN WOMEN, COLORADO SPRINGS, CO

Just when you think you have the story cornered, you'll find it's sneaked up and gripped you by the back of the neck instead.

> — BILL HUGHES, EDITOR, *DREAD MAGAZINE*

Burt relies more on atmosphere and skillful plotting than blood and gore, making his stories old-fashioned in the best sense of the term. If you think, "they just don't write them like that anymore," you'll be pleased to discover that Burt does.

> — GARRETT PECK, THE HELLNOTES BOOK REVIEW

Your kids will love these stories and so will you! Spooktacularly entertaining summertime reading! Highly recommended.

> — J.L. COMEAU, EDITOR, THE CREATURE FEATURE REVIEW PAGE, WWW.COUNTGORE.COM

If ever there was an author to rival the storytelling genius of M.R. James and E.F. Benson, Steve Burt is it.

— DON H. LAIRD, PUBLISHER, *CROSSOVER PRESS, THRESHOLD MAGAZINE*

Bram Stoker winner Steve Burt's stories have entertained—and frightened—my children for years, not to mention me. My son is in college now and still talks about stories from the *Stories to Chill the Heart* series' four collections. In fact, his scariest nightmare came about after reading one of them. You can't give a better compliment than that to a horror writer!

— DAN KEOHANE, AUTHOR, *SOLOMON'S GRAVE*

Awards for Steve Burt

Winner, Bram Stoker Award (dark fiction)

Silver Medal, Benjamin Franklin Award (mystery/suspense)

3 Ray Bradbury Creative Writing prizes

Sole Honorable Mention, *ForeWord Magazine* Award (suspense/horror)

Honorable Mention, Independent Publisher Award (young adult fiction)

Runner-Up, *Writer's Digest* Award (genre fiction)

Finalist, *ForeWord Magazine* Award (young adult fiction)

Nominee/Finalist, Bram Stoker Award (dark fiction)

Runner-Up, *Writer's Digest* Award (inspirational fiction)

Finalist, *ForeWord Magazine* Award (audio fiction)

8 Honorable Mentions, Year's Best Fantasy & Horror

2 Mom's Choice Awards (gold Teen & gold Young Adult)

Moonbeam Children's Book Award (silver Teen Horror/Suspense)

Beach Book Festival Award (gold, Best Teen)

Hollywood Book Festival Award (silver, Best Teen)

Other fiction by Steve Burt

Stories to Chill the Heart Series

Odd Lot: Stories to Chill the Heart (2001), winner of the Benjamin Franklin Award (silver) for Best Mystery/Suspense Book

Even Odder: More Stories to Chill the Heart (2003), Bram Stoker Award Nominee/Finalist (runner-up to J.K. Rowling, *Harry Potter and the Order of the Phoenix*)

Oddest Yet: Even More Stories to Chill the Heart (2004), winner of the Bram Stoker Award (tie with Clive Barker)

Wicked Odd: Still More Stories to Chill the Heart (2005), Honorable Mention for Independent Publisher Award

The four-book series is now a single eBook titled, *Steve Burt's 39 Oddest Tales,* ISBN 978-0-9741407-4-2

Inspirational books

A Christmas Dozen: Christmas Stories to Warm the Heart (2000), runner-up for Writer's Digest 10th International Self-Published Book Awards for Best Inspirational Book; and finalist for ForeWord Audio Book of the Year

Unk's Fiddle: Stories to Touch the Heart (2001)

FreeK Camp

Psychic Teens in a Paranormal Thriller

Steve Burt

Burt Creations

Norwich, CT

FreeK Camp
Psychic Teens in a Paranormal Thriller

FIRST EDITION
Copyright © 2010 by Steven E. Burt

First Trade Hardcover Edition: ISBN 978-0-9741407-9-7
First Casebound Hardcover Edition: ISBN 978-0-9741407-7-3
First Trade Paperback Edition: ISBN 978-0-9741407-8-0
Second Paperback Printing: December 2010
First Digital eBook: 978-0-9741407-6-6

Printed in USA

Inquiries should be addressed to:

Burt Creations

Burt Creations
Steve Burt
29 Arnold Place
Norwich, CT 06360

Tel: 860-405-5183
www.burtcreations.com

TEXT DESIGN BY DOTTI ALBERTINE, WWW.ALBERTINEBOOKDESIGN.COM

PREFACE

The Paranormal?

WE CAN'T HELP BUT WONDER about psychic phenomena and the paranormal, can we? We expect kids will naturally speculate and experiment, but we find that such behavior continues into adulthood. If you think about it, how can we not? Every day we brush up against that which we don't fully understand or can't exactly explain. Even with "hard science" unraveling the unknown at a fast rate nowadays, we still haven't explained everything. Mystery remains (thank goodness) and it keeps life interesting.

No wonder so many of us have a fascination with—or at least a curiosity about—the psychic and paranormal. The seeds of fascination are sown early in our lives.

As a kid, I listened to ghost stories around campfires and in classrooms. I read or heard about psychic mediums, clairvoyants, and intuitives who seemed to know the unknowable. I checked out books on famous people like Arthur Conan Doyle (Sherlock Holmes' creator), who was a popular lecturer about the spiritualist movement (communicating with the spirits of the departed) and the Maine medium and author Edgar Cayce, famous for his séances (mediums calling forth the spirits of the dead to get answers to the persistent questions of the living). At carnivals and circus sideshows I saw gypsy fortune tellers use Tarot cards, dolphin decks, and crystal balls to predict people's futures. (We kids used Ouija boards and the Magic Eight Ball.)

Television shows introduced me to dowsers (water witches), rainmakers, the Israeli mentalist and spoon-bender Uri Geller, a flying Superman who could see through walls with his x-ray vision. In my dreams, I found myself regularly flying high over the ocean and levitating 10 feet above the sidewalk.

Even church stimulated my imagination. My Sunday school classmates and I learned that when two or more believers agreed on something in prayer, they could move mountains—so we tried levitating the table. Was it only Jesus who could walk on water or pass through a solid wood door?

Months after my grandfather died, I sensed him standing beside my bed one night.

***

The word *paranormal* comes from the Latin *para,* meaning beside, alongside, or next to. We see it in our word *parallel* (railroad tracks running side-by-side without converging, soldiers marching in side-by-side columns). *Para* is also in *para*medic and *para*legal (who aren't doctors or lawyers, but have acquired the basics needed to work s*ide-by-side, next to, alongside* the professionals).

But wait! *Parallel* is a concept, not necessarily a reality, right? Can our supposedly parallel tracks ever touch? Can marching soldiers bump up against one another? Enter an earthquake, a tremor, a heavy rain or mudslide—or human intervention (train robbers with crow bars scheming to stop the mail train). Parallel doesn't necessarily mean permanently so! Tracks shift and merge; soldiers wobble and collide. Likewise, maybe the *normal* and the *paranormal* do occasionally intersect.

That's what happens in the Maine woods in *FreeK Camp*—the normal and paranormal crisscross when a psycho villain encounters psychic teens. Enjoy.

P.S. Don't forget there's a helpful Glossary of Paranormal Terms in the back of the book.

Acknowledgments

My thanks to the following people who read through the draft copy of FreeK Camp and offered corrections and suggestions: Connie Hurtt, Mary Staggs, Lorraine and Bruce Grey, Jolyn Joslin, Steven Sawan, and Wendy Burt-Thomas.

I am also grateful for my "California team" (all award-winners in their fields) for their hard work and patience with me as we took the manuscript and turned it into a real book: copy writer extraordinaire Laren Bright (www.larenbright.com), book shepherd Ellen Reid (www.bookshepherding.com), and book/cover designer Dotti Albertine (www.AlbertineBookDesign.com).

And thanks must go out to the 1960-61 women's group at the United Methodist Church in my hometown of Greenport, NY, on Long Island's northeast tip. I was in sixth grade when they provided me and my sister Nancy with scholarships to pay for church camp (Camp Quinipet on Shelter Island across the bay). There I met five other boys—all of us complete strangers on Day One—and through five days of activities and adventures, we forged deep bonds. Our trials weren't on the level of the FreeKs' trials in my novel, but that's where the seed of an idea for the novel was first planted. (Quinipet also provided the idea and the setting for my short story, "Croaker," which appears in *Wicked Odd*.)

Finally, thanks to all those fans who keep buying and reading my books.

CHAPTER 1

NO ONE SUSPECTED THERE WAS A CAMP FOR KIDS with paranormal powers in the backwoods of Maine—or that its past would put their lives at risk.

The five "different" 13- and 14-year-olds took their seats in the battered pale blue van marked *Free Camp #2* which—thanks to someone wielding a red Magic Marker two years earlier—had become *FreeK Camp #2*. Not only had no one felt the need to erase or paint over the added K, but whenever it faded, it was magically freshened up by someone under cover of darkness. Beneath the camp name someone had added a Smiley face with a third eye—like the CBS eye—in the center of its forehead. It was what Free Camp kids called the mind's eye.

Once they were in, the driver, a tiny man with curly red hair, reached up and closed the side doors, reassuring the parents and siblings in the parking lot, "Don't worry. Never lost a summer camper yet. I'll get them there in one piece." Then, with the families trying not to stare, he opened the driver's door and climbed up onto a child's booster seat. With the door still open so they could see, he strapped a pair of leg-extenders onto his calves. "Got to reach the pedals, you know!" He flashed them an impish grin. "Seatbelts, everybody," he called back to the kids behind him, and buckled his own. He slammed the door once, twice, and finally a third time. "Some days it doesn't want to latch," he said to the families. "But everything else works fine. See you back here in a week."

The odd little man eased the van out of the parking lot into the flow of traffic, encouraging his passengers to show genuine enthusiasm in waving goodbye to their families.

They were off, though to where, the kids weren't exactly sure. Free Camp's mailing address had been a post office box in rural Bridgton, Maine, in the state's western lakes region. But the actual camp, according to the brochure, was pretty far from town, more than a long hike. Still, even if it was a few miles away from civilization, a free week at summer camp in July would be a welcome change from their hometowns.

The front passenger seat was empty. It wasn't that they felt uncomfortable sitting next to the midget, as they'd begun referring to him in their parking lot whispers—he seemed nice enough—but he'd neither invited nor instructed anyone to sit there. Once they'd stowed their backpacks, suitcases, and sleeping bags in the way-back cargo area, he'd motioned them through the double side door. The Hispanic-looking brother and sister had grabbed the comfortable captain's chairs, leaving the third-row bench seat for the other three. The first in was a slight boy with long blond hair and wire-rimmed glasses. Wedged between himself and his armrest was a book, the spine imprinted with the title, *Encyclopaedia of Psychic Science,* and the author's name, Nandor Fodor. In the middle sat another boy—pudgy, pale-skinned, and freckle-faced, a raised brown Mohawk tuft spanning his shaved scalp front-to-back like the Great Wall of China. The last in was a frizzy-haired brunette in wrap-around sunglasses, dangly turquoise pierced earrings, and carved-wood peace-symbol necklace. She held a Free Camp brochure on her lap, an index finger resting on the words *those unique, special, and unusual children who, because their gifts are so very different, may feel strange or alienated from other kids.*

The five weren't yet a group, a team. But they'd become one soon, and not in the usual summer-camp way. No, for this group it would happen differently. Fate—and the biggest challenge of their young lives—would draw them closer, soon. At the moment, as they rode peacefully along on a sunny July morning, they had no way of knowing just how lucky they were—for in an hour they would arrive at Free Camp safe and sound. *Safe.*

The other van, Free Camp #1, which had picked up another five "different" kids two hours earlier, would not. That van had been carjacked by a madman.

CHAPTER 2

THE BALD MAN IN THE CAMOUFLAGE FATIGUES and Desert Storm cap drove Free Camp #1 for an hour without saying a word, not even when the kids asked, "Are we close?" or "How much longer?" Finally, wondering if the man might be deaf, the frail, pale boy behind the driver's seat tapped him on the shoulder.

Without turning, the driver raised his hand and waggled a thick finger in warning. The boy drew back as if he'd touched a hot stove, his mouth open in surprise.

Back in the third row, a tall black girl glimpsed the driver's eyes as they narrowed in the rearview mirror. She leaned forward, placed a hand on the boy's shoulder, and whispered, "Don't mess with him."

Minutes later the van swung from the narrow blacktop road onto an even narrower dirt road. After a mile or so the road looked as if it would end. They hadn't seen a house for some time, not even on the paved road. Now they saw nothing but woods.

The driver pulled up in front of a heavy chain stretched between two trees like a smile, a NO TRESPASSING sign hanging from it like a single tooth. He squared the Desert Storm cap, turned slightly in the driver's seat as if he might look back, but he didn't. He opened the door and hissed, "Stay" out of the corner of his mouth as if commanding—or threatening—a dog.

The kids froze, eyes darting around at one another, connecting them in their fear.

In what appeared to be almost a single fluid motion, he stepped out, dropped the chain, moved the van over it, replaced the chain, and slid back into the driver's seat. Then, before anyone could object, he guided them into the thick, dark shroud of vegetation that cloaked the long-forgotten logging road.

They drove for 10 minutes before the black girl got up her nerve and asked, "Where are you taking us? Is this the way to Free Camp?"

The scowl in the mirror chilled her into silence. None of the others spoke.

Their forward progress was slow. Branches and vines slapped and clawed at the van before closing behind them like a wake, sealing them off from the world. For 15 more minutes the foliage scraped the van's roof and sides. They looked around, pretending disinterest and trying to ignore the rising terror they felt deep down. Something was wrong, but then again, maybe it was just their imagination.

The black girl got up her courage again. "Sir?"

He cut her off before she could pose the question. "Almost there, kiddies."

Without meaning to, she glanced at his rearview mirror again. His yellowed teeth bared in a menacing grin. She shivered, tasting something acidic in the back of her throat.

Suddenly the overhanging branches parted and disappeared. The van broke through into a small clearing and stopped in the center.

To the right sat a windowless, one-level, concrete building. It resembled a single-car garage except it had no big garage doors. There was only a dark green walk-in door that looked fairly new in contrast to the faded gray cement. The place looked more like a concrete bunker. Its roof and walls had been camouflaged with a layer of fresh-cut branches that were woven into a layer of military-surplus netting. Someone had decided it should be invisible not only to passersby but also to the eyes of aircraft and satellites.

The driver adjusted his cap as he had by the chain and stepped from the van. He marched around the front to the passenger side and opened the double center doors.

"Okay, let's move it, troops!" he barked. He motioned them toward the heavy green door. "Day One, campers. First stop on the challenge course."

The five popped their seatbelts and began climbing out.

"What about our knapsacks and sleeping bags?" asked the chubby, red-faced boy who was first out the door. Mickey Mouse grinned from the face of his ball cap, the printed message announcing Call Me Mouse.

"Leave your gear!" the driver said sharply. "You won't need it here." He laid a steely hand on the chubby boy's bicep and steered him toward the building. "Through the green door. Play Follow-the-Leader."

"Flashlights?" asked the frail boy who had tapped the man's shoulder earlier.

"No. That's part of the challenge. And no cell phones! Hand off your cell phones as you exit the vehicle."

"We didn't bring any cell phones," the boy said. "Your camp brochure said to leave them home." He fell into step behind the first boy in the Mouse cap.

"Good job, camper!" the man said. "How about the rest of you? Girls? Cell phones?"

The black girl and the remaining two passengers, two white girls, shook their heads. "Left them home," the black girl said.

"Wonderful. Now, follow the boys through that green door." Reluctantly but obediently, the five kids filed into the concrete block-house.

"Slop bucket's in the far right corner," he said. "You'll figure out how to use it. Get comfortable and await further instructions."

Those were the last words they heard before he locked the door, leaving them in full darkness. What they wouldn't hear would be the sucking sounds a half hour later as the murky green waters of a played-out, flooded stone quarry nearby swallowed Free Camp #1, their belongings, and any evidence they were alive.

CHAPTER 3

THE SECOND VAN HAD BEEN ON THE ROAD 20 minutes when the frizzy brunette with the peace symbol under her chin could hold her tongue no longer.

"Excuse my ignorance, Mr. Twait," she said. "But . . . are you a . . . a leprechaun?"

Dead silence at first as the other four fought to hide their shock at her question, then the sound of smothered giggles.

The driver said nothing, kept his eyes on the road.

The brother and sister in the captain's chairs glanced sideways at one another and, when they couldn't stifle their giggles any longer, started to laugh. The Mohawked boy and the blond boy in the wire-rims next to him caught the bug. Even the driver laughed. The only one who wasn't laughing was the question-asker. She appeared to be waiting for an answer to what she'd meant as a serious inquiry.

The little man on the booster seat held up a stubby right hand. The noise subsided. "I get that question a lot—usually from little kids in the grocery line."

The brunette removed her sunglasses and leaned toward the center of the van so she could see his eyes in the mirror. They were soft, and she could see his face break into a gentle smile when he caught her looking.

"It's hard not to wonder," he said, "considering the fact that I'm ver-tically challenged."

No one breathed.

"Short!" he said. "Vertically challenged! Get it? I'm what they used to call a midget. But now, thanks to politically correct language, I'm vertically challenged. Comprendez?"

They breathed again and the tension dissipated.

"To answer your question, missie—Maggie, isn't it?—no, I'm not a leprechaun. Yes, I'm of Irish descent, as you may have surmised from my red hair. But I'm not a leprechaun. I'm just short—very, very, very short— around four feet. And leprechauns, unless I'm mistaken, are mythical creatures, aren't they? At least, last I heard, they were."

In the mirror she saw him grin, and his green eyes twinkled mischievously like a leprechaun's might. "Well, I don't know if leprechauns are mythical or not," she argued. "Just because most people haven't seen a unicorn or a dragon or a mermaid, doesn't mean they don't exist."

"Good point, Miss Maggie. But back to your question and some of those unspoken ones that come with it. I'm one of those extra short folks who are now sometimes referred to as little persons. In case you're wondering, yes, everything about me is normal. And yes, I'm married— to Rose, who is your camp cook. I also have a child by her, a daughter, whose name is Caroline. She's thirteen, and both she and her mother are of average height. My official title is Assistant Director of Free Camp, but I'm also one of two van drivers and a water safety instructor. As far as the name, I go by Twait, not Mister Twait, thank you, just Twait. It's a nickname. You don't need to remember my long Irish last name or my unusual, hard-to-pronounce first name. Just Twait. If you have other questions, I'm happy to satisfy your curiosity and will try not to be offended. Just ask."

His rapid-fire statements silenced them briefly, and when none of them asked follow-up questions, he said, "So, Maggie, your turn to be on the spot. You're the spoonbender, aren't you?"

The others turned to stare at the girl, their faces knotted into question marks.

She fidgeted, pursing her lips as if deciding whether to answer. But she had already shown that silence didn't suit her, and something about

Twait's own openness and vulnerability may have convinced her to trust these strangers. She let out a breath and spoke.

"Most people think spoonbending is a parlor trick. Like a magician guessing the card you're thinking about, or pulling a rabbit out of a hat, or making a coin appear from behind your ear. But it's not—at least not for me."

"What's a spoonbender?" asked the kid with the Mohawk. His voice was high and hadn't changed yet.

"Yeah," agreed the girl in the captain's chair. "What's a spoonbender? Anybody can bend a spoon, can't they?"

"I can," said her look-alike from the other captain's chair, using hand motions as he spoke, his voice gently mocking. "See? Not just a spoon, but a fork, too. Ouch, I pricked myself on that one." He pretended to set the invisible fork aside. "But a knife"—he picked up an invisible knife, gritting his teeth as he struggled to bend it—"ungh, argh, a knife's too stiff. I can't bend a knife. Maybe if I put it in a vise or got a blacksmith to help me." He grinned foolishly, but Maggie's icy glare froze him in place, and he knew he'd crossed the line. "Kid-ding," he said, stretching out the word. "Sorry." He tried to look serious, though he still had a twinkle of mischief in his eyes. "Really. Can you bend knives and forks, too, or just spoons?"

They waited to see if she'd put her sunglasses back on and clam up. She kept them in her lap as she held the black-haired boy with her indignant stare. But the curl at the corner of his mouth suggested playfulness, not malice. Sensing a potential ally in the sister, she said, "Is your brother—I assume he's your brother—is he always this—"

"Obnoxious?" the Hispanic girl said, shooting the boy an eye dagger. "Rude?"

"Actually, I was thinking funny," Maggie said. "Hilarious, even. He's quite the wit."

The boy's face brightened.

"Juan? A wit? I think you mean half wit, don't you?" After about a three-second delay, the boy under the Mohawk laughed, and she flashed him a smile. The others rolled their eyes or shrugged, the clear but unspoken consensus seeming to say, "Get back to the question."

"Spoonbender is a street term," interrupted the long-haired boy in the wire-rims. "Like Maggie says, it's often associated with sleight-of-hand tricks and illusion. But if I'm hearing her right, she's saying she can actually do it."

"Like mind over matter?" Mohawk boy said.

"Kind of, yes," Maggie said. "I've read up on it and learned there are technical words for it—telekinesis and psychokinesis. But those categories are pretty broad. They include a lot of other stuff—like levitation of objects. Street term or not, spoonbender actually fits me better. I can bend small metal objects—that's all, only metal—but I can't levitate or move things. Well, except for a shopping cart in the Stop & Shop parking lot once. That was probably because it was metal and on wheels—and there was a slight breeze. It's a magnetic thing, I figure. I can't move a block of wood or a glass of water across the table. And I can't snap a plastic fork or spoon in half or even bend it. I'm only able to do metal."

"A magnetic personality!" Mohawk boy exclaimed.

Everyone groaned, even Twait.

"Okay, okay," Juan said. "So show us. Do it."

Maggie's eyes scanned the group, ending up back at Juan. "Hey, I don't even know you guys. Do I look like some trained dog who'll do a trick for your amusement?"

But their eyes stayed on her.

"You know you're dying to show us," Juan taunted.

"Do I need to pull over for this?" Twait said.

"No, no, no. Just send back that bottle opener sitting on the console."

Twait passed it back to Juanita, who tried to relay it on to Maggie.

"No, don't let me touch it," Maggie said, her upraised palms saying no. "Just hold it out on your fingertips."

Juanita held it out for everyone to see.

Maggie closed her eyes for several seconds, seemed to gather her powers of concentration, and then opened them. She stared at the shiny object balanced on Juanita's fingertips.

The bottle opener slowly curled into the shape of a banana.

"Cool!" It was the kid beside her with the Mohawk. "Now—no hands again—can you make it open a bottle?"

They all rolled their eyes.

Juanita handed the opener to Maggie and said, "You'd better straighten it out. We may need it."

Before Maggie could clasp her fingers around it, though, it lifted off from her palm and began slowly floating at eye level through the center of the van, eventually coming to rest on the console beside Twait again. Everyone stared open-mouthed.

"Awesome!" It was Mohawk boy. "Levitation, right? How'd you do that?"

Maggie's mouth hung open too. "I didn't."

"What do you mean, you didn't?" Juan said. "We just saw you do it."

"It wasn't me. I bent it, that's all."

"Then who made it fly?" Juan turned to look back at the blond boy whose hands were still in his pouch-pocket. "You got some kind of remote controller in your sweatshirt there?"

"Hey, don't look at me. Wasn't me. Maybe it was Twait."

"Nope, not me. I told you, I'm not a leprechaun."

"Maybe it's poltergeists," the kid with the Mohawk said. "You know, angry spirits that shake and break things—like in the movies?"

The others shook their heads at him, except for Juanita, who just smiled at him.

"Twait, can we pass that bottle opener around?" Juan asked.

Twait handed it over. Everyone examined it.

When the opener got back to the blonde in the wire-rims, he managed to check it out without removing his hands from the sweatshirt pocket, gripping it through the fabric.

Everyone agreed it was too rigid to straighten by hand. But then Maggie laid it on the floor and willed it back to its original shape. Juan scooped it up and handed it back to Twait, who returned it to the tray on top of the console.

For a while they speculated on the bottle opener's flight down the center of the van, but with no one taking responsibility for the levitation, the conversation died. Most bets, though, were on the leprechaun.

CHAPTER **4**

IN FREE CAMP'S DINING ROOM a compact, dark-skinned man sat cross-legged in the lotus position on a long rubber yoga mat, his eyes closed, his palms upturned on his thighs. His features seemed a mix—Asian, Middle Eastern, Greek or Italian, perhaps even Mexican. Hollywood might have cast him in any of those parts the way they once did Anthony Quinn. He was in his meditative cool-down period following a half hour of slow but strenuous yoga exercise. His skin glistened, but not a bead of sweat showed on his face.

A very tall, matronly woman in a hairnet stuck her head through the kitchen door. "Bando?"

"Yes, Rose," the man on the mat answered softly.

"Twait's due any time with #2, but Jerry's over an hour and a half late with #1. You think something's wrong?"

Bando unfolded himself and got to his feet. He padded quietly toward the kitchen.

"If it was a flat tire," she continued, "or engine trouble—that #1 isn't all that reliable, you know—Jerry would've phoned, wouldn't he?"

Bando could see the worry in her face. She'd never hidden her emotions well, especially the worry.

"It's just that I need to know how many to plan on for lunch," she said.

Bando knew it was more than that. She felt the trouble in the air, too.

"Jerry hasn't called," he said. "I'm pretty sure he and that five won't be with us for lunch—and probably not for supper tonight or meals tomorrow. That's not for sure, but it's the vibe I've been getting."

Rose's hand went to her mouth, and Bando could see his words had put her on the verge of tears.

"Jerry will be fine," he said. "I feel sure of that." That seemed to comfort her.

"And those kids?"

"Danger," he said, and walked into the kitchen. "Let's change the subject for now. Is that tea water still hot?"

"It's hot. Two cups beside it on the counter—tea bags in them. Pour mine, too, and turn off the burner."

Bando watched her scoop up the six extra soup bowls and plates from the stainless steel counter and return them to the cupboard.

"Just want to know how many to plan for," Rose repeated, a slight catch in her voice. She kept her back to Bando, stayed facing the cupboard, her hand resting on the metal door-pull. "It's hard to know around here sometimes—how many to plan for."

He heard her stifle a sob.

"They'll all be fine, Rose," Bando said. "Don't worry."

Although she'd learned long ago to trust Bando and to not ask how he knew what he seemed to know, she couldn't help worrying. She wiped away a tear and turned to face him.

He pushed her tea toward her, and when she reached for it, he placed a gentle hand on hers.

"Jerry's going to be okay," he repeated. "And Twait's fine. He and his five will be here in a minute. They're crossing the old tin bridge now. Better hurry and drink your tea."

She smiled weakly. "You know I love it here, Bando. But there are times—like now—when it's, well, it's just plain stressful. Know what I mean?"

"I do know." He walked around the corner of the counter and gave Rose a hug. His hands barely reached around her waist. "I appreciate your patience, and Twait's, too. We both know your husband's a gem. So are you."

She stepped back from the hug and placed her hands on Bando's shoulders, towering over him. "You're a gem, too, old friend, one of a kind." She cleared her throat, tried to laugh. "Gee whiz, how is it I manage to find not one but two good men in my life, and one's six inches shorter than I am, and the other, the one I marry, is two feet shorter?"

Before Bando could answer, the screen door creaked open.

"Mom? Bando?"

"In the kitchen, Caroline," Rose answered.

A lanky 13 year-old with thick red hair like Twait's appeared at the kitchen door. Her hair was in two braids that reached her shoulder blades. "Dad's van just crossed the bridge. But where's Jerry with #1? He's way overdue."

Rose glanced sideways at Bando, then back to her daughter.

"It's just your Dad's group today," Bando said. "Jerry's been held up."

"You mean literally held up?" Her eyes narrowed. "As in robbery? Or do you just mean delayed, like engine trouble?"

Neither adult answered.

"Oh no," she said. "You think it's something worse? What?"

"I can't say just yet," Bando answered, looking her squarely in the eye. "But Jerry will be okay."

"What about the kids he picked up?" Caroline pressed, though she knew Bando wouldn't say more.

The beep-beep of Twait's horn interrupted them. They walked onto the dining hall's porch as the faded blue FreeK Camp #2 van crunched to a stop on the gravel by the steps.

The driver's door swung open and, after removing the extenders, Twait climbed down from his booster seat. The five passengers stayed in their seats, scanning their surroundings and awaiting instructions.

"Honeys, we're home!" a grinning Twait called up at the porch. He stopped at the bottom step. "Where's Jerry?" he said, alarm in his voice.

Rose's lip started to quiver, but she bit down and let Bando answer.

"Jerry's run into some trouble," Bando said flatly, his face inscrutable. "It may be awhile before his group joins us."

Twait didn't press. He knew he'd get no details this early. He grabbed the handle of the van's double doors. "Anything we can do?" he asked, with just the slightest eye movement toward his passengers.

"I hope so," Bando said. "But not just yet."

Twait caught more heaviness in Bando's tone than he was accustomed to, but there was nothing to be done for the moment. "Okay then, time to let them loose." He opened the doors. "This is the place you've been waiting for," he informed his passengers. "Everybody out."

Caroline jumped off the porch as the kids started climbing out. "I'll show them the cabins, Dad."

"I'm Rose. This is Bando. That's Caroline. We'll talk later. Leave your stuff on your bunks and take a quick peek around. Fifteen minutes to lunch. Ready or not, food goes on the table in fifteen minutes."

"Can we negotiate for twenty, Rose?" Bando said. "I need a few minutes with Twait."

"All right, for you, twenty." She forced a worried smile. "But twenty's the limit. The kitchen magician has spoken."

"Okay, gang," Twait said. "Open the back and grab your gear. Caroline will take you to your cabins and show you around. You heard Rose—lunch in twenty minutes. You snooze, you lose."

The kids unloaded their bags and, eager to explore their new digs, fell in behind the freckled redhead with the pigtails.

CHAPTER 5

THE BOY IN THE CALL ME MOUSE HAT grew tired of standing and slumped to the floor, his forearms on his knees and his back against the gritty concrete-block wall. He let out a loud sigh and uttered "Un-freaking-believable" as if it were a curse word.

Across the darkened room a voice said, "Is that you—in the Mouse hat?" It was the frail boy who had tapped the driver's shoulder.

"Yeah. Call me Mouse."

"I thought that was what Mickey was saying on your hat."

"No, my mother had it custom-printed for me at Disney World last year. She did it because everybody calls me Mouse. And you're Tim, right?" Mouse had heard the name in the parking lot and found it easy to remember. He associated it with Tiny Tim and Scrooge. The other boy was a good six inches shorter than he himself was.

"Yeah. I'm Tim."

"And I'm Celine," the black girl said. "My Mom loves Celine Dion, the singer who sang in Titanic, so she named me after her."

"Titanic, what a coincidence. Here we are, on it," another girl's voice said sarcastically, and the others chuckled nervously. When they quieted, she said, "Sorry. I get snippy when I'm nervous or scared. I'm Barbara Jean. My friends all call me BJ."

"Atlanta," the third girl said. "My sister is Georgia. Guess where we were born?"

"Duh, Vermont?" Mouse said.

"Actually, that's closer than you think—and I know you were kidding, Mouse—but Vermont is where we live now. We moved from Atlanta, Georgia to Burlington, Vermont when I was three."

After a few more minutes of getting acquainted, Atlanta said, "It's getting hot in here. How long do you think they'll make us stay?"

"They?" laughed BJ. "They, Atlanta? You don't think this is the camp's doing, do you? It's not they; it's him, that soldier guy who drove us here and locked us in this black hole. He's not right in the head. He gave me the creeps from the beginning. Can't you see he's off? He's not with the camp, sweetie, no way. We're in big trouble here, gang."

The room went silent. Finally someone—Tiny Tim again—said, "But he said this was an initiation, right? I mean, didn't he say it was some sort of challenge course?"

"Yeah, maybe it is a test," Atlanta agreed.

"Challenge course, my foot," BJ cut in, her voice edged with irritation. "Swinging on vines to cross a stream is a challenge course. Climbing a high wall with a rope is a challenge course. But this—I don't think so. Forcing five kids into in a dungeon is not something you'd even see in an Outward Bound camp. They wouldn't pull this on adults on Survivor. This is beyond creepy. Know what I think? I think we're lucky Mr. Militiaman didn't slap shackles on us or hook us all up to a ball-and-chain. Wake up and smell the mold, you guys. Middle of nowhere, concrete prison, no food, no water, no light, and maybe no air—this is a dungeon, not a camp initiation, not some weird challenge course. We're in deep trouble here. Something's wrong with this picture, really wrong."

A smothering mix of disbelief and hopelessness enveloped the room, and it was several minutes before anyone dared speak.

"Okay," Mouse said. "So, challenge course or not, we've got to either tough it out until the guy comes back—maybe overnight or for who knows how long—or we've got to do the David Copperfield thing and escape from a locked room."

"Who says it's locked?" BJ countered. Mouse remembered now that she'd had a crooked nose, perhaps broken once or twice.

"Seriously," BJ continued. "Did anybody try the door to see if it's actually locked?"

"I'm right by it," Tim said. "I'll check."

The tiniest sliver of daylight shone under the heavy metal door. No light entered around the sides or top. It was close to an airtight fit.

"The knob turns," he said, and the others drew in their breath as they listened to him tug on it. "But it won't open. It's stuck."

"It's not stuck," BJ said. "It's locked from the outside. He probably threw the deadbolt when he shut us in."

"How about the hinges?" Mouse said. "Feel them and see if they're held in place by metal pins."

"What do you mean?" Tim said.

Mouse rose to his feet. "I'm coming over. Stay where you are, everybody, so I don't trip over you." He felt and toed his way across the floor, explaining as he went, "When my little brother locked himself in the bathroom once, my Dad used a screwdriver and hammer to knock the pins out of the hinges. Once they were out, he pulled the door right out of the frame. I just need to feel the hinges."

He slid his hand along the door's edge. "Damn. Nothing."

"Could the hinges be on the outside?" Celine said.

"Looks that way." Mouse had forgotten that his father had removed the hinge pins from the outside of a door that opened out. This door had opened out, too.

"So whoever designed this place designed it not to keep people out, but to keep them in," Celine said.

They were all quiet again as Celine's observation sank in.

Atlanta said, "I wonder if others have been in here. Or did he prepare this just for us?"

No one wanted to answer that question, so Tim changed the subject. "What else can we try? Can we dig our way out?"

"The floor's concrete," Atlanta said. "Except for that door, the whole building's concrete."

"Maybe not all of it," Celine countered. "Let's not make assumptions. First we feel all four walls, see if there are any breaks or loose blocks. Then we form a chain and work our way across the whole floor—see if there's a section that's thin or maybe still dirt."

"Yeah, maybe the original plan called for a drain," Mouse added. "If so, we burrow down a ways and then tunnel toward the outside edge of the building. Check the ceiling, too. Is it wood or concrete? If it's wood, we can whittle away at it."

Atlanta interrupted. "When you're feeling the floor, if you find anything loose—a board, a brick, a big rock—hang onto it so we don't have to find it again. We may need it to pound or scrape our way out of here."

"Or use it as a weapon," piped up BJ.

That brought a deafening silence. They hadn't contemplated the possibility of weapons or necessity of violence.

"Excellent suggestion, BJ," Mouse said after a moment. "It's scary to think about, but considering our situation, it's realistic."

As the five of them set about the task at hand, Mouse imagined BJ—under cover of darkness—smiling at him.

Atlanta announced she'd found a pail in one corner. "It's empty except for a roll of toilet paper," she said.

Suddenly everyone understood what the bald militiaman had meant by slop bucket. They would all resist using it for another hour or so, but none of them had visited a bathroom since before they left Portland. Like it or not, in the pitch-black room they'd all eventually give in to nature's call.

CHAPTER 6

"THIS IS THE GIRLS' CABIN," Caroline said with a grand sweep of her hand. "The boys' cabin is just like it but across the ball field."

The small, almost square room contained four double-decker bunk beds, a weathered kitchen table that must have found no takers at a yard sale, and eight metal folding chairs leaned against the wall beside it.

Caroline unfolded a chair, turned it around backward and straddled it, resting her forearms on its back. "Bathroom and shower are in that little cubicle behind the bamboo curtain. Lucky you. That was added on three or four years ago. Before that you had to use the outhouse in the woods."

"How'd you shower?" asked the kid with the Mohawk.

"Everyone—boys, girls, staff—everybody showered in this rude out-door shower. The showerhead is really a garden hose tied to a hook on the back of the building. That's all it was—a garden hose on the wall, with a plywood stall built around it."

"So, no hot water?" the Mohawked kid said.

"Are you listening? Garden hose. No, there was no hot water. None. I can still remember using it. Ever since my parents started working here, I've spent every summer at the camp."

"Anybody still use it?" the blond boy in the sweatshirt asked.

"Just Bando."

"Bet they were quick showers in those days," Juanita said.

"Still are. Even in here. You still only have one water choice—and guess what? It's not hot."

Everyone groaned.

Caroline shifted gears. "So you're Maggie, the spoonbender," she said with a nod of acknowledgment before turning to the brother and sister. "And obviously you're Juan and Juanita. Twins, right?" They nodded. "What brings you two here?"

The pair exchanged what's-this-all-about looks, but Juanita answered for them. "Well, this is a week of summer camp, and it's free. As our Dad said, the price is right."

"You know what I mean," Caroline said matter-of-factly, her eyes panning her audience. "There's something different—special—about each of you, or you wouldn't be here. What is it?"

They lowered their eyes at first and then glanced nervously around at each other, hoping someone else might speak. It was like having a teacher ask a question when no one was sure if they had the right answer. Would the lunch bell save them?

Caroline folded her hands and rested her chin on them, waiting.

In the end it wasn't the twins who spoke; it was the boy with the hidden hands. "All right," he said, sitting on the edge of a bunk. "Let's get it rolling."

All eyes shifted to him. To them Caroline was still a camp insider, but this guy in the sweatshirt, even though they didn't really know him yet, was an outsider like them, an outsider who had taken the lead.

"We already know Maggie's a spoonbender. We saw it in action, and somehow Caroline knows it too. And she's saying there must be something different about each of us. We all read about Free Camp in a mailing or online or heard about it someplace. I have a hunch none of our parents signed us up; they simply provided us with the permission we needed to apply. But we applied on our own because something in the literature—something about the camp—hooked us, all of us. Admit it. We chose to apply. Why?"

Eyes darted nervously around the room, testing the trust level.

Who would respond first to this challenge from one of them, another outsider?

"Sometimes I see things." The voice was Juan's, and his words formed slowly. "At a distance. I don't actually see them with my eyes. But I, like, see them in my mind."

"Like hallucinations?" Maggie said, sitting up, interest piqued.

"No, not like hallucinations," Juanita cut in. "My brother literally sees what's happening somewhere else."

"But there's no sound," Juan said. "I can see the action, but—"

"In a limited way," Juanita finished. "It's like he sees through a camera viewfinder in a room, but he has no control over the camera's movement."

"I can't see what's behind me, and I can only see some of what's beside me."

"It's like he's borrowing somebody else's eyes."

"That's a form of clairvoyance," the kid in the sweatshirt said, holding up his copy of Nandor Fodor's *Encyclopaedia of Psychic Science* in front of him. "It's from the Latin words for clear-seeing. I've been reading about it in this." He was holding the book through the sweatshirt fabric, his hands still inside the wide front pocket. "In your case it sounds slightly different—like something called remote viewing. The government's been experimenting with it for spying purposes."

"And how do you know all this, mister-smarty-pants-whatever-your-name-is?" said Maggie.

"Charlie," he said. "My name is Charlie and I read all the time—everything. I read and I remember. If you check my backpack you'll find it weighs a ton. That's because I've got hardly any clothing, but plenty of books."

"And I thought I read a lot," Caroline said.

"You probably read for different reasons," he said. "I read a lot because I can't play sports or do a lot of other things."

He withdrew his hands from the sweatshirt, and when he showed them, several of the others gasped. Both hands were twisted and bent. On each hand, the thumb and mangle of fingers came together like lobster claws. Caroline and Maggie's faces pinched as if in pain.

The boy with the Mohawk seemed stunned, too, but then fumbled out some words. "So you're special because—because why? Because you can crack walnuts with those hands?"

Everyone winced as if fingernails had scraped a chalkboard.

Charlie tried to hold back, but a laugh escaped his lips. Then he laughed harder and harder, and the others found themselves drawn into it. The tension drained from the room.

Things finally calmed down, and Charlie said, "Mo, right? You said when we met in that parking lot your name was Mo, didn't you? Is that short for Mohawk?"

The others giggled.

"No," he said, straight-faced. "My name is Monroe, same as my father's. He goes by Monroe, so they started calling me Mo. The haircut is new this summer."

"Oh," Charlie said, face still flush from laughing. "Well, Mo, I appreciate your insensitivity and total lack of sympathy. Usually when people see my hands, that's all I get—sympathy and medical questions. Were you born that way? Is it arthritis? Can you hold a pen? Can't the doctors separate the fingers or do a hand transplant? But I've never had anyone ask about cracking nuts. You made my day."

The dinner bell rang.

"We've got five minutes to get seated for lunch," Caroline said. "Mom will put out the food whether we're ready or not. Juan, Charlie, Mo, haul your stuff over to the boys' cabin and drop it there for now. Juanita and Maggie, pick out your bunks. Quick bathroom stops for everybody and we meet in the dining room. We can finish this conversation after lunch."

"But wait," Mo said. "There are supposed to be other kids."

"That's a question mark at the moment," Caroline said. "Our driver Jerry had the early van and was meeting five kids at the same place my Dad met you. He hasn't shown up yet."

***

Meanwhile in the dining hall Twait reached up onto the desk for the office phone. "You know we've got to call in the State Police."

"I know," Bando answered.

Twait kept his hand on the phone but didn't pick it up. "I just wish Jerry would call."

"I know," Bando said. "Me too. Something's wrong, and it's more serious than a flat or a blown transmission. He'd have gotten word to us somehow."

"I'm really worried this time," Twait said, biting his lip.

Bando closed his eyes, breathed in deeply through his nose. He seemed to be listening intensely, as if for a faint breeze or for the buzz of a mosquito across the room. When he exhaled he said, "Jerry's okay. No, he will be okay. But those kids are in trouble."

Twait still didn't raise the phone. "We've got to call, Bando. Their parents need to know right away. The State Police need to get on top of this, find out what's going on. This isn't as simple as the stuff we've dealt with in the past."

"I know," Bando said, taking in another slow breath through his nose.

This wasn't new to Twait. Many times he had waited while his friend tuned into whatever vibrations and disruptions he could sense in the fabric of the universe.

When Bando exhaled and opened his eyes this time, he said, "This time it could turn out very badly, Twait, very badly. Make the call."

Twait picked up the phone and punched in the number for the Maine State Police.

CHAPTER 7

A RUSTING RED PICKUP EASED TO A STOP in front of the house trailer, a dirt-covered motorcycle riding upright in the truck bed. From the cab stepped a muscular man in tan shorts and a dirt-streaked tee shirt. His salt-and-pepper hair was damp and stuck to his forehead and the back of his neck.

He reached back inside and from the passenger floor snatched up an empty, rope-handled shopping bag, which he opened and placed on the floor under the steering wheel. He packed it with the items sitting on the front seat: the camouflage fatigues, the Desert Storm work cap, the sunglasses, the gas mask, and the bald actor's wig. He stuck a hand up under the driver's seat, found the nest he'd made in the seat stuffing, and removed the .45, which he also shoved in the bag. He grabbed the bag by the rope handles and started to close the door, then stopped. He almost forgot the stuffed animal resting against the passenger door. He'd taken enough trouble to get it. It was the only thing he'd removed from the camp van before pushing it into the water-filled stone quarry. He stretched across and gripped the stuffed animal by its neck. It felt so soft. Into the bag it went, on top of the gun.

With a couple of long strides he reached the cement block that was the trailer's front step. The inside door was ajar the way he'd left it, and a black cat climbed out a rip in the screen door, landing noiselessly on the ground. It sidled up to him and curled itself around his ankles, accustomed to his attention. He looked from the familiar black cat to the plush animal in the shopping bag—a cuddly brown and black puppy with warm chestnut eyes—then back again several times.

From the road-end of the driveway came the sound of a vehicle crunching from the blacktop onto the gravel shoulder—the mail truck. Walt the mail carrier waved toward the trailer and then opened the dented RFD box. He started to slide the bills and magazines into it, but stopped, pulled the mail out, and backed up enough to angle the mail truck onto the dirt driveway. He negotiated the ruts and drew up beside the pickup.

"How you doing, Donnie?" the mailman called out, and thrust the fistful of mail out the side window as if it were a carrot on a stick. "Finding any work?"

The man by the cement-block front step shook off the cat and stepped toward the mail buggy.

"Doing fine, Walt, thanks. Finished a roofing job last week. Now I'm onto a stonewall rebuilding that'll go three or four weeks. So, I'm getting by."

The driver handed over the mail. "Got yourself a new dog, I see." When Donnie appeared puzzled, the mailman pointed a finger at the stuffed animal peeking over the edge of the shopping bag. "Cute. And them stuffed ones are some bargain. Don't eat hardly nothing and you never have to walk 'em."

Donnie offered a weak smile. "Got a point there. And no vet bills." The cat wound itself around his ankles, purring, demanding attention.

"Seriously, it really is cute. Where'd you get it? Looks high quality."

Donnie hesitated, a distant look in his eye, but seemed to come back to earth. "Picked it up down to Portland." He hoisted the bag closer to his chest, where the nosy mail carrier couldn't see down into it and beneath the stuffed pup.

"Portland? Where at? The mall?"

"Actually," Donnie hemmed, "to tell you the truth, I got lucky. I found it in a parking lot."

"Yeah, lucky for you," Walt grinned. "But somewhere some little girl's bawling her eyes out."

The reaction in Donnie's eyes told Walt that what he'd meant to be good-natured ribbing hadn't been received that way. He opted for a quick escape from the faux pas. "Oh well, finders keepers, right?" he said, and backed the mail buggy into the turnaround space. He put it in gear and was about to wave and drive off, but stopped. "By the way, I notice the address label for your *Reader's Digest* there still has both your and Karen's name on it. Don't mean to be insensitive, but it's been about five years now. If it's a Change of Address card you need, I've got one here. You send it to the magazine subscription service company listed in the front of the magazine. Leave your name and address on it, but delete Karen's name. Got the forms right here. Want one?"

Donnie's face grew hard, his eyes two deep wells of pain. He squeezed the wad of mail with one hand, the bag with the other. The stuffed pup's head popped up a little, like it was trying to climb free of the bag. Under it Donnie sensed the weight of the.45.

This time Walt read Donnie's face in an instant. "Sorry. Really, I am. Didn't mean to open old wounds—just thought maybe you were ready to move on."

The stone-faced man's pain was obvious, deep, immense, and oddly fresh. He said nothing.

Walt offered a wave. "Okay then, good luck with that fence job." He guided the mail buggy along the ruts and back out to the main road.

Donnie watched him drive off, then returned to the screen door and laid a thick hand on the handle. The black cat glued itself to his black combat boot again.

On the right end of the cement step sat an aluminum milk box. It hadn't seen use in years, not since Addie was a baby and Karen had insisted they have organic whole milk delivered. What would that be— ten or twelve years ago they'd had milk delivery? Must be. Soon it would be five years since the two of them were taken away from him. Addie was ten then, almost eleven, and Karen barely thirty-five.

The cat was losing patience and hooked its claws into the flesh of his calf just above the boot top. It was demanding Donnie play their usual game. He leaned down and, using the hand holding the mail, flipped back the milk box lid. With the same hand he snatched up the cat and lowered it into the box. The mail spilled onto the dirt next to the step, and he cursed softly. When he released his grip on the cat, it curled up at the bottom of the box, and Donnie closed the lid. But unlike the usual game—Addie's game, really, in which the cat poked its head out from under the lightweight lid before slithering out, only to have her put it back in the box again and again, a game he had continued since her death until today—this time Donnie placed a loose brick on the lid.

He picked up the scattered bills and magazines and stepped up into his trailer, hungry for lunch. The rope-handled shopping bag and its contents disappeared into the closet. The stuffed puppy, his replacement pet, he set on the living room shelf where he could see it—and it could see him.

CHAPTER 8

NOBODY LIKED THE DARKNESS or the smell of the slop bucket they'd had to start using. Only being able to hear one another's voices made things bearable. They relied on the sliver of light at the bottom of the door to keep them oriented. It barely reached an inch under the door, because the door was fitted into the frame so tightly. Once the sun went down and the darkness became total in the blockhouse, it'd be hard for them to keep their bearings and even harder to keep their spirits up.

To make matters worse, everyone was hungry and thirsty. It was mid-morning now and their last meal had come at breakfast, long before they said their parking-lot goodbyes and boarded the van. If they had food now, they'd all eat it despite the stink of the slop bucket in their nostrils.

"All right," Celine said. "Seems this little dungeon is built on a solid slab—with no cracks and no drains. The ceiling is solid, too."

"The walls are made of concrete blocks," Tim added. "So far as we can tell, none of them is loose, so we can't push it out like in some prison-break movie."

"Not yet," Mouse cut in. "But we've got to try. I've got a jackknife. We pick a spot and keep working to scrape down the mortar around the block."

"I've got a knife, too," Tim said. "But it's just a small one."

"Anybody else got anything we can scrape with?" Celine asked. "I've got my peace symbol. No better time to use it."

"Save the necklace," Mouse said. "At least for now. Belt buckles will work just as well. If we pick two blocks that are side by side, that'll give us three joints to scrape if three of us are shoulder to shoulder."

Atlanta threw in a different idea. "Mouse, how about using your knife to pick the lock? They do it in the movies with plastic credit cards, so we ought to be able to do it with a knife."

"It's not that type of lock," Mouse argued. "It's a deadbolt—a metal rod or maybe in this case a thick bar of steel that slides side to side. The ones you see in movies are key locks that have a little button that goes from the door into an opening on the doorframe. The credit card pushes the button back, that's all. This one's not a button. It's a deadbolt."

"I understand that," Atlanta said, a hint of exasperation in her voice. "I'm saying, stick the point of your knife blade through the crack and press the point hard into the deadbolt. Then work it to the side. You know, wiggle it to shift the deadbolt a tiny bit? While you do it, I'll jiggle the door to take the tension off the deadbolt, so we keep it loose enough for you to slide. If we make a little progress, we get a new bite on it and work it across a fraction more. Maybe we can force it over gradually."

"You can try it," Tim said. "But I think scraping the concrete may be a better idea. I mean, what if you break the knife blade off in the door crack? Then we lose a scraper."

"See that light at the bottom of the door?" It was Celine again. "That door is a really tight fit—which means that tiny little crack under there is our only source of fresh air. I'm betting we'll run out of oxygen long before we can scrape through a cement wall that may be a foot thick. Atlanta's idea is worth a try."

Mouse and Atlanta attacked the door while Tim felt his way around the entire wall again, inch by inch. He didn't have a good feeling about the chances of moving the deadbolt. What really worried him, though, was the idea that the bald, finger-wagging militiaman—whose barely concealed rage had jumped to Tim's fingertip like a crackle of electricity when he touched the man's shoulder—might return any time. And he might be even angrier.

CHAPTER 9

N O ONE HAD TO CALL FOR QUIET when Bando stepped through the kitchen door. Everyone stopped talking as if the great and powerful Oz had appeared. He stepped in front of the serving table Rose had set the food on and faced the new campers, his fingers resting on the edge of the table behind him.

Even though there were only five kids and Caroline, they divided themselves between two round tables. They were hungry and eager for instructions.

"I see you've split yourselves in a fairly traditional way—boys at one table, girls at the other," Bando said.

The kids glanced around. Sure enough, with little conscious thought they had divided up as if in a school cafeteria—Charlie, Juan, and Mo at the table nearer the kitchen, Juanita, Maggie, and Caroline at the farther table.

"That's perfectly fine," Bando continued. "But you may find it helpful—even interesting—to mix things up. You're all here because you've exhibited some interesting and special gifts. You can choose to keep your gift to yourself, or keep the boys' gifts to the boys and the girls' gifts to the girls. But Twait, Rose, and I ask you to consider discovering, developing, and sharing your gifts in new combinations. Some gifts may complement others' gifts. So don't restrict yourselves by gender."

They exchanged puzzled looks, except for Caroline who seemed to have some idea what Bando meant.

"Take the twins, for example," Bando said. "Juan is male, Juanita is female, and each possesses a gift. Yet back in their hometown in Norwich, Connecticut, a crime was committed, and it took their combined talents to help police solve it. I'm sure they'll tell you about it if you ask."

All eyes turned to Juan and Juanita, who managed to look embarrassed and proud at the same time.

"So," Bando said. "Thanks to Rose, lunch is served. Plates and silverware on that end, so grab what you need and work your way along either side of the serving table. Drinks are over on that counter. Desserts are on the side table. When you're done, carry your own dirty dishes to the kitchen sink, scrape them into the barrel, and stack them in the plastic tubs. After that it's free time until three o'clock, when we meet back here. Questions?"

Mo raised a hand. "My cousin Atlanta is supposed to be here. I don't see her."

"Atlanta is in the other van," Twait cut in. He emerged from the kitchen and stood next to Bando at the serving table, the top of his head not quite reaching the director's chin. "Jerry is our driver. He must have had a flat or engine trouble or something. We're waiting to hear. I'm sure your cousin Atlanta and the other four will catch up with us soon, and you'll all mix in together just fine. But for now there's you five and Caroline."

"Any other questions?" Bando asked. There were none. "Lunch is served. Bon appetit."

In no time all six filled their plates and were back in their seats. They seemed to move faster and more deliberately now, driven by a hungry curiosity, and quickly arranged the two round tables together in a sort of figure eight, not quite boy-girl-boy-girl, but almost. They set it up with the twins sitting together near the center so everyone could hear their story over lunch.

"We bought an old chair in a secondhand store," Juan said, "for our tree house. It was a gray metal office chair. We took turns carrying it down the street."

"We hadn't gone very far when Juan touched it and saw a woman tied up in a chair. She was in a basement room."

"With duct tape over her mouth, and I saw a clock on the back wall, and a drunk man on a cot, and a whiskey bottle on a table, and a –"

"Wait, Juan," his sister cut in. "Those things didn't come all at once. They came in stages. You had a couple of different visions."

"Well, yeah. But the point is, I saw the crime scene. It was a kidnapping that was about to turn into a murder."

At the mention of the words kidnapping and murder, everyone's ears pricked up.

"And while Juan was touching the chair," Juanita said, "and I touched it at the same time, I heard some of what was going on—at the scene. What was weird was, I couldn't see it and Juan couldn't hear it."

"It was like she had the audio and I had the video."

Charlie interrupted. "As I said back at the cabin, what Juan experienced is technically called remote viewing, a form of clairvoyance or clear seeing. I'm not sure, but I'd assume Juanita's is called remote hearing, a form of clairaudience or clear hearing. So back to your story—you two used remote viewing and remote hearing together?"

"What'd you do?" Maggie said. "How'd you know where the crime scene was?"

"We didn't," Juanita said. "But we were convinced it was real, so we went to the police."

"I'll bet they didn't believe you," Mo said.

"Actually, the police chief is a woman," Juanita said, "and she'd worked with psychics before. She listened to us. They figured out the drunk man on the cot was selling the gray metal chairs to the secondhand shop for years."

"The chairs all had the same initials stamped on them," Juan said. "The vibes we got from the chair led the cops to the State Mental Hospital. It shut down years ago. The guy had been a janitor there and kept his keys. This wasn't the first woman he kidnapped and killed there. Everyone thought the other women left the country. He was about to do it again."

"So the cops got there in time to save her—because of you two?" It was Mo.

"Yes," Juan said.

The others chewed their food, fascinated with the twins' story.

"When we were back at the cabin," Charlie said, "you said your view was limited."

"That's the weird part," Juan said. "The whole time I was touching the chair and seeing, I felt like I was anchored to one side of that basement room. Everything I saw was from table height and from one spot."

"And whatever I heard," Juanita added, "like the woman's voice, and him breaking a whiskey bottle—was like I was listening underwater. You know how the sound is muffled when you clunk two rocks together at the bottom of a swimming pool? That's what it sounded like."

"So," Maggie said, "you're saying it was physical contact with that chair that connected you to that basement room?"

The twins nodded.

"I wonder," Maggie went on. "If you hadn't been touching that chair—which, I assume, originally came from that basement room—would you have still made the connection to the scene?"

Charlie seemed to sense where she was going with this. "I think Maggie is saying it's not only about clairaudience and clairvoyance. There's something here about locating, too. You saw and heard the crime, yes—but you didn't know where it was happening. That's different from connecting the chair to the basement room it used to be in. It's more like using an apple branch to find water. That's not remote viewing or remote hearing. It's like a form of dowsing, locating."

"But I saw what was going on in the room," Juan said.

"And I heard it," his sister said.

"I know, I know," Charlie said. "I'm just saying, maybe one of you has a gift for seeing, the other for hearing, but together you've got a very different third gift—like Bando's suggesting."

"Let's get back to the story," Caroline said. "I'd like to hear the rest of it."

"Well," Juanita said, "the cops busted in and rescued the woman. And when they did, they found a goldfish in a bowl on the side table."

"A goldfish?" Mo said. "So?"

"The goldfish had the vantage point Juan saw from."

"Which would explain why everything you heard sounded like you were underwater!" Caroline blurted.

"You're saying you two saw and heard through a fish?" Mo asked.

The others stared at him, stunned not only by his conclusion, but by the fact that he'd reached it so quickly.

"Sounds crazy, I know," said Juan. "But that's what happened."

"No joke?" Mo said.

"No joke," Bando said, suddenly appearing as if he'd materialized from a puff of smoke. "A Connecticut writer changed Juan and Juanita's names when he wrote about the case. The story was called 'The Chair' in book of weird tales for kids called Wicked Odd. Twait happened across it and sensed it was fact disguised as fiction. We tracked down the author, got the true names, and invited the twins to Free Camp."

Rose appeared in the kitchen doorway. "Plates to the plastic tubs, campers. Last call for desserts. Five minutes and I'm putting stuff away."

The office phone rang, and a moment later Twait appeared in the office doorway, calling out, "Bando! Phone. You'll want to take this one. State Police!"

CHAPTER 10

"YOUR DRIVER'S OKAY," said a deep voice on the other end of the phone. "We found him tied up in a clump of trees behind the parking lot."

Bando resisted the urge to fidget.

"He's not hurt," the deep voice continued. "Just shaken up. And worried about the kids he was picking up."

"Jerry's okay," Bando relayed to Twait at the office door.

"Rose, Jerry's okay," Twait repeated into the kitchen.

"No sign of the kids yet?" Bando asked into the phone. "Five campers and their parents were meeting Jerry in that parking lot. We always use that spot as a drop-off spot for Free Camp."

"No sign of the van or the kids," the officer said. "We'll need those names, sir—children and contact persons. Hopefully the parents can give us a description of the person who took them."

There was a momentary commotion on the other end, then the officer said, "Hold on a sec, sir. Your man wants to speak with you."

"Bando?"

"Jerry?"

"Bando, I'm sorry. I'm so, so sorry." Jerry began to cry at the other end of the line.

"I know, Jerry, I know you're sorry. What happened? Tell me."

Twait moved closer and climbed onto a chair, then onto the desk, where he sat with his stubby legs hanging over. He leaned into the receiver next to Bando's ear, straining to hear. Bando turned the phone Twait's way.

"Jerry, Twait's on the line too."

"Twait," Jerry said. "Did you pick up my kids with your van? Tell me you did. Please." He knew Twait hadn't, but he couldn't help hoping.

"No, I didn't—only my five. They were there waiting with their parents."

Jerry made a pained sound. It took him a moment to compose himself.

"Jerry," Bando said. "Start at the beginning."

First a long pause, then Jerry drawing in a deep breath. Bando and Twait waited.

"Well, like always, I got there a half hour early—around eight. I parked by the back edge of the lot near those trees. Not another car in sight. I was drinking my coffee, listening to the radio, when this head pops up by my window and yells BOO! Scared the crap out of me. I spilled the coffee on my lap. I say, 'What's your problem, pal?' when he jams this enormous gun in my face. He looks like an alien. Takes me a second to figure out he's wearing a gas mask. He tells me, 'Get out of the van.' And I can tell by the sound of his voice—and that huge pistol—that he's dead serious. So I step out. And that's when I see he's wearing one of those sand-color camouflage uniforms like they used in Iraq. Since it's just me, and the kids haven't arrived yet, I tell him the keys are in the ignition and it's got a full tank of gas—just take it. I'm praying he just wants the van, but I'm scared to death he wants to hurt me."

Bando and Twait heard the terror in their friend's voice.

"But then . . . then . . . he . . . he marches me into the woods and makes me lie on the ground." Jerry began to sob harder. "I was sure he was going to kill me."

"Jerry, you're okay," Bando said soothingly. "Jerry, he didn't kill you. You're okay."

"He duct-taped my wrists behind me and taped my ankles together. He put tape over my mouth and my eyes. I was so scared. I thought I was going to die, that he was going to kill me. There was nothing I could do."

Twait balled his hand into a fist. He gnawed the knuckle of his index finger.

"Did he make any demands, ask any questions?" Bando asked.

"No. Other than BOO, he never said a word. Just pushed and pointed with that big pistol. I was terrified and he knew it. After he tied me up, he ran more tape between my ankles and wrists and taped me to a couple of low bushes so I couldn't crawl out of the woods."

"Do you know if he hung around, or did he leave right away?" Bando pressed. "Think, Jerry. Do you remember seeing his vehicle anywhere nearby, maybe parked in the woods or up the road? Was he alone? Was there anybody besides the one man?"

"That's all I know," Jerry said. "He left me there and he didn't hurt me, and then after a couple hours, the police found me lying there. The EMTs say I'm okay, but they're worried about shock and want me to go to the hospital. And—" Jerry's speech was faster now, hyper-animated.

"Jerry, checking you for shock is a good idea," Bando said softly but firmly. "We can get by without you here. No hurry. You've been through quite an ordeal, and you need to work through it. I'm sure the police will have more questions. You rest up for now and we'll talk again tomorrow."

"But where's the van? And the kids?"

"We're all working on that. I'm sure they're fine. Can you put the officer back on the line now?"

Twait heard the phone changing hands on the other end of the line and hopped down from the desk. He pointed toward the kitchen and mouthed to Bando, "I'll tell Rose," then disappeared through the door.

"Sir?" the deep voice said. "You still there?"

"I am," Bando answered.

"Let me get this straight. Your camp had two vans deployed to pick up campers—one early, the second two hours later. Jerry was driving the first and was due to pick up five children. The later van, with your man Twait, was also scheduled to meet and transport five additional children to camp. The second van and its five passengers arrived safely at your camp, where you have them now. The first van—Jerry's—still has not arrived. Is that correct?"

"Yes, that's correct."

"We've got a description of the van from Jerry, but would appreciate your describing it, too, and license plate numbers. We also need the names of the children who were waiting for the first van, and their parents' or guardians' names and contact information. We have to notify them that their children may have been abducted. They should be able to provide us with a description of the man they handed their children over to. Time is of the essence. We need to get the word out."

"I doubt he kept the gas mask on once he tied Jerry up. My hunch is, he put on sunglasses to meet the parents, though, so they wouldn't be able to easily identify him."

"The parents may also be able to tell us if there was an accomplice. We aren't sure he acted alone. If he left the meeting place in the van, where did his own vehicle go? He had to have gotten to the parking lot somehow. We'll be checking the area."

"Good point," Bando said. "Can you check the duct tape for fingerprints?"

"We're doing that. Rest assured, we've done this sort of thing before and know what we're doing." When Bando didn't answer, the officer said, "Sir, I know this is hard. We'll do everything we can to get them back safely."

"I know you will, and thank you." Bando took a deep breath. "If you can hold a moment, I'll give you that information."

"Great. We'll have a couple of our people at your camp soon. They'll have more questions for you and the staff. Oh, and one more thing. Sir?"

Bando had sensed the question was coming. Both he and the officer knew this couldn't possibly be a random, spur-of-the-moment carjacking, nor could the abduction of five teens be an unplanned consequence. This was thought-out beforehand, planned and well executed. The man in fatigues hadn't wanted just any vehicle; he had wanted a Free Camp van. So he set it up in a way that he could get the children who came with it. He had posed as a driver so the parents wouldn't suspect, had gotten them to entrust their precious children to him, and kidnapped them.

Several questions formed in Bando's mind. Did this man want any Free Camp van, or was he aiming for the early van? Was he after a certain child? Could he be a separated or divorced parent who had lost a custody case? If so, why take the entire group of five? And why risk being recognized by the targeted child's other parent at the drop-off point? If any Free Camp van was acceptable, what could be the motive? But there was also a more basic question: If the kidnapper wasn't a disgruntled parent with access to his child's schedule, how did this man in the gas mask learn the pickup times and the meeting spot?

"Here's the question that's got me wondering, sir," the officer said. "Is there anyone you can think of who might hold a grudge against you, the camp, or another staff member?"

Bando could hear Rose sobbing softly in the kitchen. Was it tears of relief that Jerry was okay or tears of worry for the five campers who hadn't gotten to Free Camp? "Nobody comes to mind right off. But my staff and I will talk about it. You can bet we're going to think hard on that question." He said goodbye and hung up the phone. His mind was already turning over stones.

CHAPTER 11

WHILE MAGGIE AND JUANITA made themselves at home in the girls' cabin, the boys settled into theirs.

"Alright, you guys, now it's your turn," Juan said, straddling a backwards chair. He sat with his chin on his palm, trying to look thoughtful. "Spill it."

Mo glanced up blankly from a bottom bunk. Charlie lay with his eyes closed on another bottom bunk.

"Don't pretend you're asleep over there, Charlie," Juan said. "You and Mo know what I'm talking about. I see things out in the Twilight Zone and Juanita hears things there. Maggie bends spoons. What do you two do?"

Charlie's eyes remained shut. He and Mo were playing the waiting game.

"Well," Mo finally said, a playful look in his eye and the corners of his mouth curling into a smile. "Obviously I can scare myself silly so my hair stands straight up." He laughed at his own joke.

Charlie snickered but kept his eyes shut.

"Oh, ha ha," Juan said, annoyed. "Come on, you guys, fair is fair." He reached for his backpack and withdrew a package of M&Ms. He waved it slowly, teasing. "Come on, Mo. You know you want some of these."

Without opening his eyes, Charlie said, "He'd rather have the Milky Way in the side zipper pocket."

Juan's eyes grew wide. "How'd you know about that?"

Charlie ignored the question, saying instead, "And if you're going to bribe me, I'll take that navel orange in the smaller bag by your pillow."

"How the—?" Juan sputtered. "Did you go through my bags?"

Mo appeared puzzled. "What's going on, you two?"

"You know very well I haven't been near those bags." Charlie opened his eyes and sat up. "Show him what's in them, Juan. Go ahead. Let Mo see what you've got there."

Juan set the M&Ms on the table and reached into the backpack again. Like a magician pulling a rabbit from a top hat, he brought out a chocolate bar. "Just for your information, it's a Snickers, not a Milky Way."

Mo's mouth fell open. Then he recovered and said, "Snickers is fine. I actually prefer it to Milky Way."

Charlie turned and sat up on the edge of his bed. "Juan, shall I get the orange myself or would you prefer to do the honors? After all, it is your bag and your orange. And, with my hands, zippers are difficult, and an orange"—he moved one of his shriveled hands like a lobster claw—"is hard to peel. I hate to admit it, but there are some things I can use help with."

Juan reached for his smaller bag and pulled out the orange. "It's not an orange, wise guy. It's a tangerine." The two of them glared at each other.

Mo finally broke the silence. "Cool! How'd you do it? X-ray vision? Can you see through women's clothes?"

Juan and Charlie couldn't hold their serious looks in the face of Mo's goofiness. They laughed, stopping only when Mo raised the question again.

"Seriously, how'd you do it? It's got to be x-ray vision like Superman, right? Or is it ESP? Can you read minds?"

"I dreamed it. I have dreams that sometimes come true. They're not always accurate—like Milky Way instead of Snickers, orange instead of tangerine. I think my mind tries too hard to fill in the blanks, or maybe

I just misremember some of the details. That seems to be where the mistakes come from."

"Yeah, but still," Mo said, "it's pretty awesome. Maybe you could, like, win the lottery. Or see exam questions ahead of time."

"Doesn't work that way. It's kind of like Juan's remote vision. I can't pick and choose what I see. It just happens."

Juan moved his chair a little closer. "So you just dreamed the Milky Way and the orange now, when you had your eyes closed?"

"No. I wasn't asleep. I was just avoiding your questions. I had the dream back at home last night. But either it didn't seem important then, or when I woke up I kind of forgot about it."

"But you remembered it just now," Juan reminded him.

"I know. It's weird that way. Seems to be a twist on what they call precognitive dreaming. That's when someone dreams an event before it occurs, and then later it happens."

"Sounds like a fortune teller to me," Mo said. "Like one of those crystal ball gazers."

"Mine's different. With classic precognitive dreaming, the dreamer knows what's going to happen long beforehand. You dream it, you tell it, it happens. With me, though, I don't usually remember the dream until later—just as it's about to happen."

"So it's more like déjà vu and I feel I've already been through something?" Mo asked.

"Similar. But déjà vu is fairly common for many people. Mine is—well, first I dream it, but I don't experience it. If I can recall it, I have no doubt it's a dream. With some of these, though, after I dream them—like the Snickers and the tangerine—they happen, or some variation of them happens, in real life. The dream turns out to be reality. The difference between my dreaming and your déjà vu is, I get the sense I've dreamed it and I recognize it's coming true—but not until it's just about to happen. If you had asked me at lunch about the Snickers and the orange, I couldn't have told you a thing—not about how each of you looked, or the cabin, or the stuff in the backpack. But a minute ago, just before it happened, I knew. I knew just in time to tell you what was there. You two have had déjà vu experiences, haven't you?"

Juan and Mo nodded.

"You know how it feels when you can't get ahead of a déjà vu experience, can't quite predict even a second or two beforehand what's going to occur?"

"It's frustrating," Juan said. "I don't know it until after it's happened. But then something tells me it's a duplicated experience, and I can't put my finger on the truth."

"Yeah. Well, with me, I dream it first, then recognize it just before it occurs. Last night I had the dream about us and the Milky Way and the orange. I immediately recalled it when I awoke, but then I forgot it like I do with my regular dreams. But then a minute ago, just as you pulled out those M&Ms, I re-recalled it."

"But your eyes were closed when I pulled out the M&Ms," Juan said. "Which means you didn't see with your eyes. You somehow knew, but your eyesight didn't provide the trigger."

"Hmm, you're right," Charlie said. "That totally hadn't occurred to me. So it wasn't my seeing you reach into the backpack that brought it up. It must have been your action itself—whether I saw it or not—that triggered the memory of the dream."

Mo shook his head. "Hey man, I don't understand it. But it works, and it's really cool."

"Yeah," Juan said with a grin and a thumbs-up. "Déjà vu with an attitude."

"So, Houdini," Mo said. "What's Rose got in mind for dinner?"

"For you—liver," Charlie shot back without missing a beat. "She heard it's a Mohawk favorite."

"Yeah, right," Mo said. He stuck a finger into his mouth and pretended to gag. "In your dreams."

They laughed.

Suddenly the M&Ms bag made a crinkling sound where Juan had laid it. It sat up on its own, rose several inches off the table, hovered in the air briefly, then slowly made its way across the room to Mo's open palm.

"I'll trade you, Juan," Mo said, the goofy grin on his face again. "These M&Ms for that Snickers."

"It was you!" Juan exclaimed. "The bottle opener in the van. You're the one who moved it!"

Mo's eyes half closed and he flashed a sly smile. "Levitation—guaranteed to get a rise out of your friends." He raised an eyebrow and wiggled it the way a dastardly cartoon villain might. "For my next trick, I'll make an M&M disappear." True to his word, he picked one up and popped it in his mouth, then wiggled the eyebrow again, saying, "Ta-daaah!"

CHAPTER 12

DONNIE TWITCHED AND STRUGGLED in the recliner as if he'd been lashed to it. His face contorted, his chest heaved, and he gasped open-mouthed like a fish in a bucket with nothing to breathe. He tried to scream but his vocal cords produced no sound, no voice. His body convulsed as if he were strapped to an electric chair. It took every ounce of will for him to pry his eyes open and force himself awake. As he did, it was like surfacing from the ocean floor into open air—heart pounding, lungs greedily sucking down air. His hair, tee shirt, underwear, and even his cargo shorts, all felt awash in sweat. He sat up in the recliner, grabbed the warm Budweiser from the lamp table and put it to his lips, quickly draining what was left. He set the empty bottle down and shuddered.

The nightmare had been even more intense this time and, as usual lately, he wasn't sure if he was lucky or unlucky to have broken free of its spell. He lit a Marlboro from the pack on the table and walked to the refrigerator for a fresh beer.

Part of him—the broken part—wanted to die, to have the pain and grief and suffering over with. But another part, the tiny ember that had become a hot coal searing the base of his brain about where a pony-tail might form—Satan's tail, he thought— still raged and burned. That part—where a person's most unhealable memories reside—still remembered vividly the State Police knocking at the door to say Karen and Addie had drowned in the treacherous whirlpool under the waterfall.

A little girl had fallen in, they said, a camper who had slipped on the slippery stones at the edge of the pool. And Addie, always the hero at school and camp, had jumped in to save her. Both victim and would-be rescuer had been sucked into the frothing, churning swirl. Karen, the only adult volunteer and a strong swimmer with lifeguard training, had leaped in after the two girls. With a surge of adrenalin, she had miraculously thrown the first girl out of the whirlpool's grip, and the other campers had managed to drag her to shore. But Karen couldn't free herself or Addie. The pressure pinned them there, smashed and lifeless, for six hours until a police dive team finally freed them.

Donnie glanced up at the brown-eyed pup on the shelf. Next to it was his favorite photo of Addie, taken in fourth grade. She was standing on a stone wall, him on the ground in front of her, her arm around his shoulder. It had been a family trip to Vermont—the Shelburne Museum, where they'd seen the old Lake Champlain steamboat Ticonderoga and the life-sized, hand-carved, circus parade. Karen had clicked the shot with a disposable camera from the museum gift shop. Addie had on jeans and a peach-colored shirt, her hair in pigtails. He and Addie grinned with eyes half-closed against the bright sun. But what had Karen been wearing? He cursed himself for not being able to remember. But then, why should he? She was behind the camera, not in the picture. Still, he wished now he'd been paying closer attention. He touched the glass of the picture frame tenderly, then turned and gazed out the screen door.

The place had gone to hell in a hand basket the last five years. The lawnmower sat in the yard with grass high around it. The rusty Rototiller had been abandoned behind the tool shed, the blue plastic tarp that covered it now in tatters. It practically begged to be used the way he and Karen had when they first got together, raising first a garden, then the kids. But first came little Adam's crib death, and then Addie's death at that cursed camp.

He spotted the black cat near the edge of the high grass. It was creeping forward on its belly, stalking a baby bird that flopped helplessly in a rut in the driveway. It wasn't far from the apple tree Karen had planted in the side yard, where they'd seen a nest most years.

Suddenly it occurred to him the cat should still be in the milk box. He'd dropped it in there and placed the brick on the lid. He pushed open the screen door and stared down at the box. The brick lay on the ground. Had the cat gotten help from some unknown ally—another cat perhaps—or had it found the strength and leverage to lift the lid by itself? The open milk box conjured an image of the concrete block prison in the woods.

"Damn!" he swore. And from the corner of his eye he saw the cat pounce on the baby bird. "Damn! Damn! Damn!"

Five minutes later a bald man in fatigues fired up the pickup and roared down the driveway, barely missing the black cat as it bit down on the neck of its prey.

CHAPTER 13

BANDO'S PLAN TO MEET WITH THE KIDS at 3 p.m. hit a snag. He'd barely assembled them in the dining hall and filled them in about Free Camp #1 being carjacked when two police cars drove up and parked in front of the building. They needed to question Bando, Twait, and Rose, which meant Caroline was left with the job of entertaining the five campers. She decided to take them up the north trail to the waterfall.

"My cousin Atlanta is in that van," Mo protested to Twait as the group prepared to hit the trail. "I should call my aunt and my mother."

"The police are notifying the kids' parents," Twait said. "Once the police clear out, we'll give you all a chance to phone your own parents."

"But I'm worried about Atlanta. Why would anybody take her and those other kids?"

"Maybe it was just bad luck," Charlie said. "They happened to be in the early van, and the guy wanted to get it over with. Maybe if it had been us in that van, he'd have gotten us."

"Yeah, well, he'd have had his hands full," Mo said.

"Who says he doesn't with them?" Caroline asked. "You ever read 'The Ransom of Red Chief'? It's a story about a kid who drove his kidnappers crazy."

"I did," Charlie said. "It was funny." Only he and Caroline recognized the story.

"Let's get going," Caroline said. "We want to get to the waterfall and back before supper. If we don't move it, it'll be mosquito city on the way back."

The six of them set out on the trail. Except for their attention shifting to a doe and her fawn beside the path five minutes out, the kids' minds didn't relax much. It was hard not to think about their counterparts in Free Camp #1. Right now they didn't know if the others were dead or alive.

"If you hadn't made us leave our cell phones at home," Mo complained, "we'd be able to—"

"Hey, wait a minute, buster, I'm not camp management," Caroline scolded.

"Yeah, well," Mo blustered, "if camp management hadn't made us leave our cell phones home, we wouldn't be waiting to use some dumb old office phone. We'd be calling our parents right now."

"And maybe one of those kids could have dialed 9-1-1," Maggie added.

"Yeah," Mo said emphatically, prepared to keep up his tirade.

But Charlie held up a twisted hand. "Wait. What you just said."

"What?" Mo asked. "What did I say?"

"Not you, Mo—what Maggie said. Think about it. She said those other kids could have called 9-1-1 if they'd been allowed to have their cell phones. I don't know if this guy knew or didn't know campers couldn't bring them along. But it made me think—he's got inside knowledge of the camp."

"He must have," Juan said. "Otherwise he'd have never risked carjacking the van."

"It's not a carjacking," Charlie said. "It's a kidnapping. If he'd wanted just the van, he'd have taken it. I mean, once he got Jerry out of the van, he could easily have stolen it."

"But Bando said the guy tied Jerry up," Maggie said. "Which suggests he didn't want to hurt him; he just didn't want him squealing, at least not right away."

"He needed Jerry out of the way so he could wait for the parents to show up with their kids," Juanita said. "He wanted the kids, not the van.

And whether he knew the cell phone rule or not, the first thing he must have done is take them away—so they couldn't sound the alarm. Which means this was all planned ahead of time."

"By somebody who knew the van pickup time," Caroline said.

No one said anything for a while, until Mo broke the silence. "Will he come after us, too, or did he just want them?"

Nobody had an answer for that one. Not even the waterfall ahead, lovely and exciting as it might be, would be adequate to clear the fears and worries out of their young minds.

***

Back at the dining hall the police searched the camp files for clues. Perhaps the bald man was a disgruntled employee from the past? Rose asked the officer in charge if they'd considered a camper's separated or divorced parent as the suspect. The officer assured her they were already looking into that. Twait asked if Jerry had been able to give them a description or help with a sketch. They said they were working on it.

"Wherever these parents live—and we understand they're from different states," a policewoman said, "we're getting cooperation from local law enforcement in notifying them. They'll assign sketch artists. Sounds like all those parents saw the man they thought was your camp driver, so we should have a composite in the next couple of hours."

"Any other ideas on your part?" the officer in charge asked. "If it's not someone with a beef against the camp, then how about a person with a grudge against one of you personally?"

"This is only our third year running it as Free Camp," Bando explained. "For decades it was Camp Matawandi. It shut down five years ago and sat idle for two."

"Why'd it shut down?" the policewoman asked.

"A couple of people drowned," Rose said. "Not on the waterfront where the swimming beach is. It happened up at the waterfall."

CHAPTER 14

"IT'S JUST NOT WORKING," Mouse said after trying for fifteen minutes, any earlier optimism gone from his voice now. "The deadbolt must be more than just a steel bar. Maybe it's got a grip, a handle on it so you can roll it downward and into a slot." He and Atlanta sat down. "Sorry, everybody," he continued. "It was worth a try, but it didn't work. What else have we got?"

Besides being sweaty and famished, the group's hope was waning.

"Maybe it really is a test," BJ said, "only it's not about us getting out, it's about endurance."

"Yeah, maybe!" Celine scoffed. "But I don't think I want to bet my life on it. Do you really believe that guy was from the camp? What if he never comes back? Or, worse yet, what if he does? We need to keep trying."

"Wait," BJ's quiet voice said, and the others hushed. "We have the best chance over here by this corner, fifth block up from the floor."

"Is the block loose?" Mouse asked.

"No," was all BJ said.

Everyone waited for more.

"I was just over there," Tim said. "I've been over these walls three times and I didn't feel anything."

"Come over here with your knife, Mouse," BJ said. "You too, Tim, bring that little penknife. There's room for each of you to work a side of the block. It's not loose—not yet. But it's weak in places. Trust me, I can sense it. The mortar on the inside of this block is still in good shape, but the mortar on the outside of the wall is crumbling. My uncle's a mason. I know a little about it. Mortar is the glue that holds the cement blocks in this wall together. And mortar is actually a mixture—one part of cement to a couple of parts sand. You mix it up and add water. But if there's too much sand in the mixture, or if it didn't get mixed well enough, or if it was too dry—the mortar starts to fall apart. Down here by me is where the inside mortar is still strong but the stuff on the outside of the building is weaker, starting to crumble." BJ's voice was small, but she spoke with quiet authority. Nobody challenged her assessment.

Mouse and Tim felt their way along until they bumped into her. She guided their hands to where she wanted them to scrape.

"Celine," BJ said, backing out of the corner. "Can you squeeze in here too? You had that big belt buckle, didn't you? It'd be perfect for scraping the mortar at the bottom of the block they're working on. We've got to hurry. The air is getting thin and that crack under the door is too tight for enough fresh air to get in. Pretty soon we'll be breathing in more carbon dioxide than oxygen."

"We're not just running out of air," Tim added. "We're running out of time. Our guy thought we couldn't get out, but something just made him think maybe we can. He was calm, then sad, then angry, and now he's feeling really nervous. I can feel it. He's on his way back."

Celine removed her belt buckle and started scraping as Mouse and Tim, working the sides and top of the block, speeded up.

CHAPTER 15

THEY HEARD ITS MAGNIFICENT ROAR before they rounded the final bend, but even then they weren't prepared for what appeared before them. The waterfall left them speechless, open-mouthed with awe, as if they had come upon Jack's mythical beanstalk connecting earth and sky. The stream that fed it above plunged from the cliff and cascaded in a beautiful wet curtain for forty feet before it crashed thunderously into the bedrock pool it had pounded and carved out below. Even at a distance, its misty spray cooled their sweaty faces.

Finally they found their voices.

"Awesome!"

"Wow!"

"My God!"

"Incredible!"

"Look how high it is!"

"Listen to that!"

"Feel it?"

They stood close to one another, as if this were too powerful an experience to take in alone. It had to be shared.

When the falling water struck the scoured-out basin, it transformed the pool into a swirling, sucking whirlpool. Able to contain only so much water, the catch pool sloughed off the excess by expanding itself to make a broader, deceptively quieter pool. The overflow continued downhill, creating the stream that supplied the camp lake and waterfront.

Maggie and Caroline followed the trail to the right of the pond. Juan hung close behind.

Mo and Juanita clambered onto a fallen tree-trunk that bridged the lower stream. Someone had strung two thick ropes beside it for handrails.

Charlie stayed by the trunk bridge but didn't climb on.

"Come on!" Mo yelled halfway across. "It's like a Ropes Course! There's another path on the other side."

Two steps behind Mo, Juanita called back, "Yeah, Charlie, come on, try it. The log's safe."

Charlie drew his hands from his sweatshirt and held them up, clicking the thumbs against the connected fingers like castanets. "These babies aren't so great on ropes, guys. Not a very strong grip, thanks." He turned toward the other group.

"Mo, Juanita, remember what I told you," Caroline yelled. "Stay behind the wooden railings on the other side! Camp rules!"

Mo let go of the rope with his left hand so he could flash Caroline a quick OK sign. While his hand was off the rope, he faked losing his balance, but when he saw that neither Juanita nor Caroline was buying it, he gripped it again. He and Juanita wobbled the rest of the way across.

Two granite benches sat fifteen feet back from the waterfall. Maggie and Caroline sat on one, Juan on the other. A minute later Charlie caught up and joined Juan.

"Expensive benches," Maggie said. "My brother's high school class raised the money for one after a classmate was killed by a drunken driver. Who put these here?"

"They're in memory of a woman and her daughter who drowned here about five years ago. It was before Bando and my Dad took over the camp. That's why you see those railings and warning signs everywhere. The ones who drowned were trying to rescue a little girl who fell in."

"And they all drowned?" Maggie asked. "That's so sad."

"They didn't all drown—just the mother and daughter. The mother somehow got the first girl out. But the Mixmaster pinned her and her daughter against the rock."

"The Mixmaster?" Maggie asked.

Caroline pointed to the whirlpool. "It's like one of those carnival rides—the Cup and Saucer or the Tilt-a-Whirl. It spins around and the force presses you back so hard, you can't get loose. They say the divers had a heck of a time freeing the bodies. It took hours."

Maggie could picture the lifeless mother and daughter pinned against the rock by the swirling waters. She shivered. "Let's get back to the camp. This spray is cold."

She and Caroline got to their feet. Charlie rose too. But Juan sat as if glued to the bench, head down, eyes shut.

"Juan, you okay?" Charlie said.

"I'm seeing something. Get Juanita. Hurry."

Caroline yelled to Mo and Juanita on the other side of the whirlpool.

"What are you seeing?" Charlie said. "Describe it."

"I'm in a small room—a living room, I think. But I can see a kitchen table and chairs. It's like the rooms are part of the one room, like one of those really small apartments."

"An efficiency?"

"I guess. I see the sink and the window above it. To the right is the refrigerator. To the left is the stove. In the living room there's a man asleep in a recliner. He's got shorts and a tee shirt on. His hair is dark with a little gray. Heavy boots on the floor next to the chair. Beer bottle on the little table. Snoring loud. Wait, he's dreaming, I think. He's twitching now."

Caroline could see Juanita and Mo hopping onto the tree-trunk bridge. She waved for them to hurry.

"The guy is freaking out, like he's having one heck of a nightmare, maybe a seizure."

Juanita saw that both Maggie and Caroline were motioning for her to hurry, so she tried to move faster across the log. Mo tried to keep up.

"He's trying to scream. But he can't. His mouth is opening and closing. He's sweating. His body is jumping up and down in the recliner."

Juanita reached the middle of the log.

"He shook himself awake. He's drinking the rest of that beer. He's up, going to the refrigerator."

Juanita slipped. Maggie saw her let go of the rope with one hand as her legs flew out from under her. With only the other hand on the rope, she bumped the middle of her back hard on the trunk-bridge, so that hand too let go. Before Mo could react, she was in the stream. The fall caught Mo totally off guard. He tried to reach her from the bridge, but he couldn't.

Juanita flailed her arms in the rushing stream, choking as water filled her mouth.

Charlie sprang to his feet and sprinted across the clearing in seconds. With one deformed hand he clamped onto a tree root at the top of the stream bank, and with the other he stretched for the gasping girl. Without actually seeing it, her hand grabbed his wrist and held on. He pulled. Despite the excruciating pain in the thumb and fingers gripping the root, he held on, drawing Juanita out of the fast-moving waters toward himself.

The others helped drag her onto dry land, then they pulled Charlie up.

Mo stood dumbstruck on the trunk-bridge, shaking and embarrassed.

"Are you all right?" Caroline asked Juanita, who lay on the trail trying to catch her breath.

"I'm fine." Then she glanced up at her brother, who had said nothing. "What is it? What did you see?"

Juan told her and Mo what he'd seen, and the others filled in what Juan forgot.

"Any sense who or what you were seeing through?" Juanita asked. "And why do you think you saw that particular man?"

"I don't know. I was seeing at about normal eye level, and I think I had my back against a wall. I figure the connection came through that bench when I sat on it."

"What did the man do after he went to the refrigerator?" Juanita asked.

"I don't know. He probably grabbed another beer. That's when you fell in."

"Sit on the bench again. We'll do it together. Maybe we can see and hear something. It could be important."

When they tried the bench this time, even though they held hands, neither twin made a connection. Even if they'd "seen" or "heard" the room in their unique ways, though, it would have been too late. While Charlie was pulling Juanita from the stream, the man had already discovered the open milk box, cursed, changed into uniform, packed his gun, and roared out his driveway.

CHAPTER 16

ATLANTA HAD TO LOOK REALLY CLOSE to make out the sliver of light at the foot of the door. "The sun must be almost behind us now. Daylight's fading."

The others heard both her words and her meaning. Their air supply and their time were running out. And once they lost that visual reference point, they wouldn't know if their eyes were open or closed, which would add to their sense of confusion.

"We've still got a couple of hours," BJ said. "Summer days are long. The sun just won't be at the right angle to hit the door." She pressed the button to light up her watch. "It's 5:10."

"You think the police are out searching for us yet?" Atlanta said.

In the corner, over the sounds of picking and scraping, Mouse said, "Of course they are. The camp must have reported us missing when the van didn't show up. That means the cops know and our parents know too. Half the state must be looking for us by now. And with us being from different states, they probably called in the FBI."

"Our parents must be going crazy," Atlanta said. The noise ceased and the others listened. "They should be able to locate the van, right? I mean, it's got the camp's name painted all over it. Shouldn't be hard to spot. And the police will make the driver tell where we are. Won't they?"

"Look," Mouse said. "This guy may be wacko, but he's smart. He planned this out. I don't think he's the regular van driver. He somehow got a set of keys or overpowered the regular driver. He wanted the pickup to look normal, usual—to fool our parents. He must know something about the camp, because he knew where and when to pick us up. He didn't just abduct us. He was prepared for us. You saw the way he had this building all camouflaged. He knew how to make us disappear. He made sure we didn't have cell phones. But if he really worked for the camp, he'd have known the acceptance letters—not the brochures—told us not to bring them. So he knows something about the camp—the van pickup schedule, anyway—but he's not fully an insider. With this so carefully planned and executed, I'll bet he made the van disappear too, and the police aren't going to find him cruising in it."

One of the girls made a sniffling sound in the dark.

"So what's this guy want with us?" BJ asked.

No one answered until Mouse said, "I have no idea."

"I don't know what he wants with us," Tim said. "But I know he doesn't want us to escape. He needs us for something."

The chipping and scraping started again in deadly earnest. No one had any idea how Tim knew what he knew, but something in the way he said the words rang true, and they knew they were in a race for their lives.

***

It was their captor's backup plan that bought them an extra hour.

En route to the blockhouse Donnie wheeled his pickup into the wood lot he'd logged recently. Several huge tie-down tarps covered the fifty cords of firewood he'd planned to sell in the fall. Three pallets of cement blocks sat off to the side of an area cleared for parking. The wood lot made a perfect drop spot for the lumber and concrete delivery trucks that hauled in the construction materials he needed for jobs.

In front of the pallets sat a wedge-shaped trailer designed to carry snowmobiles inside it. Most snowmobilers owned these trailers now, so there were fewer snow machines riding around jammed in the beds of pickups. The trailer's wedge design cut down the wind resistance on the road, and the trailer's canopy-top door opened like a car hood so the snowmobiles stayed dry and securely locked inside.

Once he unlocked and opened the trailer, it took a few minutes to get the first snowmobile out and park it. The second one, with its temperamental ignition, refused to start. When he tried to push it on its treads, it balked, and he had to hook a hand-winch between the machine and his truck bumper so he could inch it out. Finally, with both machines on the ground, he cleared the three snowmobile suits and three pairs of boots out of the trailer. He closed the top, locked it, and lined up the trailer tongue with his bumper hitch. Minutes later, with the mobile prison visible in his mirror, Donnie barreled north, eager to check his POWs.

The back of his head throbbed. The coal in his brain was heating up.

CHAPTER 17

"**B**UT THE ROOM JUAN SAW—how do we know it's connected to the missing van?" Maggie said.

She and the other four sat down in the dining hall to wait for dinner as Caroline disappeared into the kitchen.

"We don't know it's connected to the missing van," Charlie said. "But my hunch is, whatever Juan saw is tied to this camp—probably by way of those two granite benches. The inscriptions read: In loving memory of Karen, and: In loving memory of Addie—the two who drowned. We don't know their last names, but we can ask Twait."

"Twait's gone to meet with the police." The voice startled them despite its softness. Bando rose from a beanbag chair by the wall. He was so compact and quiet he'd blended into it like a chameleon on a branch. He'd only become visible now because he'd changed backgrounds.

"Most of the other group's parents are staying in Portland—in case the situation changes. After he talked with the police, Twait was going to spend some time with them."

"And?" Charlie asked. "Has anything changed?"

Bando pulled out a chair and sat down by them. "We have a composite sketch of the man who stole the van. Here are two versions."

They crowded around the drawings on the table. One was of a bald man with eyes hidden by wrap-around sunglasses. He looked like a bug. The other was exactly the same except a Desert Storm cap covered the bald head.

"Those are copies. You can keep them. I have more in the office. The police want to know if any of you recognize this man."

They shook their heads.

"They wanted you to see the sketches in case you already knew the man from the past. But they also want you to keep your eyes peeled in case you spot him near the camp."

Worried looks appeared.

"Don't worry. They've got round-the-clock surveillance on us. There's a State Police car on the road out front, by the end of the driveway."

Their faces didn't register assurance.

"Let's try another approach. How about feelings, impressions? You're all special. Does your gut tell you anything about the guy in the sketches? Go ahead, pass them around. Don't just look at them—feel them. Can you pick up any vibes?"

They passed the two sheets around, fingering them, pressing their hands on them. In the end they all shook their heads.

"Juan? Juanita? Anything?" Bando pressed.

Juan spoke slowly. "For me the problem is—and I'm not certain about this, but I'm pretty sure, and it may be true for my sister as well—the man in the sketches hasn't touched the paper. It's like a bloodhound sort of thing. Bloodhounds need a piece of material to get the physical scent."

Bando nodded thanks. "Charlie?"

Charlie wracked his memory. "Sorry. Nothing yet."

Bando got to his feet. "Okay. Rose and I will have supper on in about five minutes. Thanks for your help."

As Bando started for the kitchen door, Caroline stepped out and walked to the table to sit with the others.

"Wait a sec, Mr. Bando," Mo called, a hint of annoyance in his voice.

Bando stopped and turned. "You don't have to say mister, Mo—just Bando, remember? Now, what's your question?"

"Well, it's not a question. It's just—just—well, okay, it's this. Maggie and I may not have any weird psychic powers like the twins and Charlie— maybe we just do our little party tricks—but we've still got opinions. You could at least ask us what we think."

Bando walked back to the table. Then, without annoyance or judgment in his voice, he said, "Mo and Maggie, I'm truly sorry if I've offended you. I believe my first question—about picking up any vibes—was addressed to all five of you. However, you may have heard it differently than I intended. My apologies. I meant to invite you all to share your impressions. But you're correct, Mo, I did not invite you to share what you thought. I can see now how you and Maggie might feel excluded. I'm sorry."

Mo gave a little nod of acceptance.

Maggie rolled her eyes at Mo's dramatics.

"Okay, you've all seen and handled the sketches. Do any of you have thoughts?"

Mo didn't hesitate. "I do. I think we need to find out the last names of Karen and Addie, the ones on the waterfall benches."

"Why?" Bando asked.

"Because Juan may be right. What if his connection did come through the benches?"

Bando's eyebrows signaled his curiosity. "A connection to who and to what? To the van and the kids?"

"Well, I-I-," Mo stammered. "I guess we're not sure. But it's worth checking out, isn't it? I mean, we really should see where those last names lead us."

Caroline cut in. "I asked Mom. She doesn't know the names. The former camp owners took the files with them when we took over."

"You can make a couple of phone calls, though, right, Mr. Bando—I mean, just Bando?" Mo said eagerly. "If we have to, we can check newspaper articles. I'm sure the drownings made headlines back then."

Bando's eyes half closed, like a cat's, as he deliberated.

"Mo's right," Juanita said, and Mo's look of surprise made it clear that her support had caught him off guard. "Seriously, Bando. If Mo thinks it's worth following up, we should."

"I agree," Juan said.

"Yep," Maggie nodded.

"We owe it to those other kids," Charlie said. "One of them is Mo's cousin. How could he not check out any possibility?"

Bando scanned their faces. Their jaws were set. They were together.

"Okay. I'll call the previous owners and see what I can find out."

Bando disappeared into the office, and once he did, Juanita patted the back of Mo's hand and whispered, "Good job."

A couple of minutes later Rose emerged from the kitchen and announced that their first dinner at Free Camp was about to be served.

***

In the woods nearly an hour distant, a cement block thudded onto the hard ground outside a concrete blockhouse. Fresh air rushed in, filling the lungs of five hungry, thirsty, gasping prisoners.

CHAPTER 18

THE KNOCKED-OUT BLOCK left an opening eight inches high by sixteen inches wide—too tight for a full-grown adult to squeeze through. But for a scrawny teenager—with four friends acting like pallbearers sliding a casket into a hearse—there was a chance.

"Who's first?" Celine asked.

"Tim and BJ are the smallest," Mouse said. "First one out unbolts the door—unless it's padlocked. If it's locked, we'll all have to crawl out this way."

Atlanta said, "If we all have to squeeze through that hole, it'll get hard for the last one, because everybody will be on the outside pulling, nobody inside lifting and pushing."

"We'll worry about that when the time comes," Mouse said. "Who's going now—Tim or BJ?"

"I'll go," Tim said. "Let me stick my arms through. Then pick me up." He put his hands and head facedown into the hole while the others grabbed his hips and legs, preparing to load him like a cannon. Just as his head was going through, he called back under his armpit, "Oh, no! He's almost here. I feel him. He's agitated. Hurry!"

Tim's torso blocked the light and the room went black again.

"Shh!" BJ whispered. "Listen."

In the distance they heard a vehicle rattling over the woods road. The noise grew louder. It was moving faster than the van had. The driver was in a hurry. They pushed Tim harder, but he wouldn't go through the opening.

"I'm stuck. My belt buckle is hanging up on the block under me. Slide me back a little and pull my belt off."

"We'll never all get out in time," Celine said. "He's coming."

They eased Tim back a couple of inches, Mouse whipped the belt off, and they pressed him back into the hole.

"Okay, listen, all of you," Atlanta commanded. "Listen closely. I have a plan. He doesn't know the block is out. We need to buy Tim some time. Mouse, here's the slop bucket. When the guy opens the door, you kick it over at his feet to keep him by the door. BJ and Celine, you stand in front of the hole and block the light. Even an extra minute will help Tim. Tim, forget the deadbolt. You run for help."

Tim's legs disappeared out the hole as they heard a vehicle skid to a stop. Its engine sputtered and died, and a door creaked open and then slammed.

"One last thing," Atlanta whispered. "You'll have to trust me on this. Eventually he'll find the hole and see somebody's gone. Tell him I got out. Whatever you do, don't tell him I'm still in here. Let him think two of us got out. Remember, tell him I got out."

Before they could answer, the deadbolt clunked.

Atlanta moved toward the door before Mouse could put a foot against the bucket. BJ and Celine backed up against the hole. The room darkened.

Suddenly the door opened outward and light blinded them. A bulky silhouette filled the doorframe.

Mouse blinked, struggling to focus his eyes, and kicked over the bucket.

The man heard the metal pail hit the floor, then heard and smelled the gush of its contents spreading across the cement floor by his feet. He recognized immediately the minefield his adversaries had laid down between him and them.

"Why, you little—" he snarled, raising the .45 and aiming it at Mouse.

"Don't!" BJ cried, stepping up to shield Mouse.

Celine was only a split-second behind. "He didn't mean anything!"

Light shone through the hole, exposing Tim's escape route.

"What the—?" The man made a false start toward them, remembered what was underfoot, and stopped. He glanced around the room, not once but twice. "Where'd the other two go?"

No one answered.

He stared at the hole and then backed out into the doorframe. He yelled into the air. "You two kids better get back here right now, damn it. I know you're out there. If you don't come back now—right now—I'll have to shoot one of your friends, then another and another. Hear me? I'll shoot them. And you'll have that on your conscience! It's your choice. Here goes the first one."

He stepped back inside, aimed first at the three terrified teens, then re-aimed at the hole in the wall, and fired. The explosion was deafening. The children winced and turned away, cowering. A chunk of concrete disappeared out of the block Tim's belt buckle had been catching on.

The man stepped outside. "Okay, that was the first friend. Do I have to shoot them all?"

No answer.

"You're making me do this! I'll give you to the count of three." He stepped halfway inside again and called to the air behind him, "One."

No answer.

"Two."

"I'm here," said a tiny, quivering voice. "Don't shoot." Tim stepped around the corner of the building, one hand raised in surrender, the other holding up his beltless pants.

The man grabbed him by the shoulder and muscled him inside. "Get your butt back in here." He scanned the semi-darkness again. Four prisoners—three inside and one recaptured. Where was the fifth?

Tim made the same observation. He couldn't see Atlanta's body on the floor.

"He didn't shoot anybody, Tim," Mouse said. "He shot through the hole in the wall. We're all okay."

"Where's the other one?" the man grunted. "There was another girl." When nobody answered, he said it louder. "Where's the other one?" He waved the .45 for emphasis.

"She was the first one out," Tim said. "I went second. She's halfway to town by now."

The man didn't move, at a loss as to what to do next. Finally he said, "Well, you've been busy little beavers, haven't you?"

BJ saw her opening and, with a hand salute, said, "You said it was Day One of the challenge course, sir. Did you expect us to do nothing? Surely you've been a camp counselor long enough to know challenge-course kids better than that."

Her question caught him off guard. Did they really think this was part of a camp program?

"No matter. Let's go. Out of the sweatbox." He motioned them out the door with the .45. "I've got other transportation waiting here for you. Walk past the pickup to the trailer."

They filed out. He followed.

He grabbed the handle on the trailer's molded-plastic shell and lifted the canopy. It flipped up easily, exposing the empty interior of the snowmobile trailer.

"Everybody in!" he ordered.

As the jaws of the whale swallowed Jonah, the mouth of the snow-mobile trailer swallowed the four kids. They heard the click of the lock and the roar of the pickup's engine as it came to life. Once again they found themselves in the dark—hungry, thirsty, and scared—about to depart again for who-knew-where and Day Two of the challenge.

Back in the blockhouse, as the pickup and trailer started out of the clearing, Atlanta floated down from her hiding place above the doorframe. She peeked around the corner of the open door and began chanting numbers. Hovering against the ceiling for 10 minutes—a mere six inches above the man's head in the room's only remaining darkness—had physically and emotionally drained her. She'd tried not to move, but the blast of the .45 had made her wince and almost call out. She'd kept it together, though, and so had her new friends. Everyone had held to the plan, and because they had, there was hope of rescue. They all stuck with the story—the lie she'd needed for a distraction—and the bald man with the gun had checked the room, not once but twice, without looking up!

CHAPTER 19

"7-8-1-4-7-6," ATLANTA CHANTED. "7-8-1-4-7-6."

She scratched the numbers and the words *Maine license plate* in the dirt outside the blockhouse door. In case she forgot or later transposed them—or, God forbid, something happened to her—she wanted to make sure they were accurately recorded somewhere. If it didn't rain, maybe somebody would find them. She also printed her name, the date and time, and *bald man in uniform has a gun and took Mouse, BJ, Tim, Celine.* Then she stepped into the growing shadows and began to walk the overgrown woods road where the pickup and trailer had disappeared. "7-8-1-4-7-6. 7-8-1-4-7-6."

***

Meanwhile, Mo, Charlie, Maggie, and the twins gathered in the dining hall, waiting to use the office phone to call home. The second van hadn't arrived, and they couldn't wait any longer. The time had come to let their parents know what was going on.

Charlie, Maggie, and Juan talked by the water fountain.

Juanita sat on the tattered couch. Mo plopped down beside her. The middle cushion had little support under it and sagged badly, so that the two of them found themselves leaning toward the center of the couch and each other. When each reached out a steadying hand, Mo's fingertips grazed Juanita's. Her hand recoiled as if she'd been zapped by static electricity.

"Hey, do that again," she said.

Mo looked first confused, then sheepish. A grin appeared.

"Not that, silly." She shook her head. "Just give me your hand." She stuck hers out to him.

He took it.

"Be quiet," she said, closing her eyes. "I thought I heard someone."

Juan, Maggie, and Charlie saw something was going on, so they crossed the dining room to the couch.

"What is it?" Juan said.

Juanita held a finger to her lips to shush him. "7-8-1-4-7-6. 7-8-1-4-7-6. It's a girl's voice. 7-8-1-4-7-6. Write it down. Hurry. 7-8-1-4-7-6."

Charlie ran and flung open the office door. A moment later he returned with pen and paper, chanting the numbers Juanita had recited. "7-8-1-4-7-6." He handed the pen and paper to Maggie, who wrote them down.

Juan grabbed his sister's wrist with one hand and Mo's with the other. "An overgrown path," he said, his eyes closed. "Woods with vines and brambles growing in from both sides. Getting dark fast. Slowing down, either because of the darkness or maybe just being cautious. Looking down at a chain stretched between two trees, about waist high. Looks like a better dirt road ahead."

"She's still saying the numbers," Juanita said. "7-8-1-4-7-6. But she doesn't say what they mean."

"Who doesn't say what they mean?" Maggie asked.

"Whoever's talking."

"You think it's one of those kids?" Maggie said.

"My guess?" Charlie said. "She's hearing Mo's cousin Atlanta. Juanita tuned in by touching Mo, who's a blood relative. It's like Juanita and Juan tapping into the mental hospital because that office chair was physically connected to the place."

"If it is Atlanta," Mo said, "it sounds like she's lost in the woods."

"Look out!" Juan cried. "On the right!" He ducked to his left as if under attack.

"She screamed," Juanita said. "Now she's crying."

"The path and woods are blurring, spinning," Juan said. "I'm being spun around, pushed to the ground. It's black, not unconscious black, because I can see the black. More like someone pulled a bag over my head or is choking me."

"Screaming, crying, begging," Juanita said. "'Let me go, let me go.' A man's voice, 'Thought you could get away, eh?' Now her again. '7-8-1-4-7-6. 7-8-1-4-7-6.'"

"The connection's gone," Juan said. "Can't see."

"No sound."

"I think he hit her, knocked her out."

"To shut her up."

"I hope that's all he did. But maybe . . . ."

Juanita pulled a hand free and clamped it over her brother's mouth.

Mo's cheeks were wet with tears.

No one breathed for a minute.

Finally Maggie said, "We've got to tell Bando."

"Yes, we need to," Charlie said, leaning close into the circle. "But we can't let our parents know what's going on—not yet. If we do, they'll want to come for us tomorrow, maybe even tonight. We can't leave too soon. We're part of this. If they take us home, how can we help Mo's cousin and the others?"

They exchanged glances. Everyone nodded agreement.

"So here's the deal," Charlie said. "We tell Bando we made the calls. We say our parents are okay with us staying here, since there are police watching the place. Okay?"

"Won't Atlanta's parents call Mo's parents? They're cousins," Maggie said.

"Our families are hardly ever in touch," Mo said, drying his cheeks with his sleeve. "Her Dad and mine are brothers, but her father lives in Hawaii; she and her sister Georgia live with their Mom and stepfather in Vermont. I live in Worcester, Massachusetts. So the family connection is mostly between Atlanta and me. We write letters back and forth. Probably nobody except us even knew we were coming to the same camp."

"Okay," Charlie said. "Here's how I see it. Juan and Juanita have no choice but to tell Bando what they heard and saw, so Bando can call the cops, who may be able to figure out those numbers. But we can't tell our parents what's going on. We have to tell them we got here safe and are enjoying camp. But we leave it at that. For tonight all we can do is sit and wait—and try to get some sleep."

Everyone agreed the twins needed to tell Bando about their psychic experience. And they agreed to fudge the facts with their parents. But getting some sleep would take more than just agreement.

CHAPTER 20

THE PLASTIC SHELL THAT CLOSED over them not only cast them into darkness again, but cut them off from the world. The lull of tires on the road warped their sense of time. They were exhausted, and in this second prison—with their only hope, Atlanta, recaptured and thrown back among them unconscious—their spirits sank to a new low.

Like most snowmobile trailers, this one was vented to avoid temperature extremes that might damage the cargo, which meant that fresh air wasn't the problem it had been in the blockhouse—but water was. They'd had no liquids since breakfast and they were thirsty and dehydrated. Cool water could also help them revive Atlanta.

The trailer slowed and made a turn, bumping and jarring them. Dust thrown up by the truck's wheels seeped through the vents.

"Dust," Mouse said. "That means we're on another back road." He pressed a button to light his watch dial. "I'll time it so we know how long it is back to the main road." The others were too worn out and depressed to respond. Mouse's watch read 8:40 p.m. It was nearly dark out.

Ten minutes later they turned onto a still rougher road, perhaps an old logging trail. At 9:10, a half-hour from the blacktop road, they came to a stop.

The pickup door slammed. They waited for the plastic pod to open. It didn't. They heard whistling. It sounded like "Whistle While You

Work" from Snow White and the Seven Dwarfs. The whistling faded in the distance.

"Is he leaving us here?" Tim asked.

"Maybe he went into his house," Celine said.

Mouse rose to a hunched position and found the vent. He couldn't see out, but he listened. Tim felt his way to a spot beside him and listened too.

From the distance came the sound of—what was that, a creak?

"Sounded like a boiler room door," Tim said. "You know, like those iron hatches inside a ship."

"It was definitely metal," Mouse said.

The whistling started again and grew louder until it was outside the trailer. A key clicked in the lock and a moment later the canopy lifted on its spring hinges.

They blinked, eyes adjusting to the moonlit night. The bald man loomed over them, backlit by an almost full moon. He aimed the .45 their way.

"We need water and food," Celine croaked. "We haven't had anything all day."

The man said nothing.

"And our friend needs a doctor," BJ said. "She's hurt bad."

He waved the .45. They stepped out onto the ground on shaky legs, finding themselves in another clearing in the middle of woods. This one was smaller than the last, and in front of the truck—up on blocks—sat a small blue-green, older-model Shasta travel-trailer. A sloppily painted sign on its door read TRESPASSERS SHOT. To the right of it in a patch of weeds huddled a gray cement mixer. Not far from the mixer a huge bulldozer with peeling yellow paint rested on tank-tread haunches. On its front end was a huge bucket, and on the rear was attached a backhoe that resembled a giant robotic digging arm. The bald man had brought his captives to a construction site.

"This way," the man said, waving the gun.

"What about our friend?" asked BJ.

"Drag her—unless you want me to shut her inside the trailer. When the sun comes up, she'll broil in there. Your choice."

Mouse and Celine each took a side, looping Atlanta's arms around their necks. Her head lolled forward. They grunted, straining to lift her on her rubbery legs. BJ and Tim linked hands under her knees and lifted too.

"It's a miracle you didn't kill her," Celine said.

"Too early."

The man pulled a flashlight from his fatigues, snapped it on, and shone it on a path that was imprinted with the bulldozer's tread marks. A little farther along, the path opened into a sand quarry. Mountains of sand had been stockpiled in a half dozen mounds. A dump truck was parked in front of a small wooden shack. They marched out past the farthest pile.

"Stop here. Set the girl down."

They tried to prop Atlanta up against the base of the sand pile as if it were a beanbag chair. Her limp body slumped back on the sand, eyes still closed.

"Welcome to the Sandpit Motel, your home away from home—but only for a little while."

They looked around and saw no motel, only the sand quarry.

"Not here. Down there." He motioned to the ground with the .45. "You five have the basement room."

They looked. Practically flush with the surface of the ground was a hatch they hadn't noticed. It looked like something from an old war movie—like the opening submarine sailors disappeared into when the captain commanded, "Dive, dive, dive." The heavy steel door had been flung open. Here was the creaking sound Mouse and Tim had heard in the distance.

A few feet from the hatch a vent pipe jutted out of the sand like an upside-down letter J.

"Is it a well?" Celine asked.

"Air supply for the school bus. The motor was shot, so I buried it way down there in the sand—a cheap bomb shelter."

"Bomb shelter?" Mouse asked.

"Bomb shelter to some, motel to you, pal. Now all of you grab your girlfriend and get down that ladder." When they didn't move fast enough, he barked, "Now! Move! I haven't got all night. Some of us have to work tomorrow."

Ten minutes later the five found themselves underground—prisoners of the dark once again—but only for a half hour. That's when BJ felt her way around the inside of the buried school bus and discovered the candles, the matches, the bottles of water, the cans of food, and the First Aid kit. She lit two candles.

Shortly after that, Atlanta came to, imagining at first that they'd been rescued. But the others filled her in as they dressed and bandaged the cut on her head. She drank some water and ate a few forkfuls of canned spaghetti, then fell back asleep.

Around midnight the others, exhausted by the ordeals of the day, snuffed the candles and slept far below ground like the dead.

CHAPTER 21

"CHARLIE, CHARLIE, WAKE UP," Juan said, shaking him by the arm and shoulder.

Charlie's eyes opened slowly, a hard sleep to wake from. On the other bunk, Mo snored on.

"You were having a bad dream, yelling in your sleep."

Charlie blinked and rubbed his eyes with the backs of his hands, trying to get the glue and sleepers out. He sat up.

"What was it?" Juan asked.

"I was by the waterfall. Someone was caught in the whirlpool."

"Alive?"

"I don't know. I couldn't make out the face. It was behind the water, like when you're looking through frosted glass."

"Maybe you were picturing that girl and her mother who drowned there. We were just talking about it yesterday, and we were right there by the falls, sitting on their bench, so it would seem logical to work it into a dream. I'm surprised we aren't all dreaming it."

"I didn't see two outlines, just one."

"Well, my sister fell into the stream that comes out of the pool, remember? Maybe your dream combined the two incidents, Juanita's plus the mother and daughter's."

"I don't think that's it. I have a hunch this may be a future event."

"Why would you say that?"

"Because right now I can't recall any of the details."

Juan went back to his own bunk and pulled a spiral notebook and pen from under his pillow. He returned and sat by Charlie.

"What's that for?"

"Try writing it out."

Charlie looked puzzled.

"Write what you say you saw. While you do it, see if the rhythm of writing pulls out some of the background stuff you don't see right now. Do it fast. Dreams fade."

Charlie looked skeptical, but Juan wouldn't take no for an answer. He opened the notebook to a fresh page and handed it to Charlie with the pen.

"Speed-write. That way you don't give your mind time to make up a bunch of fake details. Squeeze out whatever's still in you from that dream. Hurry."

Charlie pinched the pen awkwardly between his thumb and the stuck-together nest of fingers. "I love to read, but I hate to write."

"No time for excuses. Write."

As Charlie wrote out his dream in the boys' cabin, Caroline sneaked across from the Assistant Director's house to the girls' cabin.

"I had to wait until Mom and Dad were asleep," she told Juanita and Maggie when they opened the door.

"So your Dad's back?" Maggie asked.

"Got back a couple hours ago, around ten. He, Mom, and I met for a while with Bando. Dad said the police have nothing new. They're putting most of the parents up at a hotel in Portland."

"Did the parents identify the guy?" Juanita asked. "Other than helping with the sketch, I mean. They must have picked him out of one of those books of police mug shots by now, right?"

"I guess not. Dad said all they've got so far is those two sketches."

"How about the last names of the two people from the waterfall benches?" Juanita asked. "Bando told us he'd check that out tonight."

"He did. He called Dottie, who cooked here before Mom, back when it was the old camp. The mother was Karen Beals. She was a volunteer counselor. Addie Beals was her daughter, and since her mother worked here, she got to attend camp for free. The granite memorial benches came from a Mr. and Mrs. Beals. Dottie didn't remember their first names, but she thought they still lived in Bridgton."

"I guess they'd be Karen's mother-in-law and father-in-law, if their name is Beals," Maggie said.

"I don't think so. Bando said Dotty referred to them as her parents."

"So Karen was an unmarried single mother," Maggie reasoned aloud. "Which means we're not dealing with an angry husband seeking revenge."

"But we still can't rule out the carjacker having a connection to the Beals family or the drownings," Caroline reminded.

Juanita changed the subject. "What did Bando say about the numbers? He was going to have the police check them out."

Caroline looked puzzled. "What numbers?"

"Oh, that's right, you weren't in the dining hall then. Well, I was sitting on the couch and accidentally touched Mo. When I did, I heard a girl's voice repeating a series of numbers. My brother saw what was happening, so he grabbed Mo's arm. And as soon as he did, Juan saw through the eyes of someone walking down a wooded road in the dark. He thinks it was the girl who was chanting the numbers. Somebody stopped her—like, grabbed her from behind—and maybe hit her in the head. Our best guess—since we were both touching Mo—is that the message was coming from his cousin Atlanta."

"I was in the kitchen with Mom about that time. This is the first I'm hearing about it."

Juanita filled her in and recited the numbers.

"Bando didn't mention the numbers tonight," Caroline said, "at least not while I was there. But, don't worry. I'm sure he told the police. Don't let his calm exterior fool you. He's worried about those kids too. If he said he'd call the numbers in, he did."

"I hope so," Maggie said. "If it's a license plate, maybe it'll lead them to that bald guy, and they can nail him right now, tonight and . . ."

"They can find them," Juanita finished in a prayer-like whisper, then softly added, "safe and sound."

CHAPTER 22

THE NEXT MORNING, about the same time the kids were finishing off Rose's pancakes at Free Camp, two Maine State Troopers were in Casco knocking on the front door of a rundown trailer with a rusty red pickup in the driveway.

A man in jeans and a faded blue chamois work shirt came to the door. His salt-and-pepper hair was thick and full.

"Help you, gentlemen?"

"Mr. Bronson? Donald Bronson?"

"Donnie. Birth certificate's Donald, but everybody around here knows me as Donnie. I'm just about to leave for work. How can I help you?"

The exchange was brief. Without saying why, they showed him a sketch of a bald man in sunglasses.

Donnie scrunched up his face, appearing thoughtful but perplexed, then shook his head. "Doesn't look like anybody I ever seen. Hard to tell with them sunglasses."

They asked about a six-digit license plate number.

"I have no idea."

They pointed out that the six numbers matched a trailer registered to him.

He acted surprised, leaned out the door, and squinted toward his truck.

"Not the pickup. Might be one of my other vehicles, though. I've got a dump truck, a bulldozer, an old travel trailer that's no longer on the road, a motorcycle—let me see, is that the whole of 'em—oh, and one snowmobile trailer with two of my old snow machines in it. I'm not sure about the numbers on any of them, but I'm sure you fellows can radio in and check State Motor Vehicles and find out."

"It's the snowmobile trailer," one of the Troopers said.

"Well then, that one sets up to my wood lot north of Harrison gathering mold and rust. I haven't used it in a couple of years, but that don't matter—it's not a plate I'd memorize anyway, not the way I know my pickup's plate. Why? Did you find it somewhere? Somebody steal it? Is it busted up? I'd be more worried about the two snow machines inside. Are they still there?"

"We have no reason to believe it's anywhere but at your wood lot," the second Trooper said. "Just the same, can you give us directions to the location?"

Bronson gave them directions and watched them drive out the rutted driveway onto the blacktop road. This would be a day to maintain his normal routine and go to work on the wall job at the estate. It was no time to draw attention to the sand quarry and the school bus buried in it.

***

Maggie and Mo worked together clearing the dishes from the breakfast table while the others chatted.

"So what's on the schedule for this morning?" Maggie asked.

Caroline returned from the kitchen with a sheet of paper in her hand, her finger going down a list. "Bando had a team-building exercise set for nine o'clock. He also had my Dad leading a session after lunch, one on discovering your gifts."

"What do you mean, *had* them scheduled?" Mo said, chomping on a pancake he'd slathered with grape jelly and rolled into a burrito.

"I mean, Bando had to leave for Portland a few minutes ago to meet with the police and the parents, so he can't be here this morning."

"Let me guess," Juan said. "They're switching slots and Twait's going to do his thing this morning? And if Bando gets back after lunch, he'll do his session in Twait's?"

"Actually, Bando left it up to us. He said if we want to use this morning for something else we can."

"Like what?" Juanita asked.

"Like free time, or a hike, or . . ."

"Canoeing or swimming," Mo suggested.

Caroline shook her head. "Almost anything but canoeing or swimming—not mornings."

Mo groaned and the others feigned looks of dejection.

"Have we got access to a computer?" Charlie asked.

"Not here at the camp. This is only a summer operation, so the office doesn't use one. The staff cabins don't have them either. No broadband or wireless, so even if we had one we'd need to use dial-up through the office phone."

"So we hike to town," Charlie said. "There's probably a public library there, right? They should have two or three Internet computers people can use."

"I'm pretty sure they do. But it's a long, long walk, even using the shortcuts."

Mo wolfed down the last bite of his jelly-roll/burrito-pancake. The others watched him chew.

"Why do we need a computer?" asked Juan.

"For a couple of reasons. First, we can check old news stories about the drownings. If they're not on computer, the library may have hard-copy information—like an old local newspaper. It was big news for a small town. Second, we can go online and get the address and phone number for Mr. and Mrs. Beals. Sounds like we all share the feeling that Karen and Addie's deaths are connected somehow to this carjacking or kidnapping or whatever we call it—we just don't know how. Look, since we're stumped on the van, we may as well see what we can find out about the drownings."

"And third," Maggie added, "maybe we can check out Juanita's numbers. In some places you can use a phone number to get the owner's name and address."

"That's called reverse lookup," Charlie said. "Some phone books used to have a special listing in the back. You found the number and it told you who had it."

"They call it a crisscross directory," Caroline said. "I read about that in a Sue Grafton mystery. We may be able to do it on the Internet now."

"Wait a minute," Mo interrupted. "Juanita only heard six numbers, not seven. If it's a phone, we're missing a number. How can we know if it's the first number, the last number, or one of them in the middle?"

"Let's say it's not a phone number," Maggie said. "And it's not a Zip Code, because those have only five numbers."

"It's got to be a license plate," Juan said. "Hopefully from Maine and not some other state."

"Is there a reverse lookup—what'd you call it, a crisscross directory—for license plates?" Mo asked, his mouth finally free of mangled food.

"Maybe," Charlie said. "I suppose it depends whether it's considered public information or private information. We'll find out when we get to the library."

"If the library is as far a walk as Caroline says, it'll be noon before we get there," Maggie said.

"Not if Dad drives us. He knows Bando said we can use our time any way we choose. Besides, how can he refuse kids who want to spend time at the library?"

At 9 a.m. they waved goodbye to Twait from the library porch and disappeared inside.

"Pick you up around 11:30," he yelled, and drove off.

CHAPTER 23

Mouse woke up. At first he wasn't sure his eyes were open, so he rubbed them to be certain. They were open, he was sure of it. Then he remembered he and his new friends were in the gloomy darkness of a buried school bus. He pressed the button to light his watch and saw it was 8:45 a.m.

"Anybody else awake?" he asked into the blackness.

A groggy voice answered. "Am now." It was BJ. "But I can't see anything."

"We'll light a candle when everyone's awake. Got to make them last. We don't know how long we might be stuck down here."

"Awhile, I'm guessing," said another sleepy voice, Tim's. "If this guy's going to hurt us, he's not in a hurry. For now he just wants to keep us. He must have some reason."

"Money?" Mouse ventured. "A kidnap for ransom?"

"Could be," Tim said. "From down here we have no way to know if he's made any demands. We have no radio, phone, or computer to find out."

BJ spoke again. "The ransom theory doesn't make sense. Why take five of us? It'd make more sense to kidnap one person. Why mess with five?"

"I don't know," Mouse said. "Maybe because none of our parents are millionaires with enough cash to put up. Could be he thinks five families together can scrape it up."

"I don't think it's about money at all," BJ answered. "He hasn't taken our pictures, has he? Or made us write notes to our parents or speak to them on the phone?"

"Or cut off each of our little fingers," Mouse said. "To motivate them."

"Not funny, Mouse," BJ scolded. "But you do see the point. He'd have to do something to make our families believe we're still alive."

"Sorry about the finger thing," Mouse said. "It was a nervous attempt at humor."

"So why'd he take us?" The new voice was Celine's. "If we're not worth something—like, if we're not hostages so he can extort money—why bother holding us?"

"Revenge," a weak, shaky voice said. "He's angry, making a point, punishing someone."

"Atlanta! You're awake!" BJ exclaimed, and a flurry of words began tumbling out of her mouth. "How do you feel? Are you all right? Does your head hurt? Quick, Mouse, light a candle. Somebody get her a drink of water."

Minutes later they gathered around a stub of candle by Atlanta's cot, Tim and BJ on beanbag chairs, Celine and Mouse on the floor.

Mouse held up an oil lamp. "Let's try lighting this thing. Looks like the kerosene lamp my grandfather keeps in his cellar in case a storm knocks the power out." He lifted the glass chimney, adjusted the wick, and lit it.

"Look!" Tim said. "It lights up the whole room."

It was true. They could see the interior of the school bus from where they sat near its middle. It no longer looked like the buses they'd ridden. The bench seats had been ripped out. No light came in the windows. The front windshield, the windows in the folding front door, and all the slide-down windows on either side—even the back windows in and on either side of the rear emergency exit—looked as if they'd been painted black. But it wasn't black paint; it was the crushing dirt and sand pressing against the outside glass. The lantern light brightening the interior of the bus cheered them briefly, but it also illuminated their prison walls, which brought a dark sense of despair. Now they could not only see—they could perceive just how desperate their plight was.

They sat in utter silence a while until Atlanta croaked in a dry-throated voice, "I'm thirsty."

Mouse, trying to sound cheerful, affected his best movie-cowboy drawl. "Well, let's get a move on. Somebody get the little lady a drink. And let's rustle us up some grub."

They did, they got a move on. They dug through the storage closets and found supplies, then passed around a breakfast they'd always remember: a bottle of water, a large can of baked beans, and a tin of Spam luncheon meat cut into five slices. The feel of food in their stomachs rejuvenated them and made them feel hopeful again. It also helped them regenerate a few brain cells—which they desperately needed so they could figure out what to do next.

CHAPTER 24

"THERE'S BEEN NO RANSOM DEMAND," the officer-in-charge said to Bando. "Not to any of the parents, not to anyone."

"And the van?"

"It's simply disappeared. We've had bulletins posted for the New England states, New York and New Jersey ever since we found your driver. The I-95 bridge cameras between Kittery and Portsmouth show nothing. We've checked every tollbooth camera in the state, plus the Canadian border crossings. There are dozens of other secondary roads—without camera surveillance—this person could have used to cross the state line. From your photos of the van, it'd be pretty easy to spot. We also faxed and emailed images to every municipality and law enforcement agency in New England."

"How about the sketches?"

"Sent out everywhere. Also, the sketches and van pictures aired on the late news last night and again this morning, along with photos of most of the kids. They're all over today's papers, too."

"So, from what you say, the kids are likely still in the state. If that's true, either he's hidden them and the van or he's dumped the van where it won't easily be found and placed them in a secure location."

"Or—"

Bando stopped the man with a raised index finger. "I don't think so. Something tells me he hasn't harmed them."

The officer studied Bando. "Is that wishful thinking? Or do you know something I don't know? Is there something you're not telling us, sir?"

"It's just a gut feeling I have."

"Do you also have a gut feeling where we might find the van or the guy who bound and gagged your driver and drove off with his five passengers?"

"No."

"Then, when we go out to meet with their parents in a minute, unless you know something for sure about their safety and well-being, I'd ask that you consider their feelings and the delicate nature of this case, and kindly keep your gut feelings to yourself."

"I understand. And I appreciate everything you're doing."

The two men approached the door that would lead to the anxious parents.

"Almost forgot," Bando said. "Anything on those numbers?"

The officer stopped. "You gave us six numbers, so we ran them through Motor Vehicles. Zip Codes are five numbers and phones are seven or ten, so that didn't make sense. And there's the outside possibility it's an out-of-state license plate, which we're checking."

"So we're hoping the numbers make up a license plate?"

"Yes. And we do have a Maine plate that matches. A couple of our guys ran it down this morning. The owner didn't match the sketch, and the plate turned out to be an old snowmobile trailer with two snow machines in it. Looks like a dead end."

Bando looked puzzled. "How can we be so sure it's a dead end?"

"Well, we can't. But at the moment it looks like it. Remember, sir, you gave us that number out of thin air. You asked us to check it out without referencing it to anything. We have no reason to believe it's in any way connected to those teenagers' disappearance, do we?" He stared hard at Bando and added, "Do we have a reason to?"

"Not that I know of."

"All right. Shall we go and meet with the parents now?"

"First, one favor."

"What is it?"

"Can you give me the name?"

"What name?"

"The man with the snowmobile trailer."

The officer scowled. "I can't. You know that. We have no reason to suspect him. I can't just turn you loose to badger people. Besides, who says the numbers don't match an old lottery ticket?"

"Hadn't thought of that. Lottery tickets have six numbers?"

The officer gave an exaggerated eye-roll and placed his hand on the doorknob. "Ready?"

Bando placed a light hand on the man's wrist. "Just answer me this. No name, no address. Does the man with the snowmobile trailer live within an hour of Portland and the spot where the children were abducted, and also less than an hour from the camp?"

Before he could object or stop his mouth, the officer said, "Yes, about halfway in between."

Bando removed his fingertips from the man's wrist, and when he did the officer-in-charge blinked and made a face as if he were trying unsuccessfully to recall a dream. But the memory of the wrist touch and the question evaporated in an instant, and the officer simply asked, "Ready to go and meet the parents?"

"I'll follow your lead."

And they stepped through the door.

CHAPTER 25

THE LIBRARY HAD FIVE COMPUTERS, three with Internet access, the other two limited to library files. The woman behind the circulation desk said she needed to keep one of the Internet computers open for the regulars, but she let Mo and Maggie sign onto the other two. Juan and Caroline sat down together at a library-only computer. Juanita and Charlie took the other.

"Bingo!" Maggie had been logged on for about two minutes. "Here's the address and phone for Mr. and Mrs. Beals. No combination of those six numbers Juanita heard."

"No luck on the crisscross directory," Mo said. "A few states have Web sites for reverse-lookup of phone numbers, driver's licenses, and license plates—including Maine—but you have to pay to become a subscriber. It's for, like, private eyes and lawyers, I guess."

"How much is it?" Charlie asked.

"Oh, like $59.95. You register and pay online."

"By credit card?" Maggie asked.

"Yep. Anybody got one?"

Nobody had one.

"How about a search for the numbers?" Maggie asked. "Or the words *license plate* along with the numbers?"

Mo tried it, but came up empty.

"Forget that," Charlie said. "It's a dead end for now. Look online for news stories about the drownings."

"We're doing that on the library-database computers, too," Juan said.

Five minutes later, using combinations of key words like *Beals, drown,* and *Maine camp,* Maggie pulled up an archived article from the Portland Press Herald. It told them little they didn't already know, but confirmed the names and order of events.

Karen Beals and her daughter Addie had drowned while saving another little girl who had fallen into the pool at the foot of the waterfall. The girl's name wasn't mentioned, but the article mentioned how distraught Marcus Schaumburg, the camp's director at the time, was. Above the article was a black-and-white photo of the waterfall, and beside that in a sidebar was a history of the waterfall that had claimed three other lives in separate incidents over a 70-year span. Two adults had leapt to their deaths from the top; one teen had entered the whirlpool on a dare.

As the articles were printing, Juanita announced, "Found something—not the actual articles, but references to where they can be found in the Bridgton paper. Looks like two stories ran close together, just after the drownings, so they probably contain the same information as the Press Herald article. The third one mentioned is a joint obituary for Karen and Addie Beals. The fourth was published two years later and is about the dedication of the memorial benches. None of these is available on computer, but they're archived the old-fashioned way on library microfiche. According to this, the articles are here. We just have to ask."

Charlie told the librarian they were from the camp and had been assigned to do a history project over the summer, and the waterfall tragedy was their topic. She helped them install the microfiche in the microfiche reader, and once they had the hang of it, left them to pore over the articles.

"Sorry you can't print them out the way you can with computers," she said. "But you can take notes. If you really need copies, you can request them from either the Maine State Library or the Bridgton newspaper office itself. They should have back issues in their morgue."

The first article contained much of the same information that had been in the Portland Press Herald. The little bit that was different Maggie jotted in the margins of the Press Herald printout they'd made.

The second was a follow-up that had run two weeks later. It reported that a lawsuit would likely be filed against the camp. The story contained quotes from the grieving parents, Mr. and Mrs. Beals, and comments from local folks who cited the earlier fatalities at the waterfall. Two pictures of the waterfall itself accompanied the story. One had been shot looking up at the falls. The other showed the whirlpool where the victims had been trapped.

The third piece, Addie and Karen's combined obituary, offered photos of mother and daughter as well as basics like birth dates, schools attended, and associations and memberships like Brownies and Girl Scouts. The list of survivors included Karen's brother Lauriston and his wife Harriet, Karen's sisters Marie and Jessamine and their husbands John and Richard, her parents in Bridgton, nieces and nephews, Karen's high-school best friend Nina Todd, Addie's cat Scram, and Karen's "special friend" Donald Bronson. The funeral home was listed along with visiting hours and a time for the funeral service at the Methodist Church.

The article that appeared two years later was upbeat, showing a crowd of eighteen people gathered at a dedication ceremony for the two granite benches that had been placed by the waterfall. No names were given in the caption under the photograph. The article recapped the tragedy, named the basic players again—Karen, Addie, the Beals parents, and camp director Marcus Schaumburg. Only this time the writer mentioned the name of the little girl who had been saved by Karen Beals—Giselle Schaumburg, the director's daughter.

Juanita jotted the basics on the back of the earlier printout, and she and the other five teens went back to work.

"Marcus Schaumburg and Giselle Schaumburg. Search for them and see what comes up," Charlie said.

It didn't take long to find their obituaries. A few months after the dedication of the benches, Marcus and his wife Marita along with daughter Giselle and son Roland had all been killed in a 40-car pileup in the fog on a West Virginia highway. Their minivan had been sandwiched between the rear of one tractor-trailer and the front of another. It was clearly an accident with no chance of foul play.

"Sorry, kids, but time's up. I've got a couple other people who need the Internet," interrupted the librarian.

"One last search?" Juanita pleaded. "It'll only a take a minute."

"One minute," the librarian said, and walked back to her desk.

"Mo," Juanita said. "Try Karen's 'special friend's' name—*Donald Bronson.*"

CHAPTER 26

MOUSE STEPPED OFF THE LADDER. "Our host must have locked the hatch door from the outside. Looks like we're not getting out that way. But I did discover a slide-latch on the inside of it—you know, to keep out the radioactive zombies after a nuclear war. I bolted it shut."

"Why'd you do that?" Celine asked from behind the oil lamp in their midst.

"To keep the bad guy out. Maybe we can't get out, but he can't get in either."

"Keep him out?" Atlanta said weakly. "Right now he's our only hope of getting out. What if he comes back and we're all asleep, and he can't get in, so he goes away?"

"Interesting point," BJ conceded. "We can't stay here forever."

Mouse let out a sigh and sat down. "So what are you saying? Do you want me to climb up again and pull back the bolt? At least this way we've got a first line of defense. Maybe we can make some weapons out of what's here—for when he comes back. If we refuse to go up, he's got to come down the ladder. That's a bottleneck."

"And then what do we do—all jump on him and use one of these knives to stab him?" Tim asked.

"Or maybe we hold him down and slit his throat!" Celine added. "Really, though, if you think I could do something like that—forget it!"

The others shook their heads and muttered same here, me neither, and no way.

Mouse wasn't ready to go down without a fight. "Okay, how about we disable him? We knock him out so we can escape. When we get to the top, we lock him down here in his own prison until the cops can get to him."

"He's got a gun, Mouse," Celine pointed out.

"Wait, wait," BJ said. "I have a different idea."

The others hushed.

"He said he was going to work today, right? That means we don't have to neutralize him to escape. He's already out of the picture. Why don't we just do it—escape?"

"Like, maybe because the hatch door is locked," Celine said, a hint of sarcasm in her voice, "from the outside."

"No, wait," Tim said. "BJ may have something here. Mouse, you climbed the ladder. How far is it from the roof of the bus to ground level?"

Mouse tried to recall.

"Don't guess. Climb up again. Last time you went up for a different reason—to see if the hatch door was locked. This time check out the distance."

Mouse disappeared up the ladder again. A moment later he called down, "Looks like it's made of three metal barrels with the tops and bottoms cut out. The barrels are stacked end to end and welded together to make a tall tube. It's like a giant straw."

"Three barrels. Do they wiggle?" Celine yelled up. "Can you move them side to side? Try the top one closest to the surface."

"Just a second. Nope. The welds are strong, and there's probably too much pressure from the dirt around the outside holding everything in place. I'm coming back down."

"Count the barrels again on the way down," BJ said. "Just to make sure."

Seconds later Mouse emerged. "Still three."

"How tall is a barrel?" Atlanta asked.

"About three feet," Tim said.

"Seems right to me," Mouse agreed. "So it's about nine feet from the roof of the bus to ground level."

"Then we'd better get started," BJ said.

"Get started with what?" Celine asked. "The hatch is locked and the barrels won't move."

"He didn't weld the windows shut," BJ said, standing up. "They may be stuck, but some of them are bound to work. If not, we break them open. Right, Mouse?"

"Right."

"But the dirt will pour in," Celine said.

"Exactly," BJ answered. "That's what we want. If we're going to dig our way out today—before our guy gets back—the only place to store the dirt is inside the bus. The good news is, we're lucky to have a place to put it."

"What if it caves in as fast as we can drag it inside?" Atlanta asked. "Won't the bus fill up before we can take out enough to tunnel nine or ten feet up? If it's clay, the sides may hold, but what if it's sand?"

The others let BJ field the question. "The ladder comes down through the roof behind the driver's seat, so let's try the first three windows. If they all open, we work them at the same time. Maybe the barrels will provide support on one side."

No one moved.

Mouse piped up, "Okay, BJ's is the only plan we've got. We don't know how much time before the guy comes back. Tim and I will open the three windows. Grab things we can dig with or pull dirt with. Cut the bottoms out of those plastic water jugs and use them to scoop. Empty tin cans will work too. We'll need pails or something to carry dirt to the back of the bus."

The group rose, and Atlanta said, "What about the chemical toilet where the driver's seat used to be? We can use that to carry dirt."

"We may want to keep that intact awhile longer," Mouse said.

"Yeah," Tim said. "Remember the Spam and beans."

Everyone laughed. It would be their last laugh for a while.

Tim and Mouse got all three windows open, and as soon as they did, the soil began running in like sand through an hourglass, a reminder that for them time was running out.

CHAPTER 27

"WE'VE GOT AN HOUR TO KILL before Twait comes back for us," Charlie said.

"I vote for ice cream," Mo said quickly. "Preferably a scoop shop, not a packaged cone from a convenience store. Caroline, you know the turf. Where to?"

Five minutes later they were in an ice cream parlor making their choices.

Charlie handed Juanita a five-dollar bill. "Would you get me a small cup of Moose Tracks? I need to run across the street to that convenience store. Be right back."

By the time the others got their ice cream, Charlie was back. The group sat on two benches inside a gazebo in the middle of the town square.

Mo pointed to Charlie's paper bag. "What'd you buy?"

Charlie set his cup of ice cream down, reached into the bag and pulled out a Portland Press Herald, which he handed to Mo.

"Take it. My hands don't hold newspapers so well, and I want to eat my ice cream before it melts. Look at the front page."

Juanita squeezed in close to Mo as he unfolded the paper. On the bottom right of the front page was a two-line headline: CAMP VAN CARJACKED, FIVE TEENS ABDUCTED. The police sketch had been embedded in the story, which Mo read aloud to the group. It continued on page eight and included a picture of the missing van and photos of the five kids.

"There are three girls—my cousin Atlanta and two others named Celine and Barbara Jean, who goes by BJ. The two boys are Timothy, who goes by Tim, and Robert, who is known as Mouse." Though he wasn't sure why, Mo felt the need to say the names of the lost campers out loud again. "Atlanta, Celine, BJ, Tim, and Mouse."

Maggie repeated them, "Atlanta, Celine, BJ, Tim, Mouse," as if saying the names aloud might keep them alive, or at least connected to the second group.

"I'm sure all the other New England newspapers ran the story today," Charlie said. "Which means our parents will be calling the camp."

"They'll want to know why we didn't tell them last night," Maggie said.

Caroline wondered, "You think your folks will come and take you home right away?"

"Ours will," Juan and Juanita answered in unison.

"Probably mine, too," Maggie said.

"Definitely mine," Mo said. "After all, my cousin Atlanta is in the other van."

"How about yours, Charlie?" Caroline asked.

Charlie made a pained face. "I live with my grandmother. I'm not sure she'll make the connection. She's a little forgetful."

"So what do we do now?" Mo asked.

Charlie reached into the bag and pulled out a cell phone. "They haven't come yet," he said.

"Is that a disposable?" Caroline asked.

"Yeah. I bought it when I got the newspaper. I also picked up a couple of cards with minutes."

"For what?" Juan asked. "To call our parents?"

"No, not our parents. We do need to make a couple of phone calls, though—like Mr. and Mrs. Beals. And thanks to that last search Juanita suggested, we've now got a number, address, and MapQuest directions for Karen's 'special friend'—Donald Bronson. These leads may not turn up anything, but we need to check them out. First thing to do is figure out what we're going to ask once we get them on the phone."

Mo tore out the newspaper story. "We should have these kids' pictures in case we spot them."

Juanita held up a photocopied sheet with writing on it. "We've got the notes we made on the waterfall drownings."

Caroline took the newspaper from Mo. "Let me have the rest of it. While you make the phone calls, I'll read the other stories. Maybe there's more in another section."

"We'd better hurry," Maggie said. "If our parents do decide to come soon, we haven't got much time."

Ten minutes later Juanita handed the phone back to Charlie. "I feel terrible, lying to Mrs. Beals that way."

"You didn't really lie. Telling her the camp's new management is considering a follow-up to the benches' dedication makes sense. Maybe Bando's been thinking about it."

Juanita frowned. "Pretty lame, Charlie. You know very well nobody's planning it. We're just pumping her for information."

"I guess Mrs. Beals hadn't read about the carjacking?" Maggie asked, ignoring Juanita's protest.

"If she did, she didn't let on."

"What did you learn from talking with her?" Charlie asked.

"That the loss of her daughter and granddaughter is still painful."

"And?" Charlie pressed. "What else?"

"She isn't crazy about Donald Bronson, her daughter's 'special friend.' When I asked if we should include him in a memorial service, she could hardly say his name. I don't think she and her husband approved of him, which is probably why they only listed him as 'special friend' in the obituary."

"Anything else?"

"She was confused about whether we meant a rededication service this year or next—because this is such short notice. I said it might be next year, but everything was still very tentative, that we were just new campers trying to see if there was interest. I feel terrible reopening her wounds."

"Short notice?" Charlie asked. "Check the notes. When did the drownings happen?"

Juan and Maggie scanned the notes.

Juanita, visibly shaken, walked away.

"The anniversary date of the deaths is tomorrow, Wednesday," Maggie said. "How could we not notice that?"

Mo ran his hand over his Mohawk, visibly excited. "So it's probably no coincidence the carjacking and kidnapping are close to the date of the drownings."

Charlie pointed to the sketch in the newspaper article Mo had torn out. "Which could mean our bald-headed guy hasn't sent a ransom note because it's not about money—it's about something else. Know what I think? I think nobody's heard from him because he's waiting for tomorrow to do something."

"Tomorrow? For what?" Mo said.

"I don't know. It scares me to even speculate. Maybe some sort of grand finale, with lots of fireworks."

Nobody uttered a word until Charlie said, "Maggie, your turn. Call Donald Bronson. Use the same story Juanita used. Maybe he can point us toward our carjacker."

Maggie punched the numbers into the cell phone. Nobody answered until an answering machine picked up after the fifth ring and a man's voice said, "Donnie Bronson, handyman. This is my home and business phone. Leave a message and your number after the beep. I'll get back to you."

Three seconds later came the beep. It caught Maggie off guard. She wasn't officially representing the camp and didn't know what to give for a return phone number. Should she hang up or leave a message? She finally fumbled out, "Um, Mr. Bronson, I'm very sorry about the loss of Karen and Addie. I know it happened a couple of years ago, but I only read about it this morning. I'm so sorry for your loss." She clicked off.

Charlie, Juan, and Caroline stared at her but said nothing.

Mo said, "You only just read about it this morning?"

"So?" Maggie said.

"So, while that's true that you read about the deaths today, you didn't read about them in this morning's paper. Those stories were five and three years old—on microfiche—remember? The only story we read this morning was about the missing van and the other kids."

"I heard every word," a girl's voice called out loudly. It was Juanita, coming across the lawn. "You don't have to tell me what you said. I heard you, Maggie. I was way over there, but I heard you as if I was on the other end of the phone—in that man's home or office or wherever his phone is."

"Did you hear anything else?" Juan asked.

"No, only Maggie. It sounded like she was leaving a message on an answering machine."

"I was. Donald Bronson wasn't there. I panicked and left a stupid message."

"Juanita," Charlie said. "Did you hear the man's recording, his voice?"

"No."

"Quick, Juanita, take the phone and hit Redial," he said. "Listen to his voice. We'll all link arms in case there's some other psychic connection, too. Maybe Juan can catch a vision."

As Juanita was about to call Bronson's number, Caroline appeared with the newspaper in her hands. "In the classified section they published a special prayer called a novena. It's got the same two photos we saw in Karen and Addie Beals' obituaries."

"Does it have the name of the person who submitted it," Charlie asked. "Was it Mr. and Mrs. Beals?"

"It says: your loving Donnie."

"Link arms with us, Caroline. You're part of this group, too. We'll explain in a minute. Juanita, hit Redial. When it comes time to leave a message, say, 'Donnie, we need to talk.'"

Juanita hit Redial and held the cell phone to her ear. Juan leaned close as everyone drew into a tight huddle under the gazebo, listening as if their lives—or someone else's—depended on it.

CHAPTER 28

"HOW ARE YOU FEELING, JERRY?" Bando asked.

Jerry was in his bathrobe and slippers, sporting a day's growth of heavy beard stubble. The still shaken driver mumbled something and invited Bando in, motioning him to a rocking chair.

"Tea? I know you've never been big on coffee. I've got some unsweetened vanilla chai tea that's not bad."

"The chai sounds lovely, thanks."

Jerry ran cold water into a kettle, set it on a burner, and turned up the flame. "I remember you like it heated slowly on the stovetop too, not in the microwave."

Bando nodded and Jerry sat down.

"How am I feeling, you ask? To be honest, I feel terrible. Not physically, but mentally. I'm heartsick about losing those kids."

"You never had them."

"You know what I mean. They're in danger, or they may be dead or subject to torture—all because I let some wacko grab my van."

"It couldn't be helped. For all you knew, the man simply wanted to steal a ride. You couldn't know he'd wait for those parents to hand their children over to him."

Jerry looked up, and a little of the guilt seemed to melt from his shoulders.

"This was well planned and executed. The man did a lot of preparation. It's not everyone who thinks to hide their identity using a gas mask."

Jerry nodded, this line of thinking new to him. Another layer of guilt sloughed off.

The kettle whistled.

"Stay seated, my friend," Bando said, his voice soothing. "I know where the cup is and where the tea is. Take a couple of deep breaths and relax. I'll pour you a cup of the chai too. To share a cup of tea between friends is one of life's little pleasures."

Jerry nodded, and before he knew Bando was gone, he was back in the rocker. As if by magic, two cups of tea had appeared, one in Jerry's hand, the other in Bando's.

Bando sipped. "Feeling a lot better, aren't you? Calmer."

"I am." Jerry sipped too. "It reminds me of those times you led the camp staff in meditation."

Bando set his teacup on the side table. "Would you like to try a relaxation technique?"

"Sure. I can already feel myself slowing down, and we haven't even started yet."

"Close your eyes. Take ten slow, deep, cleansing breaths—in through the nose, out through the mouth. Listen to my voice as you do it, and I'll guide you."

Two minutes later Jerry was completely relaxed.

"Jerry, may I ask you a few questions?" Bando's voice had a stroke-the-cat quality, something that said trust me.

"Yes."

"At different times we all pick up the camp telephone and field questions. On one of the occasions when you answered, did someone ask about the time and place we'd be meeting the campers and their parents? Take your time and think deeply before you answer."

After a long moment Jerry said, "No."

"How about the same question, but not at the camp—maybe someone you met someplace else?"

A long pause, as if Jerry were leafing through old file drawers in his head.

"A month ago I stopped at Danny's Irish Pub for lunch. I had the Free Camp van parked out front. I sat at the counter and ordered my usual Angus burger and fries. A minute later this guy in jeans and work shirt walks in and sits next to me. 'I'll have whatever he's having,' he says. My food hasn't come yet, so this guy has no idea if I've ordered food or a beer. There's a pool table in Danny's, and the guy challenges me to a game of Eight Ball. He mentions seeing the camp van in the parking lot and wonders if I'm one of the regular drivers. I say yes, and he asks how the kids get to camp—do parents drive them all the way or is there a gathering location where I meet them? I tell him I meet the families early in the morning at a convenient spot in Portland, and the kids travel with me in groups of five or six. He wonders where in Portland, suggesting he might know an even better spot. When I tell him our meeting place, he agrees it's already the best spot. Last thing he asks is when the first day of camp is. I win the pool game, and even though we're not betting, he picks up the tab for both meals. I don't think he had but two or three bites of his lunch."

"That's very helpful, Jerry. Now I'd like you to go a little deeper into your relaxation. Are you comfortable?"

"Yes, very comfortable."

"Good. Now put your hands on your knees, palms up. I'm going to place my own palms very lightly on yours, so lightly in fact that it may feel a bit ticklish. You're going to release a little electricity to me, transfer a little energy. But it's energy you'll feel better about getting rid of. Are you comfortable?"

Jerry nodded.

"Trust me?"

"Yes."

"Okay, here we go."

Bando held his fingertips above Jerry's hands, creating surface tension.

"I know Danny's Pub is dark, even at lunchtime—but the area

over the pool table is well lit. I want you to remember that pool game. Remember it?"

"Yes."

"Did he tell you his name?"

"Hannibal. 'Like Hannibal the Cannibal,' he said."

"Left-handed or right-handed?"

"Right."

"What did his hands look like?"

"Rough, calloused. Like he worked outdoors, maybe construction."

"Ring on his finger?"

"Don't recall one."

"Accent?"

"Local Maine, close by here or maybe Mid Coast. Not Down East, though."

"Height and weight?"

"My size, heavier. Muscular."

"Beard? Hair color? Eye color?"

"No beard, no mustache. Never really saw the eyes clear for color. Lots of thick brown hair, but not shoulder length or anything. A touch of gray—salt and peppery—around the temples, I think."

"Age?"

"Mid to late forties, maybe early fifties."

"You see his vehicle?"

"No, he left before I did."

"Okay, that's great, Jerry. Now I have one last thing. You ready?"

"Yes."

"Get a straight-on picture of this fellow in your head, like a driver's license photo. Got it? Got the image?"

"Got it."

"Good. Now imagine your head is one of those old Polaroid cameras that took a picture and then pressed out a print. Remember them? The image came out blank at first, but then when it hit the air, it developed right before your eyes, and you had to smear this tube of sticky stuff over the image to preserve it."

"I remember those."

"I want your head to snap that driver's license picture of the man you met at Danny's, and let your hands be the slot where the print comes out. When I say Click, you do it. Okay?"

"Okay."

"Here we go. Good clear image. Click!"

Twenty seconds later a man's face projected itself onto the screen in Bando's mind.

CHAPTER 29

Donnie Bronson's answering machine picked up again, his recorded voice droning the same message, urging the caller to leave a message after the beep.

"Donnie, we need to talk," Juanita said, and hung up.

The huddle broke up and everyone found a place in the gazebo to sit down.

"Well, Juan?" Charlie asked.

"While the guy was speaking on his machine, I saw the same room as yesterday when I was on that bench by the waterfall. I was seeing it from the same spot, only this time I could make out the light blinking on the answering machine next to the phone. Whatever eyes I'm seeing through, they aren't moving. They don't shift side to side like normal people's eyes. These eyes are stuck—like a doll's or a teddy bear's. They give me wide peripheral vision, but they can't move."

"No man in the recliner this time?" Maggie asked.

"Nope."

"Juanita?" Charlie asked. "You hear anything?"

"I'm not positive, but the guy on the answering machine might be the guy I heard yesterday—the one in the woods who said 'Thought you could get away, huh?'"

"And what about the girl's voice in the background?" Caroline asked.

The others turned her way, puzzled.

"The girl, very faint. Her voice comes between Bronson's sentences. You heard her, right?"

Juanita and Juan shook their heads no.

"I hear strange things," Juanita said. "But there was no girl's voice, just the man's, and then me leaving a message."

"I don't hear strange things, just regular voices," Juan said. "All I heard was the guy."

"What did this girl say?" Mo asked.

"What did she say?" Caroline said, exasperated. "I can't believe you didn't hear her! She whispered it. It was eerie, distant. She said, *Dad, don't, please.*"

"That's it?" Charlie asked. "Nothing more?"

"What do you mean, nothing more? She said it three times—first before he spoke, then after his first sentence, and then again at the very end, before the beep. She was pleading."

The others looked at each other, then back to Caroline.

"I'm not crazy. I know what I heard."

"I've got to support her on this one," Juanita said. "I've been through what she's going through. The first time it happens, you can't believe it yourself."

"I'm with my sister," Juan said. "Let's give Caroline the benefit of the doubt."

"Sorry, everybody," Mo said, "but I'm still skeptical."

"How about if we call him back and listen again?" Maggie suggested.

They agreed.

"Juanita, you and Caroline share the phone," Charlie said. "Juan, stand close so you can hear, too. We all keep a hand in the middle, like a basketball team, maintain contact."

Charlie thrust a twisted hand into the middle, and they each piled a hand on top.

Caroline held the phone up so she and the twins could hear. She pressed Redial and waited for Bronson's voice.

"Hello," a man's voice said. When neither Caroline nor Juanita said anything, he repeated, "Hello? Hello? Who is this?"

Both girls were too stunned to say anything.

"I can hear you breathing!" Bronson hissed. "Who is this?"

Caroline whispered loudly to her friends, "She's saying, *Dad, don't, please!* Can't you hear her? *Dad, don't, please!*"

But Caroline's hand wasn't over the mouthpiece, and the others weren't the only ones who heard what she said. Donnie Bronson heard her, too, heard her parrot the words in a pleading whisper, "Dad, don't, please!"

"Who is this?" Donnie Bronson roared. "Who's there? Damn you!"

Charlie used his free hand to signal the girls to hang up. Before they could, Mo, acting as if someone else had taken over his mouth, leaned in and said, "You can't hide us forever, Mr. Bronson. She wants you to let us go."

Startled, Caroline hung up.

Seconds later, before they could talk about what happened, Twait beeped and guided the van into a parking space by the library. With hearts still racing, they walked to FreeK Camp #2 and piled in for the ride back.

CHAPTER 30

THE DIGGING GOT OFF TO A DIFFICULT START. Even with the three windows lowered, the openings were narrow. Bronson had removed all of the original bus seats, so the three diggers had to stand on the chair, the table, and a wooden box. It was awkward reaching through and scooping dirt inside. But they managed, and slowly three piles of soil and rocks accumulated at their feet.

Then they ran into another roadblock.

"Now what do we do?" Mouse climbed off the box that had allowed him to work his digging spot. "We've reached and scooped as far as we can from inside. All we've got is a little cave beyond the three windows."

Celine and Tim climbed down. Everyone sat around the lamp.

"The dirt we're running into now is pretty hard-packed," Celine said. "It's time to start chipping up instead of out."

"Which means," Tim said, "somebody's got to squeeze through one of the windows into that little pocket."

"It isn't safe," Atlanta said. "Sooner or later it'll cave in. There's a lot of dirt above the digger. If it all drops at once, there's no way to pull the person out."

"And there are no boards or braces to shore it up as we go," Tim said, "the way they do it in mines."

The five of them sat looking glum. Occasionally one of them would glance around their cell, as if what they needed to help with the tunnel might suddenly jump out at them. Nothing appeared.

Mouse walked toward the chemical toilet Bronson had set in place of the removed driver's seat. The others' eyes followed him at first, but then they realized he might need some privacy. Celine lowered the wick of the lamp to dim it.

"Wait. Turn that back up," Mouse said.

The room brightened again.

"There's a little tool box by the gas pedal."

"Any shovels?" BJ asked.

"Don't see any." Mouse rattled through the contents. "Just the usual suspects—hammer, screwdrivers, pliers."

"While you're up there," Celine said sarcastically, "see if the key is in the ignition. If it is, start the engine, sit on the potty and drive us out."

Nobody laughed. Desperation was setting in. They hung their heads.

"Okay," Mouse said, still hunched over the toolbox. "Time to go to Plan B."

They heard him grunt as if launching a karate attack, after which came a series of smack-smack-smacks. Their heads snapped up and they watched Mouse, claw hammer in hand—insanely, almost gleefully—strike blow after blow on the high, wide windshield.

"Cave-ins," Mouse shouted through his breathlessness as he smashed, "welcome."

The others caught on, and with everyone except the injured Atlanta working, it took less than fifteen minutes to demolish and remove the front windshield. The opening gave them a broader, higher excavating area, and the scooping came easier. When the dirt did cave from time to time, the overhanging roof protected them. The diggers might get a face full, but at least they weren't buried under tons of earth. Thanks to Mouse's great idea—or his temporary insanity—the dirt delivered itself to their doorstep, lots of it.

They scraped and pulled platefuls and pots full of earth through the windshield, layering it across the bus floor. The room began closing in on them from the bottom, but in front, things were looking up, literally. Now it was a race against time as they clawed, scratched, and scraped their way out, hoping to reach daylight before they had to face their dark, angry captor again, the man whose name they didn't know.

CHAPTER 31

"Dad?" Caroline said, buckling herself into the front passenger seat.

"Yes?" Twait said from his booster seat.

"I was wondering, have you or Mom ever heard—"

"Hold that thought." Twait leaned out the window to check traffic. When the coast was clear he swung the van into a U-turn. "Okay. Now, what about hearing voices?"

Caroline's lips began to move, but stopped suddenly. "Wait. Dad, I didn't say anything about voices. I said, 'Have you or Mom ever heard—' And before I could finish, you interrupted me."

The others tuned in.

"Are you sure? I'd swear you asked about voices."

"No, she didn't," Juan said.

Juanita confirmed it. "Nope, I was listening too."

Twait tried to wait them out. It didn't work.

"Well?" Charlie said. "Either you have a gift for reading minds and finishing sentences—which, according to my books, would make you an intuitive—or you have some form of clairaudience. Or maybe it's not you, but Rose. If one of you has a gift for hearing voices, you must have figured there'd come a time it might show up in Caroline—and she'd ask about it. Which is it? Did you intuitively read her mind just now? Or has Caroline's time arrived?"

There was no sound except the tires on the road. Twait pulled to the side of the road and shut off the engine and turned toward Caroline.

"Lately your mother has been hearing a woman whispering—usually when she's on the phone. The woman's voice is in the background. It happened when she was talking to the fruit and vegetable delivery guy. The woman whispered, 'He's coming.' When Mom asked the delivery guy about it, he said he didn't hear anybody. It happened another time when she was on the phone with me, but I didn't hear it either—I only heard Mom. But I believe she heard it."

Juanita interrupted. "You said usually it's on the phone. When are the other times?"

"When she put on the headphones for her music. She listens when she does her treadmill. That's why she hasn't been wearing them lately. It's the voice."

"Does she recognize the voice?" Mo asked. "Is the woman living or dead?"

"She can't be sure. She tried asking the woman her name. But it's not a two-way conversation. She hears the woman. The woman doesn't seem to hear Rose—or, at least, she doesn't answer."

"Has she heard other voices, Dad?"

"Not in years. When she was a teenager, she heard a man's voice. It went on for months, kept whispering ferry dock. When it wouldn't stop, she told her father, and he called a cop friend who took her seriously and checked the missing-persons reports.

"Earlier that winter a sailor from the Sub Base in Groton, Connecticut failed to return to his sub. It was assumed he'd gone AWOL. His family insisted he hadn't, and he'd never shown up at home or called them.

"There's a ferry that runs from New London, Connecticut to Orient Point, New York. Back then, it didn't run in the winter months. Still, the cop had a gut feeling about Rose and that young man's voice, so he had divers check the waters around the ferry dock. They found his car on the harbor bottom off the end of the dock. There was nothing blocking the loading ramp, and he must have driven off it late at night. With the ferry out-of-service for the winter, and the company staff all being off, nobody had reason to check there. Nobody knows if it was suicide or accident, but he drowned in his car."

Twait's story left them all deep in thought.

"Dad, I think I know who Mom's voice is. I'm almost positive it's Karen Beals—from the waterfall."

"Why would you say that?"

Charlie answered for her. "Caroline heard the daughter, Addie, in the background of a phone conversation."

"Something big is about to happen here," Mo said. "Something bad."

Caroline looked at her father. "I think Mo's right, Dad. And whatever's about to happen, I think Karen and Addie Beals are trying to stop it—Karen talking to Mom, Addie to me. They need our help."

"They need it soon," Charlie said. "Before any new voices join them in the whirlpool."

CHAPTER **32**

ONNIE BRONSON FOUND IT DIFFICULT to think clearly. His brain had been buzzing like a beehive since the phone call, and the burning pressure at the base of his skull was growing again. It felt like a sharp spike slowly entering the back of his neck, making it hard to focus on anything else.

How in the world could a boy phone him from the buried school bus? He'd dug the hole and lowered the bus with a construction crane back when he, Karen, and Addie had faced the threat of Y2K and the millennium change. He'd been no different than the thousands of other survivalists around the country who built hideouts and underground shelters. Karen hadn't liked doing it, but he'd convinced her and Addie to stay in it with him for nearly a week when the calendar jumped from 1999 to 2000.

These kids from the camp van were 10 to 15 feet under the earth, locked in. They had food and bottled water but absolutely no phone. There was no way they could contact the outside world. Even if they had managed to smuggle in a cell phone, there was no way it could pick up a signal. Besides, he hadn't given his name, so they couldn't know who he was. And he was sure he'd left no documents in the bus, so how had they gotten his phone number?

Impossible as it seemed, one of the two boys had just phoned him at home and warned him that he—Mr. Bronson, the boy had called him—couldn't hold them there forever. He was certain he'd heard it. It was a boy, not one of those other voices he sometimes heard when the burning spike pressed into his skull. This had to be one of those boys—either the runty one or the one in the Mickey Mouse hat. Whichever boy it had been, there must be something strange—demonic—about him. How else could he get his voice into the telephone lines?

And what was with the other voice—the girl's? Twice she'd said, "Dad, don't, please!" She had to be one of the three from the bus, didn't she? Or was hers one of those stray voices you sometimes heard in the background of a phone call—the ones that made you wonder if someone else was listening in? Who was the Dad she was referring to?

Bronson rubbed his forehead, suddenly tired, sleepy. He plopped down in the easy chair. Before he could close his eyes, he noticed the blinking light on the message machine. He pressed the button. It was a another girl's voice—a different girl—offering condolences for his loss of Karen and Addie. She'd only just now learned of it, five years later. But she left no name or number. What was going on?

Donnie massaged the nape of his neck with his hand and reached for the aspirin bottle on the side table. He popped four tablets into his mouth and chased them down with the half-bottle of warm flat beer from the side table. His burning brain was too tired to figure things out right then, so he lay back and closed his eyes, hoping for the escape and relief of a nap.

Behind him, on the living room shelf, crouched the brown-eyed puppy, glass eyes forever lifeless but wide open.

CHAPTER 33

"I F I CAN HAVE EVERYONE'S ATTENTION, please," Bando said before the group could dig into lunch. "Rose tells me some worried parents called this morning—not last night but this morning. They've just now read about the missing van in the newspapers or heard it on TV. Strange as this may sound, they failed to hear about it last night—when you were supposed to have called them."

None of the campers responded.

"They're worried," Bando said.

"But we're fine," Mo answered. "We have a State Policeman out front guarding us."

Bando crossed his arms across his chest. "Some of your parents want to come and take you home."

A long silence ensued and the kids looked worried.

"They can't," Maggie objected. "Not yet. We need to stay here. We have to help find the others."

Bando sat down at their table, motioning Twait and Rose to join them. "The police are working on this. Why would you five need to be involved?"

"Six," Charlie corrected. "You forgot Caroline."

Bando said nothing, simply closed his eyes and folded his hands as if praying.

Rose picked up the conversation. "I stalled your parents." All eyes except Bando's shifted to her. "I told them you were safe, that your activities were keeping you busy, and you were unaware that the other van and those kids had been taken."

They stared at Rose in disbelief.

"Did they buy it?" Juan asked.

"I also mentioned the police protection. That helped."

"Thank you, Rose," Maggie said, fingers rubbing her peace symbol necklace as if it had brought good luck. "But why would you lie for us?"

"To buy you a day, which is the best I could do. Given the circumstances, none of them would let you finish the week. Mo, your mother is coming tomorrow afternoon. Juan and Juanita, your parents can't make it until Thursday. Maggie, Thursday for you too."

"What about me? Did my grandmother call?"

"Not yet, Charlie. I'm sure, once she sees what's happened, she'll be in touch."

The kids looked around the table. Bando's hands remained folded, his eyes still shut. He said nothing about the fact that, the night before, they'd let him believe they'd informed their families about the van and the other five kids—but hadn't.

"They can't come for us yet," Maggie whined.

Twait cleared his throat, drawing their attention. "We know. That's why Rose stalled them."

The kids looked confused.

"You're beginning to use your gifts and to develop into a team," he continued. "We trust that the same is true for the other kids. The police will be important in all this, of course, but Bando, Rose, and I sense that we need your help."

"But time is short," Rose said. "We have a long way to go, and there's no guarantee it'll all come out okay."

"So let's share what we know or suspect," Bando said, eyes now open but hands still folded. "I'll go first. You eat as I talk."

They dug in.

"First, I don't believe the man in fatigues was bald. He probably wore a bald wig, the kind actors use. He wore a gas mask when he surprised Jerry, so Jerry wouldn't recognize him. Jerry must have seen him before and could identify him—maybe visually and also by voice, both of which the gas mask would hide.

"At an earlier time, Jerry inadvertently told this man the details of the meeting place. After he tied Jerry up and hid him in the woods, he removed the gas mask so he could meet the parents and the five kids. He could pose as a camp driver, because they'd never met him or Jerry before. But he didn't want them to be able to give a good description of him to the police later, so he put on the bald wig and sunglasses, then added an Army uniform, knowing their attention would focus more on details like a uniform than on his face and body. That's why the police artist's sketch has produced no sightings. People need to look through the disguise to see the person."

Charlie said, "Sounds like you're saying you can see through his disguise."

Bando looked down at his plate through half-closed eyes and plucked something quickly from it. He shielded it with his palm. "What am I hiding in my palm?"

"How would I know?" Charlie answered.

"You saw me pick it up, didn't you?"

"No," Mo said. "We didn't. You did it before we were paying attention."

The other kids nodded their agreement.

"Try it again and we may be able to tell you," Juan said.

"I don't need to do it again. You already saw it. You just don't know that you saw it."

The kids appeared perplexed.

"Is this what you call a teaching moment, sir?" Charlie asked.

"Perhaps. If you learn and answer correctly, we'll know it was."

"We're listening," Maggie said.

"A moment ago you were watching me close my eyes and clasp my hands. Although you didn't realize you were paying attention, you were. True or not?"

No one answered.

"While you were pretending not to pay close attention to me, you were unintentionally observing—and not just me but whatever was in your snapshot of vision around me. For example, Mo, what is missing besides what I took from my plate?"

Mo closed his eyes for several seconds, then opened them and said matter-of-factly, "Your spoon."

"Yes. And where is it?"

"It's to the right of you, on top of Juanita's spoon, where it hardly shows because it looks like only one spoon."

"Correct. And how did it get there? Did Maggie, our spoonbender, move it for us?"

Mo closed his eyes again and reopened them. "No, you did it as you were sitting down. One hand pulled out the chair and the other sleight-of-handed the spoon."

"Exactly. And how do you know?"

"I saw you do it."

"But I thought you didn't."

"I did. But at first I didn't know I saw it. It was like replaying videotape from a surveillance camera. I went back in my head just now and saw it." Mo grinned and ran his hand lightly over the top of his Mohawk.

"It's not just you, Mo. It's a gift you can all develop."

"So exactly what did you pick up from your plate?" Charlie asked. "That was the original challenge."

"Let's ask Mo, who seems to have a handle on this. Mo, what food item did I palm?"

"A mushroom," Juanita said.

"A carrot," her brother said.

"A grain of rice," Maggie guessed.

Bando smiled. "Charlie? Mo?"

Charlie closed his eyes as Mo had done, took a deep breath, opened them, and said, "Nothing."

"Nothing? Are you sure?"

"Yep. The spoon was the trick, the distraction. But my surveillance tape shows you took nothing."

Bando turned to Mo. "You agree, Mo?"

Mo closed his eyes, paused, and opened them. "Charlie's right. Nothing."

"So you're certain, the two of you, yet the other three still felt the need to guess. As you are learning, we see more than we think we see, and there are more ways of seeing than we imagine. So, to answer your earlier question, Charlie—I have seen this man even though I have not seen him face to face."

The kids appeared simultaneously pensive and puzzled.

"Caroline, what about you? We have three guesses about what I took from the plate, and two others who say I removed nothing. What do you say?"

Caroline closed her eyes, but almost immediately they flew wide open in surprise.

"Mom," she said, looking down the table at Rose. "Did you hear the girl? Just now?"

"No, but I heard the woman again. I think you're right—it's the mother."

"This time the little girl said don't hurt him."

Twait placed a hand on top of Rose's. "What did the mother say, Rose?"

"He's on the move again. He's going back for them."

CHAPTER 34

"So," CELINE SAID. "Now what?"

Mouse's great idea was partly a success. The pocket they carved outside the front windshield was bigger than the one by the three side windows. But they now faced the same problem—the limits of a safe reach. They'd stretched and scooped as far out as they could from beneath the roof's protective overhang. Soon someone would have to step into the exposed pocket and start scraping upward. At any moment tons of dirt might thunder down and bury the digger. Even the nimblest of them couldn't jump back fast enough to escape the sledgehammer of so much earth, and the others would never be able to remove it all in time to save the person from suffocating. That might not matter anyway, for the sheer weight of the dirt would probably crush his or her chest and lungs.

They discussed the dilemma and all understood the risk. They looked first at each other, then at their elongated prison cell.

BJ spotted the cot. "I have an idea. Grab that toolbox and let's take apart the cot."

Nobody asked why. They just did it, their trust in one another growing. Besides, nobody had offered up a better idea.

It didn't take long to remove the nuts and bolts, and soon the bed's disassembled skeleton lay on the dirt-covered floor.

"These two side rails are about six feet long," BJ said. "They'll give us longer reach. We can poke the dirt ceiling from just inside the bus. They're metal and they're heavy, which means we'll tire pretty fast using them.

Our shoulders are going to hurt from lifting and stabbing overhead. If we take turns and work in pairs, I think we can gain some ground."

"Hand me that rail," Mouse said.

Celine stepped up next to him. "Give me the other one."

"Keep under the overhang," BJ cautioned. "Don't get caught with the pointed end of the rail pointed at your body, not even your feet. If—or when—the ceiling caves, it could drive the rail right through you."

Mouse hefted the rail and prepared to attack the dirt ceiling. "There's a delicious thought. Mouse-ka-bob."

Nobody laughed.

***

Donnie Bronson awoke from his nap. He went to the kitchen, made two sandwiches and wolfed them down. He thought about his prisoners again. He'd planned to leave them another day, but after the phone call—what should he do? They'd already worked their way out of one impregnable fortress. Maybe they could do it again. Why couldn't they just stay put?

He didn't dare wear the bald wig and uniform when leaving the trailer this time. He hadn't seen a cop since the questioning about his snowmobile trailer, but that didn't mean they weren't keeping an eye on him. Now he'd have to go back to work so he didn't arouse suspicion. But he had to somehow get back to the bus to double-check his security. They'd almost outsmarted him at the blockhouse, and he didn't want to risk it again with the bus. He needed to hold them one more day. The mystery bugged him—how had they phoned him from underground? And if they could phone out, why hadn't they called for help?

Bronson grabbed his Red Sox cap and pulled the stuffed pup down from the shelf. It was cute and soft, felt somehow comforting in his hand. The soft brown eyes reminded him of Addie's. He rubbed its fur across his cheek. Where had this stray pup come from? How had it gotten on his shelf? How long had it been there? He couldn't remember buying it for Addie.

A shard of broken memory arose—something about a van sinking beneath dark green water. The van transformed itself—becoming Addie and Karen. They were pinned in a frothy swirl of water. It was like viewing them through a frosted-glass shower door. They didn't scream or cry. In his dreams they had always screamed and cried to him for help, but this time they'd ceased their struggles. Their faces were almost peaceful, the way they'd looked in their caskets at the wake. Oddly though, he found he preferred the dream version—the struggling—for it left room for the hope he might save them. Now though, their faces appeared slack, exhausted—dead. They were prisoners of the waters that—no matter how hard or how many times he wished, prayed, or begged—refused to release them back into his care.

The demon riding his shoulders bit deep into his neck, and the stabbing pain shot through his brain into the backs of his eyes. He winced and shut them. But blocking out the light didn't block the terrible vision, didn't provide relief. He opened his eyes, grabbed the bag containing the wig and fatigues, and tucked the puppy under his arm. He strode to the pickup, lit a cigarette, and climbed in. He'd drive to the stonewall job he'd been on that morning, in case they had a tail on him. But he was already devising a plan to slip away.

He placed the pup on the dashboard facing him, fired up the pickup and drove off, feeling secure with his .45 in its nest under the seat.

CHAPTER 35

BANDO HAD GATHERED EVERYONE at the ballfield after lunch.

"Kickball? You're kidding, right?" an exasperated Mo said. "Shouldn't we go track this guy down? You have a picture in your head, sir, and we've got a Map Quest from the library that'll get us to this Donald Bronson's house, so we know where to find him. If your mental picture matches Bronson, he's our guy, isn't he?"

"Mo, the State Police already have Mr. Bronson under surveillance. So far, they have no reason to suspect him of anything."

"But everything we know points to this guy!" Mo insisted.

"About that you are correct," Bando said calmly. "However, you must remember, we see things in different ways than the police. Consider this—Donald Bronson doesn't match the sketch or any of the witnesses' descriptions. The six numbers of his trailer plate are just that—six numbers that have no official connection to this case. Yes, the police were kind enough to search out the plate and the owner—Mr. Bronson—but we've given them no credible source for the numbers. All we've learned is, those numbers make up an actual Maine license plate. To the police, though, the numbers seem to have appeared out of thin air."

"My sister heard them!" Juan argued. "She didn't pull them out of thin air."

"Wait!" Maggie said, stepping in. "Bando's got a point. The police know nothing about remote hearing or remote viewing." She tapped her temple with her index finger. "Most of what we know about this guy, we know in a different way than most people—not normally but para-normally. To anybody besides us …us FreeKs … those numbers were dreamed up."

Nobody spoke. Their faces said it all. This was the first time they'd heard themselves self-described as a special group, a team working together on a mission. And it was the first time they'd heard themselves called FreeKs—and they liked it.

Maggie continued. "We get a lot of our information in different ways than the police do. Forgive me for sounding like a TV cop show, but they still require facts and evidence and proof."

"Everything didn't come to us this way," Mo said, tapping his own temple with an index finger. "How about Bronson's connection to the camp. We learned that by old-fashioned amateur detective work at the library."

The others nodded agreement.

"So Bando can legitimately call the State Police's attention to that," Maggie said. "But it doesn't give him a motive to kidnap. In fact, we still have no idea why those other kids were grabbed."

"Revenge," Mo said. "Against the camp."

"Maybe," Charlie said. "But revenge would seem to call for something like burning down the dining hall, wouldn't it? There are other motives besides revenge—like, he grabbed them so he could sell them into slavery."

Mo gave an exaggerated eye roll. "The word for that is *facetious*."

"Gee, you think?" Juan added.

"Yes, Mo, I was being facetious," Charlie said. "And I apologize. I'm simply saying there's no sure way to know the motive."

"And," Maggie added, "there's nothing to prove he's our bad guy. He's got a trailer and a connection to the camp, that's all."

"Which is why it's time to play kickball," Twait said, changing the subject. "Give your minds a rest. Okay, here's the teams: staff and Caroline against the newbies."

"That's five of us against only four of you," Mo said, his eyes glancing from the redheads Twait and Caroline to stocky Rose to diminutive Bando. "It's not fair."

"True enough," Bando said, eyes twinkling. "We'll try not to run up the score. Your team kicks first."

"Ooh, we're so scared," Mo mocked, rising to the challenge.

Everyone had a blast. The ribbing was good-natured. The game stayed even until the sixth inning, when Twait kicked one that hung suspended high above the infield for so long, the little man was able to strut around the bases and tag home before the ball started down. When it finally dropped toward Mo on the pitcher's mound, it descended slowly, as if it might land like a bird.

The kids froze in place, mouths and eyes open in wonder.

"Call for it, Mo!" Twait joked. "This one's yours."

Mo stuck out his arms, expecting it to alight softly on his palms. But when his hands tried to close around it, the ball had the weight of a bowling ball and passed through, landing with a loud thunk at his feet. Mo stared in disbelief, then looked to his teammates for support—or answers.

"Levitation, Mo?" Juan asked.

Mo shook his head. "Not me."

"I believe we win by one run," Bando said. "You played well for newcomers."

Twait smiled, but not smugly. "That was fun, wasn't it? And it got your minds off everything else. Ah, the joys of camp life."

They had to agree. It had been fun, and it reduced their tensions.

"How'd you do that, Twait?" Mo said as he walked in from the pitcher's mound. "How'd you make it so heavy at the end?"

Twait winked. "Who said I did it?"

Bando walked past. "Told you we wouldn't run up the score. Okay, everybody, free time until four o'clock. Meet at the waterfront."

CHAPTER **36**

BANDO AND TWAIT LEFT THE BALL FIELD and disappeared into the dining hall.

"Nappy time," Juan said, and he and Charlie headed across the field toward the boys' cabin.

Mo didn't join them. He hung back near Juanita.

Caroline asked if anyone was interested in hiking to the waterfall.

"I'm up for it," Maggie said.

"I can use a break from the kitchen," Rose said. "If you don't mind an adult tagging along."

"Mo? You in or not?" Caroline asked.

He bit his lower lip, stalling. Finally Juanita rescued him.

"Didn't I see a ping-pong table somewhere?" she asked.

"There's one folded up in the back corner of the dining room," Rose said. "It's against the wall. Paddles, net, and balls are in the cupboard to the right."

"If you only fold half of the table down," Caroline said with a teasing smile, "you can play by yourself—like handball against a wall."

"Alone?" Juanita asked.

"I know how to play," Mo volunteered quickly.

"You any good?" Juanita's eyes narrowed.

"The girls at school say I am."

Juanita deliberated, then chirped, "Okay." The two of them walked off the field toward the dining hall.

"What was that all about?" Caroline asked.

"It wasn't about ping-pong," Maggie said.

"Definitely not ping-pong," Rose agreed.

***

Twait sat on a sagging loveseat in the office, sipping a glass of iced tea. He heard the hot-water kettle whistle in the kitchen. A minute later Bando came in with a cup of hot tea and settled into an overstuffed chair.

"You think the kids are right about tomorrow?" Twait asked. "You think this guy's got something planned?"

Bando took a sip of his tea. The question weighed heavily on him. "Yes."

"So we haven't much time left."

"No."

"Do we have a plan?"

"Not yet. But this group is gifted and smart. They've learned to work together quickly."

"And the other group?"

"Their gifts are quite different. We may not know what they're facing, but they're smart and resourceful. I have a feeling they're learning to work together, too."

Twait swigged his iced tea.

"You know what I didn't see coming?" Bando said. "Caroline. Somehow I assumed she'd turn out more like you than her mother. Maybe it was the red hair. I was starting to think I'd seen it all. But she surprised me. I hadn't expected her to hear like Rose does."

"I thought you knew everything."

"If I did, I'd get those other kids back today. This is killing their parents."

"Yes, it is. And there's no guarantee it'll all turn out okay, which really scares me."

"Me too. But you, Rose, and I, and the others from our own group, we know how important it is to—pardon the *Star Wars* reference—Trust The Force."

Twait groaned and rolled his eyes.

Not 75 feet away, at the opposite end of the dining hall, Mo and Juanita pulled out the ping-pong table. They set up the net and lobbed a few shots back and forth. From the very start the effort was more collaborative than competitive, and they never did find out if either of them was any good. It was more important to bat the ball back and forth mindlessly—together. When someone missed a shot and the ball bounced along the floor—regardless of who flubbed it—Mo would gallantly chase it down.

Finally, when he was reaching under a chair for the ball, she said, "Why don't you just float it back to us, Mo—you know, levitate it? For me?"

The ball suddenly reversed direction and rolled toward her feet. When it was still ten feet away, it lifted off the floor like a plane from a runway, and moved directly toward her nose. She resisted the urge to duck aside, knowing—trusting—that the ball would veer aside like a bird dodging a windshield. Or Mo might playfully stop it an inch from her face.

It crashed into her nose, fell to the floor, and bounced away.

"Hey! You hit me!" She blinked in surprise.

"Oops! Sorry."

Her hands went to her hips. "What happened?"

Mo looked sheepish. "I haven't worked out all the bugs yet." The ball came to rest by the couch.

Her mock anger dissipated quickly. "Lucky it wasn't a freight train."

"I couldn't lift anything that heavy."

"What's the biggest thing you've levitated?" She set her paddle on the table and sat on the couch.

"The biggest? A beach ball—but it was light. I couldn't do a bowling ball—maybe a volleyball or a basketball. It takes a lot of mental effort—tires me out. I think the heaviest was a six-pack of Coke—not empty, either. Full. I moved it from one end of our dining room table to the other. Kept it up about six inches. Okay, it drooped some by the end. After that, my brain was mush for a half hour."

"How'd you discover you could levitate things?" Juanita patted the couch cushion next to her.

Mo sat. "My parents noticed it first—when I was in my crib. One morning when the windows were closed and there was no breeze in my room, the merry-go-round mobile kept spinning over my head. I wanted those horses to run in a circle, only the windup mechanism had broken, so I took matters into my own hands—or should I say my own mind?"

"Then you're here to develop it? I mean, I'm sure you've gotten better over the years just by doing it, right?"

"I don't use it much. I haven't figured what it's good for. My parents don't want me to tell anybody or show it off. They're afraid I might become some lab's guinea pig. As far as why I came to Free Camp, I really don't know. The application just showed up in the mailbox one day, and it sounded interesting."

"That's funny. Mine came as email. And Maggie said her Mom found a coupon in with her newspaper."

"That is funny. Charlie told me his grandmother heard about it through her Meals on Wheels driver."

Juanita and Mo exchanged puzzled looks.

"So, anyway, yesterday when we saw you float that bottle opener in the van, was that your first public appearance?"

"Pretty much, yeah—except for my best friends who think it's a magic trick I learned from a book. I threatened them with a gruesome death if they told."

Juanita laughed. For the next 10 minutes they talked about their families, their schools, their towns, and their interests.

"You want something to drink?" Mo asked when the conversation reached a lull. "Rose said there are cans of apple juice in the fridge."

"I can't drink a whole one, but we can split a can."

Mo walked to the kitchen and returned a minute later with an aluminum can and a paper cup. He popped the top, poured some juice into the cup, and handed it to her. In the exchange their fingers brushed each other's. Juanita shut her eyes as if wincing in pain.

"Don't let go of the cup," she whispered.

Mo didn't know what to say and didn't dare move. Finally he croaked, "Are you okay?"

"I hear someone." Juanita's eyes remained closed, the lids fluttering slightly. Their fingers were still barely touching as they gripped the cup. "Put your free hand in mine."

Mo sat beside her and did as he was told. It looked like a strange courtship ritual.

"It's a different girl. She's kind of giving orders—take apart the cot, use the bed rails to dig and stab overhead. We've got nine or ten feet of dirt to tunnel up through. And she's warning them to stay under the safety of the overhanging bus roof."

"It's not my cousin Atlanta?"

"I don't know. I just know it's a different voice than the one saying the numbers."

"So what's it mean?"

"I don't know. Maybe this girl is touching your cousin, and your cousin's my transmitter. Looks like it works because I'm touching you on this end—you're the receiver. What matters is, a voice is coming through."

"It's like a magnet picking up a long string of linked nails."

"All I know is, I'm overhearing this second girl's part in a conversation. I doubt she knows I'm tuned in. They're buried in a bus."

"Who is?" called a voice from across the dining hall. "Who's buried in a bus?" Bando moved their way from the kitchen door.

Startled, Mo and Juanita broke contact, not only with each other, but also with the transmitter in the bus.

CHAPTER 37

ON HIS WAY TO THE STONEWALL REPAIR JOB Donnie Bronson stopped by the gas pumps at a Dead River convenience store. He inserted the fuel hose into the throat of his truck's gas tank, started the flow, and walked inside.

"Two packs of smokes?" asked the young woman behind the counter, reaching overhead for Donnie's usual.

"Three this time. And take out for a coffee." He handed her a fifty.

"Gas?"

"Yeah, but I'm not using cash for it today. Your pump out there is siphoning money from my debit card as we speak. So, just the cigarettes and coffee."

The woman took the fifty and made change that included a ten. He pocketed the change except for the ten-dollar bill, which he held out to her.

"If you do me a favor, doll, you can keep this ten." His fingertips tapped the wrinkled bill on her palm.

She folded the ten and tucked it into her shirt pocket beneath the stitched name Bobbi. "What's the favor?"

He leaned in closer.

"I've accumulated a few too many parking tickets, and being the handsome and dashing desperado I am, I fear a gun-toting meter maid or man may be on my trail—a cop. I'm going to go finish filling the pickup and the motorcycle in the back. Then I'm going to pull out the little gas can I use for my generator. After I fill the can, I'll accidentally leave it behind between the two pumps. I'll boogie on down the road. Before I get a mile away, I'll remember I left it here, and I'll turn around and come back for it. Your mission in the meantime—see if the posse's tailing me. When I come back, I won't come in. I'll just sneak a look your way, and you nod yes or no. Then I'll pick up my little gas can and go to work."

"That's an easy ten. And here I thought you were going to ask me out."

"Bobbi doll," he said with a wink, his Maine accent making the words sound like Barbie Doll, "if I wasn't getting married tomorrow, I would."

Less than ten minutes later, Donnie pulled the truck up to the pumps again, got out, and picked up the can he'd left behind. He glanced toward the window, held up the tank, and grinned foolishly as he waved to the cashier, as if saying, "Stupid me, I've got it."

His answer came. She raised not one but two fingers—two cop cars. He set the can in the truck bed and drove off toward the job. As his father had often quipped: Plan your work and work your plan. It was time to work his plan.

The wall job was on a heavily forested, thirty-acre estate. The owners, a British couple, spent two weeks there each fall. Their live-in caretaker was exceptional with lawns and gardens, and was adequate when it came to basic maintenance. But he lacked expertise in masonry and the repair of ornamental stonewalls, and the rear and side ones needed work, so he'd called on a local handyman, mason, and stonewall artisan.

Bronson turned into the entrance of the estate and stopped as soon as all four tires hit the driveway. He climbed out, hammer in one hand, cardboard sign on a stake in the other. He located a conspicuous spot and tapped the stake into the ground.

DONNIE BRONSON, local
- **Jack of Most Trades,**
  Master of Some
- **Quality Work**
- **References**
- **Satisfaction Guaranteed**

Tel: 207-555-1555

At the bottom of the sign was his phone number. He stepped back and held up a thumb the way artists did in movies—in case anyone was watching, so the posse would know exactly where he was. A moment later he and his truck disappeared past the front-gate pillars and up the long driveway into the pine trees.

A quarter mile in either direction sat the two State Police cruisers on stakeout duty. The Troopers weren't happy they'd lost visual contact with Bronson, and both were relieved when five minutes later the pickup appeared again at the end of the driveway.

Bronson parked it just inside the pillars where it was easy to see, and then walked back down the driveway with a shovel on one shoulder and a tool belt slung over the other. The cops were too far away to hear Bronson whistling "Whistle While You Work," and neither of them noticed the motorcycle was gone from the bed of the pickup. It was waiting for Bronson to push it a long ways into the woods before starting it and hopping aboard.

CHAPTER 38

"HEY, HEY, IT'S OKAY," Juan said, shaking Charlie. "It's just a bad dream."

Charlie blinked himself awake from the nap. His hands shook as he put on his glasses. He scanned the room, as if checking to be sure no ghouls or monsters lurked.

"It was terrible—a nightmare. I was tied to a tree, watching that bald guy with sunglasses race around a parking lot on a motorcycle. He had five kids blindfolded and tied to posts. He stopped, glared at them, then revved up and took off. He had something bigger than a machete—like one of those Samurai swords—and as he passed each of them, he lopped their heads off."

"Was it the other kids? Or us?"

"I don't know. I couldn't tell. But it was horrible."

"You think it's something that's really going to happen?"

"I have no idea." Charlie's hands still trembled.

Juan grabbed his notebook. "Here. Write down as much of the details as you can, before you forget."

Charlie took the pen and began to write. And as he did, Juan closed his eyes and said, "Hey, I'm seeing something—a motorcycle."

"Don't screw around, Juan. My dream was awful."

"I'm serious," Juan said, eyes still shut. "It's a motorcycle. I'm looking out the rear window of a pickup into the back of it."

Charlie stopped writing.

"This is the guy I saw in the easy chair, I'm sure of it. The tailgate's down and he's rolling a dirt bike along a plank onto the ground. He put the kickstand down. Now he's lifting the tailgate, latching it. He's coming around the driver's side, getting in. I can see him to my right."

"What kind of motorcycle? Can you see the license plate?"

"The truck's moving forward, but my eyes tell me I'm moving backward. I must be on the dashboard. The motorcycle's growing smaller over the top of the tailgate. No license plate on the front. Maybe Maine only has it on the back. Now the bike's gone. I can't see it. Lots of trees around me. Looks like we're on a blacktop driveway. I can see a yellow barn or garage back by where the motorcycle was, and a wall made of rocks beyond that. I think we're going toward the road. He's parking, getting out. I can see him walking back up the driveway toward the barn and the motorcycle. He's disappearing. He's gone. Now it's black, like a TV that's turned off. I must have been seeing through something on the truck's dashboard."

"What was he wearing?"

Juan opened his eyes.

"Blue jeans and one of those soft blue work shirts. He had a shovel on one shoulder, a tool belt over the other."

"Anything else?"

"Let me think. Oh, after he set the kickstand he stuffed something into the saddlebag."

"No Samurai sword?"

"No sword. Not even a little machete."

Charlie breathed a sigh of relief. He ripped out a sheet of paper from the notebook and handed it to Juan.

"You write down your vision while I finish writing about my nightmare."

"But we've got to tell Bando and the others," Juan said.

"I know," Charlie said. "In a minute. First get the details written down."

Juan and Charlie both wrote. When they finished, Charlie scrunched up his face.

"What's wrong?" Juan asked. "You okay?"

"There was something in my dream—something on the edge of the parking lot—and I've got to remember it. I was so focused on the guy riding the motorcycle, I almost missed it."

"Start writing again. Maybe your hand can remember what your mind can't. Write fast and don't let yourself edit."

With Juan peering over his shoulder, Charlie scribbled as quickly as his clumsy hand would allow: the man racing toward them, and off to the side there were lights flashing—first blinking yellow, then blinking red. Warning. Warning. Children. Stop. Stop. He put the pen down.

"Sounds like a stop light—yellow for caution, red for stop," Juan said. "Or a school crossing."

"No, it's not. A traffic light would be solid red, then solid yellow for a few seconds, and then switch to solid green. This was alternating yellow—two yellow bulbs taking turns, back and forth, back and forth. Then it changed to red, with the two bulbs alternating—red, red, red, red."

"So what is it?"

The Aha moment hit Charlie. "It's what we see every day—a school bus. I think our guy is either moving them around in a school bus or he's hiding them somewhere in one."

***

Maggie, Caroline, and Rose reached the waterfall and sat on one of the benches.

"So, what is it we're doing, Mom? Are we communicating with the dead?"

"Not communicating," Rose said. "That would be two-way. This doesn't even seem to be one-way. They're not talking to us. We're overhearing them. They're trying to communicate with someone else. Think back to what you heard."

"She heard a little girl pleading with her father," Maggie said. "It may have been a ghost. It could also have been a flesh-and-blood girl whispering in the background when the man recorded his answering machine message. We have no way of knowing which it was."

"For the sake of argument let's assume the voice came from someone not alive," Rose said. "The girl wasn't talking to Caroline. She said *Dad, don't, please.* She was talking to her father—whoever that may be—and Caroline was an eavesdropper on the line. None of you others could hear her—only Caroline—though you would have if it was a flesh-and-blood voice, right? It sounds like Mr. Bronson—who may or may not be the father, we don't know—he couldn't hear her, or he'd have responded."

"But, Rose, you heard a voice too, didn't you?" Maggie asked. "You heard a woman's voice in your phone lines that said *he's coming.*"

"Mom, whoever that woman is—or was—she wouldn't say *he's coming* to the guy, would she? It sounds like it was spoken right to you, or to us, or to anyone who might be able to hear her—as a warning."

"I hadn't thought of it that way then. It didn't make any sense at the time."

"Twait said you didn't just hear the voice in the background when you were on the phone, but in the headphones," Maggie said.

"That's why I stopped using them—to stop the voice."

"When did you hear it, Mom?"

"I've been hearing her for weeks."

"Weeks?" Maggie pressed. "How many times? And what did she say?"

"Eight or ten times. I keep a journal. I could check. Twice she said *he wants us back. He wants us back.*"

"That's it?" Caroline asked.

"No. The last couple of times she said *he's sick. He wants to trade.*"

The three of them sat quiet, and then cocked their heads slightly, straining to hear something above the roar of the waterfall. Could it be an engine far out in the woods?

"Kids," Rose said, "on dirt bikes." She and Caroline shivered for no reason.

"So, if we go back to camp," Maggie said, "you can both try the earphones." When Caroline and Rose looked at her anxiously, she added, "You have to, you know—for those kids."

Somewhere off in the distance, they heard the dirt bike again. It revved up and moved away. As the noise grew fainter, the waterfall dominated again, except that under its thunder Rose and Caroline heard two voices whispering—*hurry*.

CHAPTER **39**

When Rose, Caroline, and Maggie returned from the water-fall, they walked into the middle of a media circus. TV cameras and reporters were everywhere, not just local stations but the big net-works—CBS, NBC, ABC, CNN, MSNBC, even the court and crime channels—all asking questions, shooting footage, and offering commentary. It had been thirty-one hours since the carjacking and abduction. It was a wonder the authorities had been able to keep a lid on it that long.

The police sketch and the missing children's pictures had been in the newspapers and on last night's and now this day's news. Still, no demands or ransom note had surfaced, and there had been no sightings of the van, the five kids, or the bald carjacker. It was as if they'd disap-peared off the face of the earth.

With no apparent progress in the case, the viewing public's interest had grown. Soon it would become an insatiable hunger. Not just the local Maine and regional New England stations but the big national net-works were starving. They didn't want just the usual official statements from the State Police spokesperson; they wanted interviews with Bando, Twait, Jerry, the kids' parents and grandparents, local townsfolk on the street—anyone who could give them a few sound bytes. Information was appreciated, but in the absence of information, emotion was in demand.

They roamed the camp freely, filming footage of everything— the dining hall, the cabins, the waterfront, the canoes and kayaks, the swimming float, the volleyball court and ball field—any images that would arouse the TV audience's sympathy and create a viewing addiction to the story.

A CNN newswoman stood before a backdrop: Today's Fire Danger Moderate. As the cameras rolled, she referred to a brochure in her hand, offering viewers a bit of historical background on Free Camp, and then commenting on its mission and purpose. Lacking any real understanding of the camp, she made it sound like those "gifted children" who attended were like those "gifted and talented" schoolchildren with a knack for math or science, music or art, or had superior verbal and writing skills that needed to be further developed. She took the brochure's reference to "special kids and their unique gifts" to be an IQ thing.

In addition to TV trucks and vans jamming the parking spaces, there were six police cars—some State, some local. Officers in wide-brimmed hats strolled through the media hounds like lifeguards among sunbathers, arms folded across their broad chests as they watched and kept order.

Two television reporters spotted Rose, Caroline, and Maggie coming off the waterfall trail. They seized the moment and ordered their camerapersons to capture some footage, then approached the hikers and peppered them with questions. Before anyone could answer, Twait stepped in, shouldering his way between the waists of two cameramen. He held up a finger to his lips.

"Don't say a word, you three. The officer in charge will do the talking."

Rose's face drained of color when she saw the media swarm. Fearing the bad news had come, she blurted, "Oh no, have they found them? Are they—?"

"Nothing's changed," Twait reassured her. "They haven't found them. Now follow me. We've already got Juan and Charlie, Mo and Juanita in our staff cabin. Just ignore these people. Let's go."

The reporters pressed microphones into their faces and tossed out a torrent of questions, but Twait waved his arms dismissively. "Getting back from a hike. Just a hike, that's all. Let us through, please."

The footage of the three coming off the waterfall trail would later show up on an evening show along with Twait's sound byte about "getting back from a hike." The public was so ravenous they'd swallow it as news.

Suddenly everyone's attention turned to the porch of the dining hall. A State Police spokesperson had bellied up to a portable lectern that held a bouquet of microphones.

Bando stood behind the spokesperson, and nine adults stood grim-faced beside Bando. The officer leaned into the mikes and cleared his throat. The crowd drew in close and quieted.

"Who are those people with Bando?" Maggie asked Twait.

"The families of the missing kids. The police asked a couple of the parents to make an appeal to the kidnapper. From what Bando told me, there are no new developments."

"These poor parents," Rose said.

"I know," Twait answered. "This will rip everybody's heart out. But remember, Bando says we don't talk to the TV folks until the kids and we can powwow. Just keep moving toward our cabin."

The officer tapped a microphone to be sure it was working. The shuffling of feet stopped and the crowd held its collective breath.

But this wasn't a perfect silence, and it made Maggie pause for a second. What was that puck-puck-puck sound? She'd heard it before, near the waterfall. Now she heard it again, but from where? It was coming from the trees perhaps halfway up the trail they'd just descended. It reminded her of a weed whacker or a chainsaw—no, this was more like the idling motor on some neighborhood kid's ATV—or dirt bike.

The rider had paused at some spot near the trail for a view of the camp. That way he or she could see from under cover of the trees, but couldn't be seen. Maybe it was simply a dirt-bike rider wondering about all the commotion on the camp's grounds—the swarm of media trucks, cameras, and personnel. And now that mysterious observer could sit and hear loud and clear what came over the microphone, without being heard in return—except for the puck-puck-puck of the idling motor.

That explanation made perfect sense, of course, but part of Maggie's brain—that little voice she was learning to trust more and more—didn't buy it. It was the part of her brain that right now was giving her the creeps.

CHAPTER 40

CELINE'S AND MOUSE'S SHOULDERS and biceps ached from stabbing the metal rails up into the dirt. The others had taken their turns too, and everyone was worn out. It was a wearying process—knock the dirt loose from the cave's ceiling, scrape the loose stuff into the bus, carry it back from the windshield and spread it around. They were sweaty and grimy, caked with dirt.

"It's getting hard to breathe in here," BJ said. "My lungs wheeze when I try to suck down air. Anybody else noticing it?"

"It's the dust," Atlanta answered. "It's thick, like pollen affecting an allergy."

"Actually," Mouse countered, "it's not dust. This dirt is moist and clumpy."

The candles flickered.

"Hey, look at Tim," Celine said.

Tim sat propped against the bus wall on the discarded cot mattress, eyes closed.

"He's exhausted," Mouse said. "He's a lot smaller than the rest of us."

The candles flickered again.

"The problem's not dust," BJ said. "It's the air. It's thinning out. There's only that one vent pipe. Our guy didn't design this shelter for this many people—and we're using up the oxygen even faster now that we're exerting ourselves in the digging."

"So what are you saying?" Celine asked. "That we should slow down? Or dig faster?"

"I'm not saying anything, except that—exerting ourselves or not—that pipe he installed may not be enough for five of us in the long run."

The others—except the sleeping Tim—stared blankly, dead tired.

"There's only one solution," Mouse said, and the others turned his way. "We've got to dig faster, risk stepping out from under the protection of the roof into the cave. Forget Tim for now. Sleeping, he'll use less air. Two of us at a time will have to punch up as hard and fast as we can. The dirt ceiling's two feet above the roof, which leaves six to eight feet of dirt to get through to reach ground level. The dirt's hung up, stuck there. When it finally caves, if it buries one or two of us, the other two dig us out."

BJ opened her mouth to protest, but before she could, Mouse shushed her and said, "We've got to do it." He climbed through the windshield into the cave and began poking overhead.

A moment later Celine was shoulder to shoulder with him, ramming her rail up into the dirt, daring it to collapse.

They worked almost blind, trying not to look up so they wouldn't get smaller particles in their eyes. Small clods and rocks pelted their heads and shoulders, and even with BJ and Atlanta raking the accumulation back as fast as they could, the two main diggers were soon up to their knees in soil.

After half an hour BJ said, "Okay, time to change places. Leave the dirt piled where it is, so Atlanta and I can stand on it. The ceiling's getting higher and harder to reach."

Celine leaned her rail against the wall and climbed back under the protection of the bus roof. Mouse refused to quit and kept prodding.

"We're almost there," he huffed. "I can feel it. We're so close."

"Mouse," Atlanta said, "the lack of oxygen is getting to your brain. Play time's over. Time to come in."

But Mouse was angry, and he just had to stab the ceiling a couple more times, muttering as he did, "It's ... got ... to ... come ... down. It's ... got ... to ... come ... DOWN."

Atlanta grabbed Mouse's pants leg just as the ceiling gave way. Small chunks rained on him for several seconds, from which he instinctively ducked away. Immediately behind them came larger chunks that pounded his exposed back and drove him to his knees. Then—whump— the rest of what was above came down on him, collapsing into the hole and spilling into the bus.

Celine was suddenly waist deep in the overflow, and the spillover inside reached Atlanta's and BJ's knees. They had no time to react.

"Mouse!" Celine screamed. "Mouse! She struggled to free herself and began clawing back the dirt that blackened the window, digging toward the spot where she'd last seen Mouse.

Tim was awake now and helped free Atlanta and BJ. The three of them grabbed whatever they could dig with and scrambled in next to Celine.

They quickly uncovered a hand and wrist. Luckily, Mouse's ducking away from the first chunks had turned him toward the windshield, and the tons of soil that hit his back and shoulders had forced him even closer to it. Had he fallen the other way, they'd have been pulling his ankles and he'd have quickly suffocated.

They dug feverishly, burrowing like rabbits. But as quickly as they scooped the sediment away from their friend's arm, it seemed more replaced it.

Mouse's hand didn't move.

They scratched and clawed with their fingers and pulled dirt back with their forearms, crying and sobbing as they dug with their forepaws like dogs after moles. Finally they cleared Mouse's elbow, a minute later his shoulder, and then his face.

He wasn't breathing.

BJ cleared his nose and mouth, then tried mouth-to-mouth.

"There's too much dirt on his chest," Celine said. "It's the weight. He can't inflate and deflate his lungs. We've got to dig him out. Dig! Dig!"

They swept the dirt toward themselves and off Mouse, finding him on his side in the fetal position, legs and feet farthest back in the cave-in. After another frantic few minutes, they freed his torso of the pressing weight. Celine and Atlanta worked to free his legs and feet while BJ returned to her mouth-to-mouth.

"Let me press his chest," Tim said, and placed his hands on Mouse's breastbone. "His heart may have stopped. I can't remember now how many compressions per minute, but some must be better than none." He pressed the area around Mouse's heart as BJ breathed her breaths of life into their pigheaded hero.

A moment later Mouse sputtered and coughed, then gulped down the thin air that had been running out. He saw BJ staring down at him, tears in her eyes, relief on her face.

"Welcome back," Tim said.

They stopped their labors and sat down, breathing heavily, everyone sweating like they'd been shoveling coal all night in Hades. No one said a word for a full two minutes. They simply sat, as survivors of disasters do, trying to take in what they'd just come through.

Celine finally broke the silence. "Idiot." She shook her head.

They freed Mouse and dragged him to the mattress. Then the four of them returned to the cave-in and attacked it anew.

Before long they felt a tiny stream of air leaking through a fist-size opening. With it came a hint of daylight. Freedom beckoned, if they could overcome their exhaustion. Another five minutes of digging and they'd be able to crawl through and—hopefully—up and out.

CHAPTER **41**

GOING OUT FOR SUPPER was Twait's idea.

"These kids need time away from the media. We all do," he told Bando. "I'll take them to Kingsbury's Drive-In. They can get burgers, fries, plenty of comfort food."

Bando's brow furrowed. He placed the knuckle of his forefinger against his lip then nodded ever so slightly. "I like the idea. But let's not have all these reporters tailing you. You get in the van. Make it clear you're going to town for supplies. Then a couple minutes later Rose and Caroline jump in the car and say they're going home for the night. You and Rose hide the two vehicles so you're out of sight, and wait for us. The five kids and I will sneak off and follow the stream down to Granger Road by that cement culvert. Meet you there."

An hour later the six kids and the three adults were chowing down at an oversized picnic table behind Kingsbury's. Rose's car and FreeK Camp #2 were parked where they couldn't be spotted from the road.

Mo sat across from Maggie, the two of them playing an odd game with the metal tops they'd unscrewed from four salt-and-pepper shakers. Maggie would mentally drag a shaker top along the tabletop toward herself or push it away. Mo would mentally lift one a few inches above the table and move it toward or away from Maggie's plastic fish-fry basket—a game of soccer or hockey. At one point there was a tug of war, with Mo levitating a metal cap toward her as she pushed it back. Then while Mo grimaced and practically broke a sweat from his exertion, she suddenly ceased resisting and the cap flew past her elbow, landing on the ground. Both Maggie's and Mo's eyes widened in surprise, and then they broke into laughter.

From the other end of the table Bando and Twait glanced up at the laughter. Bando tapped his plastic spoon on a waxy paper cup, drawing the group's attention. "As your official camp director I'm obliged to ask this question. What have you learned so far in your camp experience?"

No one had a word to say at first. Eventually Juan ventured an answer.

"We all have different gifts." The others nodded agreement.

"But we're not exactly sure how to use them yet," Maggie added honestly. "I mean, like, look at us." She held up a shiny salt-and-pepper top. "Mo and I know how to use our gifts, and we're playing games with them, but we're not sure how they can help. We aren't helping much in finding those other kids. Caroline and Charlie's gifts, and Juan and Juanita's, seem to be better suited to helping. I guess I'm saying I feel kind of useless."

Mo nodded.

Bando didn't try to explain or make them feel better. "What else have you learned?"

"It's fun working as a team," Charlie said. "What we dug up together at the library was pretty good stuff, I think."

Bando and Twait nodded. "Okay," Bando said. "Anything else?"

"Things take time," Juan said. "You've got to Trust the Force."

"And each other," Juanita added. She looked at Caroline. "I've also learned that those people we think have the gifts may not be the only ones possessing them. Caroline surprised me with hers."

"It surprised me too," Caroline said.

"Maybe certain gifts run in families," Maggie said. "Like Rose and Caroline hearing ghost voices."

"I've learned there's more to this world than meets the eye," Mo said, "maybe another whole dimension." The others nodded.

A police car pulled into the gravel parking lot. Mo noticed it first.

"Psst. Smokey Bandit in the parking lot."

Bando never turned. "She's just doing an evening check to make sure things are calm. She can't see the van or the car, and she doesn't know we're away from the camp. Keep eating and talking like we were."

The group resumed their activity and the police car turned onto the main road again before disappearing in the distance.

"How'd you know?" Charlie asked.

"How'd I know what?"

"How'd you know it was a lady cop? You never looked."

"Was it a lady cop?" Bando smiled.

"You know it was," Juan said. "I saw her too."

"Maybe I saw her reflection in someone's glasses."

"Did you?" Maggie asked.

"Maybe," Rose cut in, "it's the same woman Trooper who cruises this parking lot every night. Maybe we see her whenever we come out for ice cream."

Bando wiggled his eyebrows. "Mysterious, aren't I?"

A moment later they were sharing information and comparing notes about dreams, visions, voices, and sounds—of waterfalls, dirt bikes, license plates, and the pleadings of disembodied spirits.

"So, what's next?" Caroline asked. "Sneak back to camp the way we sneaked out?"

"Some of you have to go back," Bando answered. "Two or three of you have to walk around camp so you'll be seen. You'll cover for those of us who aren't there, so we don't arouse suspicion."

"I'll drive the van back," Twait said. "Three of you and Rose can ride with me to the culvert and then hike back by the same trail. They heard me say I was going for supplies. I'll drive in the main driveway alone."

"What about the car?" Juanita asked.

"A couple of us need to take a ride," Bando said. "To gather data."

"So who do we go with?" Maggie asked.

"My sister and I will go with Caroline and Bando," Juan said. "You, Mo, Charlie, and Rose go in the van with Twait."

"Who died and left you in charge?" Mo asked.

Juan turned to Bando. "I believe my seating chart is correct, isn't it?"

"Yes, Juan, exactly right."

"It is?" Mo asked, astonished. "But how'd Juan know? Did you tell him ahead of time?"

Bando smiled and his eyes half closed. He shook his head no. Everyone waited.

Finally Charlie cleared his throat. "I told Juan ahead of time. It was in one of my dreams."

"Which I urged him to write in this notebook," Juan finished. "This afternoon."

"I even know what you're going to say next, Mo," Charlie said.

Juan opened the notebook to a page of Charlie's scribbles.

"Aw, this isn't fair," Mo complained. "I thought we were a team."

Juan pulled out a pen and circled something near the center of the page, then passed the notebook to Mo. The circled passage read: "Aw, this isn't fair. I thought we were a team."

After that, they all begged to read the three paragraphs following. When they passed the notebook to Bando and Twait, the two men said, "Already seen it."

Without argument they quietly took their assigned seats in the two vehicles. The van left the parking lot and headed toward Free Camp. The car went the opposite way.

Thanks to their early meal the group in the car still had two hours of daylight to gather data—whatever Bando meant by that.

CHAPTER 42

BANDO FOLLOWED CAROLINE'S MAP QUEST directions from the library, and soon he and the twins and Caroline were near Donnie Bronson's house trailer. They pulled off the pavement a little ways from his driveway.

"Looks like nobody's home," Juan said. "No truck. No lights in the house."

"He could come back any time," cautioned Juanita.

Bando sat with eyes half-closed, as if waiting for directions from the universe.

"So, what are we going to do?" Caroline asked. "Just sit here?"

Bando said nothing.

"Well?" Caroline asked impatiently. "You're the boss, aren't you?"

Bando's eyes opened as if her words were the sign he'd been waiting for.

"I'm not the boss. What do *you* think we should do?"

"Me? Are you asking me, or are you asking the three of us?"

Bando shrugged.

Caroline and the twins searched each other's faces.

"Here's an idea," Juan offered. "I've got that cell phone Charlie bought. Let's call Bronson's number and make sure he's not home."

Caroline and Juanita agreed and Bando didn't object.

Juan punched Redial and held the phone away from his ear so the girls could hear. The answering machine picked up. After the beep, Juan let it go for a while—in case Bronson was again late picking it up. Then he clicked off.

"Looks clear."

"Did you hear the girl's voice this time?" Juanita asked Caroline.

"No."

Juan opened the door. "Let's go. With any luck, he'll have left the place unlocked."

"Wait," Bando said, placing a hand on Juan's arm. "When you get in, make sure there's a back way out, in case you need it in a hurry. Leave the cell phone with me. If he comes back, I'll hit Redial to warn you."

Juan handed Bando the phone and slid out of his seat.

"You're not coming?" Juanita asked Bando.

"I can't," he answered without explaining. "Make sure you don't disturb anything. Just gather data. See and hear what's to be seen and heard."

When they got to the porch, they knocked. No one answered. They knocked again and tried the door. Locked. A black cat wrapped itself around Juanita's ankles, purring.

"Now what?" Juan said. "Either of you pick locks?"

"Probably no need," Caroline said, leaning down and reaching past the cat. "This is Maine." She picked up the aluminum milk box. There, where the box had sat, lay a key. She picked it up and fitted it into the door lock. It turned. She replaced the key and set the milk box back in place.

Juan stepped inside first.

"This is it. This is the place I saw. There's the recliner, the side table, the kitchen. Ashtray, beer bottles, refrigerator. The phone's right there, and the answering machine too."

They split up, looking but not touching.

It was a very old two-bedroom trailer, and the resident was a messy housekeeper. One bedroom held a single bed, the other a double. The kitchen, the living room, and the bedroom with the double bed had over-flowing ashtrays. The bedroom with the single bed looked like it hadn't been used in years.

"Hey, look at this mail," Caroline said. "It's mostly for Donald Bronson, but this *Reader's Digest* is addressed to Karen Beals."

"And check out these pictures," Juanita said, pointing to the shelf in the living room. "It's the mother and daughter from the obituaries, Karen and Addie Beals. Here's a family portrait—the three of them." The picture had been taken on a concrete dock with a lake in the background. The little girl, about seven or eight, was grinning and holding a large fish. Donnie Bronson and Karen and Addie Beals squinted in the sunshine, appearing to be very happy.

"I'm guessing that's our guy," Caroline said. "Looks like he and Karen Beals lived together as if they were married. They had a daughter, Addie. The elder Beals couple in Bridgton, Karen's parents, must have disapproved of the living arrangement or of Bronson himself. So they accepted their daughter and their granddaughter but snubbed him. That's why they only named him a special friend in the obituary. They were embarrassed to have their friends and community know."

"That guy in the photo—it's Bronson, I'm sure—is the one I saw in the recliner and with the dirt bike," Juan said. He walked closer to the shelf with the pictures. When he reached it, he turned and focused on the armchair as if lining up a camera shot. "I saw it from about here." His fingers rested on the empty shelf where the stuffed pup had been. "I have a hunch that our Mr. Bronson moved whatever was on the shelf here to the dashboard of his pickup today."

He turned to Caroline. "Remember how Juanita and I told you about that kidnapping we helped the cops with back home, how I saw and she heard through this little goldfish in a bowl where the woman was being held? I think it's like that here—except my viewfinder's been moved. That's why I was able to see the motorcycle through the truck's back window. I saw it through the eyes of whatever was on this shelf last night."

Juanita said, "So he's not in his truck. The truck is parked somewhere, and he's on his motorcycle."

"Yep. And I'll bet it's an off-road dirt bike that's registered for the road, so he can use it legally as well as in the woods."

"You know something?" Caroline said. "When I went to the waterfall this afternoon with Mom and Maggie, we heard a dirt bike. Whoever was on it may have stopped near the top of the waterfall and watched us."

"You didn't see anybody?" Juan asked.

"No. But we heard a bike drive off."

"And Maggie said she heard a dirt bike just before the parents took the microphones," Juanita said. "It was just as the State Trooper started to speak. All those media people were there."

"You think that's what he was looking for?" Juan asked. "You think he needs the cameras so he can go ahead with his plan?"

"His plan?" Juanita asked.

"Well, sure. He didn't just grab those kids spur of the moment, did he? He hasn't sent a ransom note, so it's not for the money. But he has some twisted reason. I think he's angry about Karen and Addie's deaths." Juan pointed at the framed picture of them by the lake. "Maybe he blames the camp for destroying his family."

Juanita shook her head. "Why take the van and the campers? Why not go after whoever he blamed?"

"You can't go after them," Caroline said. "The camp had a different director and different owners then. The article we found said the director and his whole family were killed in that chain-collision pile-up."

"If he was after them, and they died, wouldn't Bronson let it end there?" Juanita asked. "Why seek revenge on a new, totally different camp?"

Juan made a puzzled face. "Not really sure. But I'm afraid he feels like he's got to hurt or kill some kids—some weird exchange or sacrifice. You know, like throwing the maiden to the Volcano god or staking out a beautiful woman every full moon to keep King Kong from destroying the superstitious natives' village."

"You think he's about to get violent, Juan?" Caroline asked. "He could have hurt or murdered those other kids already."

"I don't think so. None of us sense that. We somehow all know—in an intuitive way—that they're out of sight but in great danger. We're finding that we know those sorts of things. It's part of why we came to Free Camp."

"But you still think he's going to act out in some horrible way?" Caroline repeated.

"Yep. Just not quite yet."

"You're sure it'll be violent?"

"Yes," he said with certainty, and shared Charlie's dream about the motorcycle Samurai charging the kids bound to stakes.

Bronson's phone didn't ring, and for that they were thankful. They'd uncovered all they could, left by the front door, and rejoined Bando. As the car started down the road, they spilled their theories and fears out to him.

Bando listened well, as he always did, but he didn't have any answers. Most of the answers would have to come from these three and the others back at Free Camp.

CHAPTER 43

THEY WERE ALL WEAK FROM DIGGING. Climbing out wasn't going to be easy. To make things worse, much of the soil that had collapsed from above was sandy, so the hole was shaped like the upper half of an hourglass. This wouldn't be like recreational rock climbing; the sand underfoot would shift constantly, and the firmer sides farther up would offer no handholds or footholds.

"Drag out anything solid," Celine ordered. "That little table, the chairs, the mattress, anything we can climb on. We've got to make some sort of ladder or stairs."

It didn't take long to drag everything out.

"It's not enough," Tim said.

They sat in the hole staring up. The sky was graying. They had maybe an hour and a half before dark, two at most.

"Use that table as a base," BJ said. "Set the chairs on it and we'll lay the mattress over them. After that we make a pyramid like cheerleaders do. If that's not enough, we try making a ladder—one person's feet on another's shoulders. Tim, you're the lightest, so you go last. You'll be the one to go over the top."

The plan offered more hope than promise, but seemed worth a try. They first stacked and braced everything into a makeshift platform they could stand on, which gained them only a few feet. Then they cobbled themselves into not a pyramid but something more like a pair-on-pair house—Mouse and Celine the first floor, BJ and Atlanta the second, Tim the roof peak. But he was still two feet shy of ground level, and even if he managed to reach the ragged edge, it would crumble in his hands. They disassembled their human house.

"What's left?" Mouse asked. He sat down on the loose dirt that had nearly snuffed out his life.

"Instead of standing two, two, and one," Celine said, "we'll have to try two, one, one, and then Tim." She didn't see enthusiasm on anyone's face, only dirt and exhaustion.

"Then we have the same problem we had at the blockhouse," Tim said. "Even if I get up onto the ground, how do I get the rest of you out?"

"You go for help," Celine said.

"But first see if you can open the hatch cover from the outside, and we'll climb up the ladder," Mouse said. "Maybe it's a lock you can smash with the hammer from the toolbox."

"Or, since this is a construction site," BJ reminded, "maybe you can find a ladder. There's bound to be something, maybe a rope."

"I'll go," Atlanta said, and the others turned and stared at her as if she'd said, "Oh, I'll just fly up there."

"Is that your head injury talking?" Celine asked.

"What? I'm serious. Now that I'm hearing these possibilities for everybody getting out, I'm willing to go up."

"But you're heavier than Tim," Mouse said. "Why would we put you at the top? Tim's the logical choice."

"You don't have to lift me. I'll go up by myself."

"And just how are you going to do that?" Celine asked.

"Same way I did it at the block house. I'm going to levitate."

Mouse cocked a skeptical eyebrow. "Levitate? You mean fly?"

"Not exactly fly, but float, kind of like a hot air balloon."

"You said *same way I did it at the blockhouse.* But didn't you hide behind the door there?" Mouse asked.

Her expression didn't change. "No, I didn't hide behind the door. I hovered above it—above him—in the dark."

"You didn't!" Celine exclaimed.

Mouse stared at Atlanta. "I think she did. Remember how the guy checked the corners and didn't see her—and how we convinced him she'd gotten out before Tim? She couldn't have hidden behind the door—because it opened out. Thing is, he never looked up. And neither did we."

"That's right," BJ said. "She's the one who had you dump the slop pail. It was a distraction."

"So he'd have to keep looking down around his feet," Atlanta added.

Celine was annoyed. "If you can levitate, why didn't you tell us fifteen minutes ago when we were doing our human ladder?"

"Because I couldn't see how getting me out would get us all out. In my mind it was all or none—not just me."

"Well, get going. Float up there and hammer open the hatch," BJ said, "or find a ladder or a rope. Then we'll all leave together. If something happens, though, you have to go for help—understood?"

"But I can't leave you after all we've been through."

"You were willing to try at the blockhouse," BJ said.

"So much has happened since then. It's hard to separate myself from you."

They sat in a moment of near reverence, on the verge of tears. Atlanta was right. The bond their captivity had forged was a powerful one, but that bond now threatened to be their undoing. The Musketeers' motto—One for All and All for One—sounded noble, as did the soldier's promise to leave no comrade behind, but neither made sense under all circumstances, especially now. They had to risk separating.

"Okay," Atlanta said. "Here's the plan. When I go up, you stay inside the bus. If he comes, hide on the ladder. Since we've got the hatch door latched from our side too, he won't be able to open it and find you there. If he calls, don't answer. You just have to stay quiet. When he sees the junk piled in the bottom of the hole he'll assume we escaped. I doubt he'll put a ladder in the hole and come down to check it out."

Everyone agreed on the plan. But Atlanta didn't move. As they waited at the bottom of the hole for her to rise, she said, "Would you mind going in the bus now? I've never done this in front of anybody. I'm feeling . . . um . . . shy."

"Shy? Why?" Mouse asked. "Do you have to take off your clothes to make it work?"

They all laughed, except Mouse.

"I was serious," Mouse said. "I thought maybe the clothes meant extra weight."

"Mouse, she didn't take them off at the blockhouse, did she?" Tim asked.

"Actually," Atlanta said, "I never thought about that before. Mouse may have a point."

"Really?" Mouse said, as if to say to his friends, "See? It wasn't such a silly idea after all."

"No, Mouse, not really," she said, shaking her head and rolling her eyes. "I'm kidding. Now just go into the bus, all of you, please, and look the other way for a minute."

They did. And when they looked back two minutes later, the pit was empty except for the junk pile they'd made.

Tim, closest to the windshield, cocked his head. Somewhere in the distance he heard an engine that sounded like the whine of a model airplane. As it came nearer he recognized it. This was a sound he'd heard in the hills near his home—a throttled-up dirt bike. For a split-second he considered yelling to the rider for help, or getting the other three to join him in making enough of a racket to attract the cyclist. That strategy might work if this was some kid coming to freewheel it up and down the quarry's sand piles.

But this wasn't such a kid. Tim knew it, knew it in his gut. And suddenly he felt the approaching rider's anxiety—the carjacker's anxiety, his fear—that the prisoners had escaped, all of them this time, and he wouldn't be able to recapture them. This angered him because—for his wild plan to work—the carjacker needed them, needed their innocence.

Tim turned from the windshield to the others. "Hurry, up into the tube. Move fast. He's here."

CHAPTER 44

LEVITATION HAD NEVER BEEN a fast mode of travel. Now, under
pressure, Atlanta felt like a mini-Goodyear blimp. It took more
than a minute to rise to ground level, where she almost made the mistake
of standing up. That would leave a trail. She hovered two feet above the
surface and glanced over at the hatch.

"It's locked!" she yelled into the hole. "I'll look for a ladder. If I can't
find something, I'll go for help!"

She floated, drawing herself along the tread-marked path with her
fingertips, until she reached the clearing where the bulldozer and cement
mixer sat. Beyond them she saw the old Shasta travel trailer.

Suddenly she stopped. From the distance came the whine of an
engine. The sound was vaguely familiar. An image of two older neighborhood boys flashed through her mind, and then she had it—motocross.
This was a dirt bike with its throttle opened up—and whoever was driving it was headed her way fast.

She had to risk walking, but the ground was soft and impression-
able. The mixer was close, so she dug her fingers in and went for it. It felt
like it took forever—like running in water—but she made it and put her
feet down in the weeds. No tracks. Neither the mixer nor the bulldozer
offered a good hiding spot. The trailer was better, so she dodged behind
it, and not a minute too soon.

The dirt bike slowed as it came into the construction site. Atlanta heard its blatta-blatta as it turned in by the trailer and idled. Was the rider looking for someone or something? Had he seen her duck behind the trailer? She crouched by one of the concrete-block pilings holding it up and stole a quick look underneath, clear through to the bike. The rider was still straddling it less than 25 feet from her. What was he waiting for? Why didn't he rev it up and move on? Was he about to dismount and go into the trailer—or worse, walk behind it?

The rider cut the ignition and the idling engine stopped. The thought crept into Atlanta's mind that he might suddenly round the corner and pistol-whip her again. She had nowhere to hide. If she lay down under the trailer, he'd see her, and there was too much open ground to risk a run for the woods. Her options were limited. She took a breath and made her decision.

She levitated. But it was like an older submarine having to blow the heavy seawater out of its ballast tanks so it could rise—it took time. Up—slowly, gradually—up. Rising—roof level. Up a little more. She was fifteen feet above the ground with an eye on the corner of the trailer in case he came around it. He didn't. What could he be doing?

Hovering slightly above the edge of the flat roof, she placed her fingertips on it and—as if playing Itsy Bitsy Spider—used them to slowly maneuver herself forward. She didn't dare lie on the roof for fear it would creak and give her away. Her only option was to hold her position dead center over the flat roof of the trailer.

What was he doing? He hadn't opened the door to go inside—she'd have heard the door or felt its vibration. He hadn't started for the bus— she'd have seen him in the distance. She inched forward and peeked over the edge.

The rider was standing by the dirt bike in his tee shirt and underwear. Was he simply someone who had stopped here to change from his riding clothes into street clothes? Atlanta noticed he was muscular like their abductor, but he wasn't bald like the militiaman—this guy had a healthy, full head of hair. Had she been wrong about this rider? Maybe this was a man who could help them. Should she trust him?

She strained hard to stay aloft, and the lingering ache in her head pounded now. She still wasn't sure about this man below, and it took all her concentration to stay up. This was a long hover for her anyway, but more so because of her exhaustion and the head injury. She yearned to close her eyes and sleep again. But she and her friends needed to be rescued. She had to call down to the man, didn't she?

Something stopped her—instinct, intuition, self-preservation? No, it was loyalty. That was it. Her friends were counting on her a second time and she didn't want to blow it again. She kept silent and watched.

The man set a rope-handled shopping bag on the ground and withdrew a uniform.

Atlanta nearly gasped out loud.

He put on the pants and shirt—camouflage fatigues—and set the cap on the bike seat. Then he pulled from the bag something a clown might wear—a bald wig—except without the bright-orange fringe hairs that poke out above a clown's ears. This wig was just plain bald. He fitted it tightly over his own hair, donned the Desert Storm cap, and squared it away using the bike's handlebar mirror. The last item to come out of the shopping bag was a gun, which he tucked into his belt.

It took all of Atlanta's willpower to not collapse on the roof. Somehow she stayed up and carefully retreated back to the center of the roof, from where she'd wait for the dirt bike to start up again.

But it didn't start up. A moment later she caught a movement out of the corner of her eye—the militiaman marching down the path toward the bus.

She wanted to scream a warning, but held her tongue, praying that the others would stick to the plan.

The man was soon out of earshot, and as soon as he was, she relaxed on the creaky roof, drained. It beat climbing into bed after a marathon. She was too tired to go for the woods. Now she'd have to resist the urge to fall asleep before he returned, changed clothes again, and roared away on his dirt bike.

***

On the path, Bronson spotted the huge hole near the buried bus. He broke into a trot. What could have happened—an earthquake, a sinkhole? He approached the edge and looked down. It looked like everything from the bus had been dragged out and stacked at the bottom of the hole to make an escape platform. The little moles had dug their way out. He had to hand it to them; they were resourceful. Had they actually made it, though?

It took him a few minutes to realize there were no footprints at the top, around the edge of the hole. And it was quite a stretch from the piled-together junk to ground level. Even standing on one another's shoulders, it would be almost impossible. *They're still in the bus.*

He called down to them. No answer.

"Campers, I know you're in there. You're doing a great job with these challenges, learning valuable lessons, right?"

Still no one answered.

Bronson put his face close to the ground. He could see partway in past the knocked-out front windshield, but he couldn't see very far into the shadows of the bus.

He tried his most persuasive voice. "Okay, kiddies, who wants to sleep in a nice dry camp cabin tonight, in a really comfortable bunk bed? There's hot food in the dining hall, too."

No response.

He walked to the hatch door. Still padlocked. He wondered again how they'd made the phone call to him at home, how they'd gotten his number, and how they'd gotten a cell phone. If they'd concealed a cell phone earlier, they'd have used it to call for help from the blockhouse. And if they had one now, why wouldn't they call 9-1-1 instead of calling him at home? But even the idea of it was absurd. What kind of cell phone could get a signal from inside a bus buried more than ten feet underground? Maybe they'd phoned him by getting a signal by standing on top of the pile of bus furnishings at the bottom of the hole. Was that the purpose of the hole—not for escape but for communication? No, that didn't make sense either, because there were no police here, no parents, and no helicopters overhead homing in on a cell phone signal. None of this made sense.

Bronson unlocked the hatch and yanked on it. It didn't budge. He tried again, then once more without success. They had found the inner bolt and slid it shut to keep him out.

"Okay, okay, very clever, campers. But it's time to open up. Don't make me get my ladder and come down into that giant rat-hole you dug."

No sound. Just quiet.

"Come out, come out wherever you are." He banged on the hatch cover with the .45.

Still no response.

Bronson's head throbbed, not just with impatience and anger—something real, something organic was exerting pressure at the base of his skull. Some demon was using it as an incubator, a womb, and the time was almost ripe for something nasty to burst forth and wreak havoc on the world.

"Remember the gun from the other building? I've got it right here and I'm ready to use it again." He aimed the .45 at the broken-out windshield. "Here's the deal. You'll want to pay attention down there. One shot now, another after the count of five. It's bound to ricochet inside the bus, so duck your heads. These are live rounds, not blanks."

He fired. Boom!

From the roof of the trailer Atlanta heard it. She picked her head up and in the distance could see the tiny figure in fatigues standing by the hole, gun pointing into it. She knew he was speaking, but she couldn't make out what he was saying.

The kids hiding in the passageway heard him.

"You've got until five. One. Two. Three. Four."

"Wait!" a small voice cried out. "Wait! We're coming out."

"Holding my fire! Show yourselves."

One by one they climbed down from the safety of the barrel passageway and showed their faces in the windshield.

"Where's the other one—the girl who got out the last time?"

"She's not here," Mouse said.

"Where is she?"

None of them answered.

Bronson raised the .45 again. "I asked you a question, campers. I expect an answer. Where is she?"

BJ spoke. "She went for help. About two hours ago."

Bronson digested the statement and carefully crafted his response. "I don't think so—not two hours ago. If she had, she'd have brought my compatriots, the other camp staff, back by now. I think she's still down there hiding."

"No, she's not," Mouse insisted. "She really did leave. More like an hour ago, I'd say."

Bronson looked thoughtful. "I need to be sure. Unbolt the hatch from the inside." He pointed to Tim. "You, runt of the litter. You climb up and unlock it." He waggled the gun and Tim's face disappeared from the broken windshield.

A minute later the hinged hatch door flipped open and Tim's head popped up.

"Back down there, runt. I want to see all of you in the bottom of the hole."

When Tim reappeared in the hole with the others, Bronson descended. At the bottom of the ladder, he stepped onto the dirt-covered floor.

"Where is she?"

"We were serious," Mouse said. "We made ourselves into a ladder and she climbed up us to the top. She's gone."

Bronson lit the oil lamp and searched every corner. He even kicked the piles of dirt. "What's this?" he asked when he discovered the first excavation site outside the three drop-down windows.

"False start," Mouse explained. "Sorry we made such a mess of your survival shelter."

Bronson's eyes softened ever so slightly for just a moment, but something snuffed that out quickly.

"I'll never use it now, anyway." His mind seemed to drift, and the look in his eyes said he was speaking more to himself than to Mouse.

"What now?" BJ asked. "For us, I mean."

"You sit tight, that's what. I'll be back for you in the morning. Last leg of the challenge course."

He climbed up the ladder, closed the hatch, and locked it.

Five minutes later they heard the bulldozer engine cranking over. It caught, and in less than half an hour Bronson pushed tons of sand from the nearby piles into the hole.

Before leaving, he opened the hatch for a moment. "I wouldn't play in the sand if I were you. I parked the bulldozer on top of it." Then he locked it once more, leaving the four children to their gloom.

On the roof of the trailer Atlanta whispered another plate number— the dirt bike's—committing it to memory, praying she'd live long enough to tell it to someone.

CHAPTER 45

BRONSON RAN THE BIKE HARD and got back to the worksite 45 minutes before dark. He came in the way he'd left, through the tall pines, stopping only to hide the disguise and .45 in a hollow tree trunk where he could easily retrieve them the next morning. He didn't dare carry them in the pickup now.

He parked the dirt bike behind the barn. Even if the cops found he'd been out biking, it wasn't a crime to enjoy an outdoor sport. The explanation was simple. He'd finished work early and gone off for a ride. But with the pickup in plain sight all afternoon, it was more likely the cops saw him as a typical Maine handyman putting in extra hours while the days were longer.

He grabbed his gear, walked down the long driveway, climbed in the truck and headed home. No sign of a tail at first, but when he turned down a road shadowed by a canopy of high trees, he had to turn the pickup's headlights on. So did the police car when he made the same turn. It didn't matter. Donnie already knew he'd again slip the tail in the morning without any trouble. Despite the minor setbacks with the kids, his plan was well underway.

***

Bando sensed something in the air and pulled Rose and Twait's car off the road before reaching the camp driveway.

"Sir?" Juan asked before they braked to a complete stop. "The man in the pickup is moving again. But there's no motorcycle in back. He didn't put it back in."

"What else do you see?"

"I think a car without its headlights on is following the pickup. I'm pretty sure it's a police car. Oops, the lights just came on."

"Are you getting a good look at the driver of the truck?"

"It's the guy from the trailer."

"Okay, let me cross-check," Bando said. "Place your palms on mine and keep looking at him."

Juan rested his hands on Bando's.

"Perfect. I see him. Same guy Jerry met in the café, the one who asked him about Free Camp pickup locations."

Juanita interrupted. "I'm hearing numbers again, from the same girl who gave them before. I thought I heard her awhile back, but it was such a soft whisper I wasn't sure. Mo's cousin, probably."

"Same numbers?" Caroline asked.

"No. Different ones." Juanita repeated them several times and Caroline wrote them down.

"Bet they match the motorcycle," Juan said.

"Something tells me you're right," Juanita said. "The police can check it."

"Anything else you hear?" Caroline asked.

"Nope. But she's reciting the numbers like they do at boot camp. I can hear her breathing harder, like she's walking fast."

"So let's assume she's seen the motorcycle," Caroline said. "Recently."

"And she's loose," Juan added. "Loose where there's nobody around."

"Like lost and it's almost dark," Caroline said. "Remember, she doesn't know we're listening. So she's not saying the numbers for us. She's saying them to remember them, so the numbers can help someone find the others."

"How do we know the others aren't with her?" Juan said.

"There's no talking in the background," Juanita said. "Nobody else is chanting the numbers with her. And she's not saying anything to anybody else. She's alone."

"So we know she's alive," Juan said, "but we aren't sure about the others, right?"

"They're alive too," Bando said, starting the car. "We've got to get back to the camp. The police need to know about this plate number."

"What they need to do," Caroline said, "is watch for a girl who's about to walk out of the woods."

***

By eleven o'clock the media circus—having nothing new to report—had left the grounds of Free Camp in favor of local motels and campgrounds. Almost everyone else was in bed—Juan, Charlie, and Mo in the boys' cabin; Juanita and Maggie in the girls' cabin; Twait, Rose, and Caroline in their cabin. Two State Troopers walked the area around the cabins.

Back at Bronson's sand quarry, Mouse, Tim, Celine, and BJ—totally exhausted—slept like the dead in their underground prison.

Atlanta had made it from the construction trailer to a blacktop road that was so lightly traveled after dark, she couldn't flag down any oncoming cars. Oddly, she found herself shrinking and hiding from their headlights' glare. Her vision wasn't normal, it was strange, and the lights frightened her. Worn out from the digging, from the extended hovering, and from the hard walk, she hid from the very lights that might offer rescue. She grew dizzy and began to vomit. She couldn't know that Bronson's blow to her head the night before had caused a concussion. She staggered across a driveway overgrown with weeds to a falling-down bus-stop shelter for the schoolchild or children who once lived down the driveway. She curled up on her side and passed out, drifting into an unconsciousness that would last for hours.

Elsewhere, two others were awake.

Donnie Bronson reclined in his easy chair and watched the late news, his side table littered with four empty beer cans and half of another. On his lap rested the family portrait from the shelf. On the TV screen flickered two newspersons behind a desk, a sketch of a bald man in sunglasses behind them.

In the camp director's cabin Bando sat cross-legged on the floor, eyes closed, hands on knees. He looked as if he might be praying that his upturned palms would act like satellite dishes, gathering whatever information the universe might choose to share.

CHAPTER 4 6

THE SUN HADN'T BEEN UP VERY LONG when muffled screams woke Juan. He opened his eyes and sat up on one elbow.

The strangled cries were coming from Charlie, whose body twitched and jerked.

"Charlie, wake up," he said, not too loudly. "It's a nightmare. Charlie, wake up, it's just a bad dream."

Then Charlie began to gurgle, and by the time Juan got to his side Charlie was choking, flailing his arms.

Juan shook him. "Wake up! It's a dream!"

Charlie's eyes flew open. The gurgling and choking stopped.

Mo was awake now, and had climbed out of his bunk to sit by Charlie's feet.

Charlie tried to shake away the sleep and the trembles. His face was white as a sheet of paper.

"First you were screaming, then you sounded like you were drowning," Juan said.

"I was. I was drowning. Maggie and I were in a car starting across an old bridge that had washed out. We crashed through a sawhorse barrier and flew through the air. The bottom of the car smacked the water. We bounced once and started sinking in deep water. Our seat belts were chains, and we couldn't get out of them. The windows were open and water poured in. We screamed, but there was only one person on shore to hear us. He had an Army uniform on and his arms were crossed on his chest. No face under the hat, just that stupid police sketch. Our mouths filled with water. We were drowning. It was terrible."

Juan grabbed the notebook. "I know it's hard to shift gears right now, but you've got to write down what you can remember." He handed Charlie the pen.

"It was late afternoon," Charlie said. "Don't ask me how I know, but it was late afternoon. And it was today."

"Put down what you can," Juan repeated. "Details, background, feelings, impressions, colors, smells, tastes, sounds, whatever comes into your mind."

Charlie gripped the pen clumsily and began to write in shaky script.

***

Meanwhile, at Twait and Rose's cabin, Caroline awoke from a dream of her own. She got out of bed and knocked on her parents' bedroom door.

"Mom? Dad?"

"What is it, Honey?" Rose called. "Come on in."

Caroline opened the door, went in, and sat on the edge of the bed.

"This time I saw her. I didn't just hear her, I saw her—the little girl. But it wasn't a dream—it was real. I was lying in bed with my eyes closed, listening to the birds. And I knew she was there, in my room. When I opened my eyes, there she was, standing at the foot of the bed."

"And she had her bathing suit on?" Rose asked.

"How did you know?"

Twait sat up against the headboard. "Mom just had a similar experience. The girl's mother came to visit."

"Did she speak?"

"Yes," Rose said. "How about the little girl?"

"Yes. She said *Dad's coming to un-drownd us.* She even repeated it. *My Dad's coming to un-drownd us.*"

"So she spoke directly to you this time?" Twait asked. "You weren't overhearing something."

Caroline shook her head.

"The mother had on hiking boots," Rose said, "tan cargo shorts, a green shirt, and a fanny pack. I'm guessing it's what she had on when she jumped in to save her daughter and the other little girl."

"How about you?" Caroline asked. "What did the Mom say?"

Rose sat up, put a hand in Twait's, the other in Caroline's. "The mother said *Tell him they can't bring us back. Tell him we'll wait for him.*"

"Tell him *they* can't bring us back? Didn't she mean *he* can't bring us back?"

"She said *they*," Rose answered.

Caroline looked thoughtful. "Mom, Dad, just what is this thing we do—hearing and seeing dead people?" She looked first at her mother, then at her father.

"Not Dad. You and me."

Twait shrugged as if to say, "Sorry."

"Dad doesn't hear or see them. But he believes that I do—and now he believes you do. And to answer your question—some think it's a form of dowsing."

"I thought dowsing was about finding water with a tree branch."

"That's what everybody thinks," Rose said. "But there are also dowsers who find lost cats and lost keys and lots of other things. Since I was your age I've had occasional contact with ghosts. I don't exactly dowse for them, but occasionally I seem to find them—or maybe they find me."

"Some folks call them earthbound spirits," Twait said. "For whatever reason, certain ones get stuck and can't move on to wherever it is they go. They usually need to resolve something."

Caroline sat taking it all in. "What could this mother and daughter have to resolve?"

"Who says it's them?" Rose asked.

Caroline fidgeted. "You think it's the carjacker?"

This time Rose shrugged. "Could be."

"Did you see or hear the mother before the van was stolen? Or the daughter?"

"I've never been visited by the daughter. The mother started a while ago—as a voice. This morning is the first time I've seen her. The problem is, I didn't know then who she was, and I had no way of knowing about the plan to take the van and those kids."

"But you knew something would involve Free Camp kids?"

"Yes."

"Something that would put them at risk?"

"Not exactly. Dad and I knew they'd be involved, but we didn't know there'd be this much danger."

Caroline pulled her hand out from under her mother's. "But you knew it wouldn't be a plain old summer camp experience for anybody, right? Free Camp never is." Her voice grew louder. "You and Dad let it happen anyway. And now we've got five missing kids who—for all we know—may be dead."

"Caroline," Twait said, trying to calm her with his voice. "This gift is new to you. We didn't know when—or even if—it might appear in you. Honey, I know it's hard, but you've got to learn to trust the universe."

Caroline's cheeks flushed with anger. Her eyes smoldered and she backed away from the bed. "It's not such a great gift if we can't use it to stop things from getting out of hand early on," she snapped, and stalked out of the room.

***

Donnie Bronson was up early, too. For the first time ever he fed the cat outside, making sure it had plenty of food and water. He made the bed, washed the dishes, and straightened up the trailer. He placed the framed portrait on the kitchen counter and left a note beside it: *I'll always love you.* Then he dressed for work, jumped into the pickup, and stared briefly at the trailer that had once been a joy-filled home.

On the way to the estate job he stopped at Dead River for coffee and donuts, and a while later he parked the truck where he had the day before. He grabbed his shovel and tool belt and walked up the driveway toward the barn and the dirt bike hidden behind it.

To the cops watching from down the road, this was just another workday for a local mason employed by a rich out-of-state couple. The cops wouldn't see or hear the dirt bike once Donnie pushed it into the woods and started it. Nor would they suspect the man under surveillance would be riding it to a U-Haul dealership to sign out the box truck he'd reserved weeks ago for one day only.

CHAPTER 47

THE KIDS ARRIVED AT THE DINING HALL to find the two round tables pushed together again and set with orange juice, butter, and small clear-glass pitchers of maple syrup. The sweet smell of bacon and sausage wafted out of the kitchen, setting everyone's mouth to watering as they passed the serving window.

"The place settings are already on the tables," Twait said, motioning the kids past the pass-through. "Rose has two pans of French toast ready to come out of the oven. The sooner everybody sits, the sooner we eat."

A minute later, Rose and Bando came out carrying two big oven pans, which they set on the table.

"Anything else?" Rose asked, and when nobody answered, she and Bando sat at one end of the table, Twait at the other. "Dig in," she said, and everyone did.

It didn't take long to get Rose and Caroline talking about their early morning visitations. Then Charlie shared his sinking-car dream.

"I was in the car with you?" Maggie asked. "What was I doing?"

"Screaming, mostly. We were sinking, remember—chained to our seats, about to drown?"

"Yes, I heard that part, but why me specifically? What was I doing there? Why not Mo or Juan or Juanita or Caroline?"

"I don't know." Charlie nudged a piece of French toast into in a tiny pool of maple syrup. "It's not like either you or I—or any of us—has the power to do anything. I don't think it mattered, Maggie, whether it was you or somebody else stuck in the car with me. The point is, there was no way to get out."

"I'm not so sure, Charlie," Bando said. "For some reason, the intuitive part of you placed Maggie in that dream with you—specifically in that sinking car. We may not know why it did that, but it may be that both you and Maggie will play important parts in what happens. There's some connection between you two."

"Hmm! Charlie and Maggie. Maybe there's an afternoon wedding we don't know about," Mo joked.

"Oh, too funny!" Maggie said, rolling her eyes. "Not! Now come on. We're running out of time. Today's the day, the anniversary. Our guy's going to do something. What else do we know?"

Bando sipped his tea and set the cup and saucer down. "The State Police ran the new numbers Juanita heard. They match a motorcycle plate registered to Donald Bronson. Simply matching the trailer and motorcycle plates to him doesn't prove anything, though. It's strong enough for them to name him a Person of Interest—but not a suspect."

"And we pointed out to them the Bronson-Beals camp connection," Twait added.

"Did you point out today is the fifth anniversary of the drownings?" Maggie asked.

Bando nodded.

"They should take him in one of those interrogation rooms with the one-way mirrors and make him tell where those kids are," Mo said.

"I'm sure they'll question him," Bando said. "Don't forget, he's a Person of Interest, not a suspect. He hasn't tried to flee, and he hasn't tried to make contact with those kids. For all the cops know, the van left the state Monday morning with those kids in it. And Bronson's camp connection may be coincidental. They don't know it's him."

"It's him," Mo said.

Bando set his cup down. "They say he goes to work and he goes home."

Mo shook his head. "If it wasn't for us, the cops wouldn't even be making the tie-in to this guy."

"Mo—and the rest of you," Twait said. "Listen. We mustn't get too puffed up. There's a danger in thinking that it's only our—um, what shall we call it—unusual information—that matters. Remember, this is a crime, not a game, and the kidnapper is armed and dangerous. It's the police who are trained to deal with these situations, not us. Three camp staff and six kids aren't equipped to storm some hole-in-the-wall hide-out under a hail of bullets."

Bando cleared his throat softly. All eyes turned his way. His own eyes were closed, his fingers making a steeple under his chin. "This is what I know. Five lives are at stake. What lies ahead will require cooperation, not competition."

"The police are doing plenty," Twait said.

"Like what?" Mo asked.

"Well," Bando said, still not opening his eyes, "this morning they told me they met with our driver Jerry last night and showed him a driver's license photo of Mr. Bronson. Jerry positively identified him as the man who pumped him for information at the cafe."

"See?" Twait said. "Testimony that's admissible in court."

"But because the guy had a gas mask on when he grabbed the van," Mo added, "Jerry can't say for sure it was him, right?"

Twait had no answer to that.

"Okay then," Maggie cut in. "How about the parents? Have the police shown Bronson's driver's license photo to them?"

"They have," Twait answered. "Unfortunately, they couldn't I.D. him either. The driver they met was bald, in an Army uniform, wearing sunglasses."

"But we all know it was Bronson in disguise," Juan said.

"Maybe," Twait said. "Probably. We know that, but it's not provable yet."

"Oh, come on! It was him. I saw him—several times—in his recliner, in his living room, and when he was unloading the motorcycle from his truck."

"But," Bando corrected, eyes still shut, "you only saw him as himself, not as the bald kidnapper. And while your gift for remote viewing may count with us, Juan, it's not enough for the police or the courts. They'd say the fact is, you've never actually seen this Bronson in the flesh—either as himself or in his disguise."

Mo tried to interpret. "In court, Juan, Bronson's defense attorney argues you saw only his picture in the library's newspaper archives, and that's the source your imagination drew from so you could view him."

"Well put, Mo," Bando agreed, opening his eyes. "Mo, either you've been watching a lot of law-and-order TV shows or you're developing a lawyer's mind."

"Maybe both," Rose said. "If there's nothing new to contribute, are we ready to clear the dishes?"

"First, how about telling us what's in store today?" Charlie asked.

"All right," Bando said. "It looks like this will be a warm day. So this morning you've got free time until nine o'clock. Then it's waterfront with Rose and Twait. They're both lifeguards and swim instructors. You can pull down the canoes, kayaks, and paddles from the racks at the boat shed. You must wear a life preserver to go out in them. Finish waterfront and put everything away by eleven-thirty. Change into dry clothes and meet here at noon for lunch."

No one moved.

"How will swimming and canoeing get those kids back?" Maggie asked. The others' heads nodded agreement.

"I don't know," Bando admitted. "But this is still summer camp. Let your minds relax for a few hours. Everything points to a vortex later this afternoon. See you at lunch."

No one thought to ask what Bando meant by vortex, but the instant he said the word, all six kids' minds conjured up an image of an ominous black funnel cloud bearing down on them—swirling and screaming like a banshee crossing the moors at midnight. Advancing, it ripped up all the trees, houses, barns, and silos in its path, spitting out dirt and debris. On its edges each of them spotted a splash of color—egg yolk yellow—that appeared and disappeared as if struggling to break free, something that looked like it might once have been a school bus. Except now it was gripped by the vortex's huge deadly fist, waiting to be flung high into the dark sky until it was dashed to earth again. Even with the morning warm and the dining room dry, the kids shivered in the damp, cold moment projected in their minds. Maybe Bando was right, maybe they did need to enjoy the morning before they could face the afternoon and the coming vortex.

CHAPTER 48

JUST BEFORE EIGHT THAT MORNING Tim struck a match and lit a stub of candle. "Anybody else awake?"

The four of them had slept eleven hours in the pitch-black bus.

"I am," BJ said softly. "Maybe fifteen minutes now, or it could be half an hour."

Neither Mouse nor Celine stirred.

"I'm worried," Tim said. "Something's wrong with Atlanta. She's out there and she's either asleep or unconscious. I don't think she made it to get help."

"You saying that because the cavalry's not here yet?"

"No, I'm saying it because I sense people's feelings."

"What—you're sympathetic? Or is the word empathetic?"

"Well, you're on the right track. Let me explain. If my dog dies, you feel bad for me—sorry. That's sympathy. But it doesn't affect you, does it? Now, let's say we're old friends, and let's say you too have a dog you love. When my dog dies, you'll feel more than sympathy; you'll share my feelings. You may even cry. See? That's not sympathy, it's empathy."

"Sounds normal to me."

"It is. But my sensitivity goes deeper. I'm what they call an empath. Sometimes I pick up certain people's moods and feelings the way satellite dishes pick up TV signals—even at a distance."

"Which is why—several times now—you knew the guy was agitated, right?"

"Yes, and that he was coming our way."

"So you've been tuned in to him."

"And now I'm tuned in to Atlanta." In the candlelight Tim could see BJ's lips trying to form a new question, but nothing came out.

"You just went from being curious to being nervous," he said. "Something's on your mind. You're wondering if you should tell me what makes you different. You feel you can trust me because your gift—a special sensitivity—has similarities to mine."

"Yes. Remember when we pushed that block out?"

"You told us where to scrape."

"And none of you questioned me."

"One spot was as good as another."

"No, it wasn't, that's my point. The mortar around that one block had already started to crumble on the outside of the building, so all we had to do was scrape the inside seal and push it out. It was the one block in the entire wall that could be knocked out. I knew it. I knew it the same way you knew our guy's feelings—and Atlanta's. I felt my way around inside that blockhouse until I sensed the one weak spot."

Now it was Tim who sat quiet.

"Wrap your hands around one of those cans," BJ said. "Don't show it to me. Pick any can."

Tim reached behind him for a can.

"Okay, now hold it out in front of you. I'm going to place my hands around yours."

He held it out. She placed her palms on the backs of his hands.

"It's chicken rice soup. It has chicken stock, chicken, rice, celery, carrots, salt, even sugar in it, plus the usual blend of unpronounceable preservatives."

"You sure it's not black beans?" Mouse asked, sitting up and stretching.

"Or sliced peaches?" Celine added, rising up on one elbow now.

"Read the label," BJ said. She removed her hands from Tim's.

He held the candle close and read aloud, "Chicken stock, chicken, rice, celery, carrots, salt, sugar."

"I never touched the can," BJ said.

"Maybe you have a photographic memory," Mouse suggested. "You saw all those can labels earlier and memorized them."

"Honestly, Mouse, I have no idea what those labels look like or what the fine print says. I don't know the manufacturers. I was just telling you the ingredients I felt inside the can."

"You did that through Tim's hands and through the metal?" Celine asked.

"Yes. I can also tell you the soup spent some time in Georgia. Could be it was processed there, or canned there, or maybe the chickens were raised there—or maybe it was just stored there briefly during shipping."

Mouse thrust another can her way. "Try this one."

BJ placed a hand on it. "Small beans. New Mexico. Natural juices, water, a little salt. The can was made from metal from Minnesota."

"Cool," Mouse said.

"And a little weird," BJ added.

"Okay, weird but cool," Celine said. "Still, it helped get us out of that blockhouse."

"What's it called?" Mouse asked. "It's not like an X-Men power."

"I think it falls under psychometry," Tim said. "I came across it on the Web when I was checking out empaths. You tell something about an object by touching it."

"BJ didn't even have to touch it," Mouse said. "Hers is even better. She felt it through Tim's hands."

BJ sat up a little straighter at Mouse's affirmation.

"So, Tim and BJ, you two have unusual powers," Mouse continued. "And Atlanta can levitate. What about Celine and me? What do we do—besides dig, I mean?"

Celine shrugged.

"Maybe you just haven't discovered your gifts yet," Tim said.

"Besides," BJ said, "how is psychometry getting us out of here? If we were all levitators like Atlanta, we'd be out by now."

Nobody had an answer. After a glum silence Mouse said, "Might as well open those New Mexican beans. Maybe together we can blow the lid off this can!"

They all laughed long and hard, a welcome relief.

A few minutes later, while they were eating, Tim said, "This is weird. Our guy is excited, really looking forward to something. He's like a man waiting for the plane carrying his girlfriend—that kind of anticipation."

"Is he coming?" Mouse asked.

A sudden hammering on the hatch answered Mouse's question.

CHAPTER 4 9

B RONSON PARKED THE U-HAUL near the bulldozer that sat on top of the filled-in hole. He raised the rear rollup door. The cargo area was empty except for the dirt bike strapped to the interior wall. He walked to the hatch door and banged on it with the .45.

"Rise and shine, campers!"

He unlocked the padlock and tried opening the door. It didn't budge. The occupants below had decided it should remain bolted.

"Troops, this is the sound of reveille!" He pretended to play the wakeup call as if he had a bugle. "I know you're down in the hold, sleepy-heads, so listen up. This is your one chance to get above ground again and move on to your next phase of the challenge course. Bang on the ladder so I'll know you heard me."

No answer.

"Okay, one more chance. Knock on the ladder and I'll give you fifteen minutes to grab some chow and do your duty. After that, you have a choice. Either you unlock and come out or I plug the air-supply pipe and drive away. Should you decide to accept these terms and move on to the next challenge, I have your transport vehicle standing by. This is your last chance to knock and let me know you heard me. Then you have fifteen minutes."

Quiet.

"I assume no one is in charge and you're talking it over. Take one more minute to decide, that's all."

Down below, the only one who argued against leaving was Mouse. He wanted them to play dead, so their captor would drive away as he'd threatened.

"For all he knows, we're already dead down here, with the door latched from the inside. And don't forget, we've got a chance with Atlanta going for help, right? But even if something happened to her, whether he closes off the air supply or not, the four of us dig again in the same spot. The dirt he pushed into the hole is looser now, which means the digging will be easier, with less chance of a cave-in. If the bulldozer is sitting on top, it'll force-feed the dirt our way even faster. We can climb on the bulldozer like it's a ladder." It was clear that Mouse had done a lot of thinking about their predicament.

He got no support from the others. They were bone-tired and simply didn't trust the current air supply to hold out even if their captor didn't cover the breather pipe.

Bronson heard a weak banging on the bottom of the ladder.

"If you are ready to proceed according to plan, knock three times."

Three answering knocks.

"Okay, fifteen minutes to get yourselves ready. Eat, clean up, look sharp. Fifteen minutes. Knock twice if you understand."

Two knocks.

Bronson walked to the U-Haul, opened the passenger door, and set the .45 on the floor. He changed into the bald wig and uniform. He adjusted his cap in the truck's side mirror and slid the .45 into his belt. The pain in his skull flared, and for a moment the entire quarry looked as orange as the truck. The voice that came with the hot pain assured him he'd only need the disguise a while longer—until Addie and Karen came back. He reached for the bottle of aspirin in his side pocket and swallowed five. The pain in his head had intensified through the night, and he'd already taken more than ten since bedtime. He knew it was eating away at his stomach walls, not helping his ulcers, but the burning at the back of his skull demanded it.

He tipped the backrest of the seat forward and removed the canvas bag he'd stashed there. He carried it back to the step bumper and climbed into the U-Haul's cargo area. There he set the bag down and unpacked a length of chain he'd fitted with wrist shackles he'd welded in his shop. He wrapped the chain through the wooden rail on the wall a couple of times.

Next he fished five key-type padlocks out of the bag and attached them to the shackles. He'd planned for five, but now it looked like he'd only need four.

Bronson stepped back and admired his handiwork. It looked so medieval, so Grand Inquisition, like there should be a rack set up in the truck too, on which to stretch bodies. *This is necessary*, the voice whispered, *if you want Karen and Addie back.*

He still wasn't sure whether four or five campers would emerge this time. Before he'd bulldozed the hole, and when he'd inspected the bus, only four had shown themselves. There were no tracks above the hole—which had to mean the fifth kid hadn't gotten out. Either he'd missed her hiding spot in the bus or she'd been buried by the cave-in—and they'd wanted him to believe she'd escaped to run for help.

It didn't matter now. If one tried to stay and hide, there'd be no later escape once he locked the hatch again. He'd give her one final chance, one final "Come out, come out wherever you are—or you'll be sealed in here for eternity." If she were there and alive, she'd give up.

Bronson knew his sacrificial lambs wouldn't like the shackles, but he had the .45, and they'd do what he ordered them to. There was only one more stop for them. Part of him felt sad—after all, they were just kids, about Addie's age—but, as the voice assured him, this was necessary. It had to be done.

He walked to the hatch, pulled the .45 from his belt, and tapped on the door.

"Time's up, campers. Your transport is ready. Let's move it. On to the water challenge."

At the foot of the ladder, Tim didn't like what he felt. He couldn't help shuddering. A moment later, with his hands shaking, he drew back the inside bolt and opened the hatch.

CHAPTER 50

BRONSON STEERED THE U-HAUL and its human cargo from the dirt road onto the blacktop. A quarter mile down the road he passed an overgrown driveway with a fire-gutted shack still visible at the far end of it. Just back from the road stood a rotting bus shelter that once protected school children from the elements while they waited to be picked up.

If Bronson had looked closely at the shelter, he'd have noticed Atlanta waking up on its dirty floor. And moments later, if he'd checked the view behind him in his side mirror, he'd have seen her stumble out to the road. But he didn't. He had his sights set on the lake.

Atlanta had barely enough strength to propel herself forward, with no mental energy for levitating. Her rescue hopes depended on finding an occupied house or flagging down a passing car. The only thing on her mind now was getting help for her friends in the underground bus.

***

Back in the boys' cabin at Free Camp, Juan, Charlie, and Mo dug out their bathing suits.

"Charlie, you going to canoe with me?" Juan asked.

"I've never been canoeing before." Charlie held up his odd hands. "You sure you want to try it with me?"

"If you can hold a pencil, you can handle a paddle. It's just thicker."

"Why don't you ask Mo? He'd be good at it."

"Actually," Mo said, clearing his throat. "I was kind of—you know—thinking maybe I'd pair off with Juanita." He blushed.

"What if she says no?" Charlie asked.

"I already asked her."

"Oh."

"So, Charlie," Juan said, "if Mo goes with my sister, maybe you should go with Maggie."

"I don't think so." Charlie's cheeks reddened. "I'd hate to stick you with Caroline. Besides, who says it's got to be a boy and a girl in each canoe?"

"What makes you think I wouldn't like paddling with Caroline?" Juan asked.

"Well, if you did mind," Mo cut in, "you could take a kayak. A kayak is something you can paddle by yourself."

Just then Twait knocked at the cabin door. "When you come down to the waterfront, meet me by the canoes. Rose and Caroline will work with the girls on kayaking while you three learn canoeing with me. Then Rose and I will switch groups."

"Um, wait," Charlie said. "Mr. Twait? I mean Twait."

Twait opened the screen door again and stuck his red mop-top in. "What is it?"

Charlie took a deep breath and exhaled loudly. He pursed his lips. "I might be able to canoe, but I don't think I can kayak."

"Why not?"

"It'll feel too tight. I have a hard time with confined spaces."

"Claustrophobia? Panicky in elevators, tunnels, closets?"

"No, not like that. It's more about restricting my legs, I think. It's hard enough to do things with these hands, so I rely on my legs for my sense of freedom. That's why I don't sleep in a sleeping bag, and I can't sleep with the sheets or blankets tucked in at the bottom of the mattress.

When I have only my hands, I feel trapped. In a canoe my legs would be free."

"I see. Is that all, or is there more?"

Charlie's face showed his discomfort.

"Well, um, I-I also fudged a question on my application."

"And?"

"I can't swim. I never learned."

Twait made a face and scratched his head. "You can't swim, but you'd be willing to go canoeing?"

"The water's shallow, right? And I'd have a life preserver on, so that'd hold me up."

Twait shook his head. "One of the basics you have to learn—and practice—before canoeing is what to do if you tip over. I'm glad you told me."

"So now what? No canoeing?"

"Is there anybody else here who can't swim?" Twait looked first to Juan and then to Mo. "If so, speak now."

"I swim like a fish," Mo said.

"Me too," Juan said. "My sister's the same. We're pool rats."

Twait rubbed his beard stubble as if trying to pull his chin down to a point.

"Okay, here's the plan. You two fishies meet us at the boatshed as planned. Charlie, meet me at the waterfront in five minutes. I'll give you a crash course in swimming."

"Alone? Just me?"

"No, not just you—you and me. I work wonders."

After a long moment, Charlie nodded. "Okay. My life is in your hands."

"Five minutes," Twait reminded, the screen door slamming shut behind him.

"Five minutes," Charlie echoed.

When Twait was out of earshot, Mo said, "So, you think he'll rat you out to Bando about lying on your application?"

Charlie was about to speak, but Juan beat him to it. "This is Bando we're talking about. What makes you think he doesn't already know?"

***

A man driving with his grandson to a trout pond came across Atlanta sitting in the middle of the road. She babbled enough of her story so the grandfather realized she was one of the missing kids. He drove her to the nearest store, where the clerk phoned the paramedics and State Police. The paramedics transported Atlanta to the hospital. Word reached the Officer-in-Charge, who phoned Bando.

It didn't take long for the State Police to find the sand quarry and close in on the hatch. They used bolt cutters to snip the padlock, flipped open the hatch, and called down the ladder. When no one answered, two officers with flashlights descended into the buried bus.

"Looks like they were here," one of them yelled up. "But they're gone now." The bus no longer held its precious cargo.

The order went out to arrest Bronson. One team closed in on his trailer while another surrounded the estate where he'd parked his pickup. But they found only the truck—no Bronson. Where had he gone? He wasn't at his sand pit, at home, or at the work site. One child was safe, four were unaccounted for, and no one had a clue where Donnie Bronson was. They suspected he was on his motorcycle, but weren't sure. He might be driving something else. And they didn't know where he was heading—or why. The man had disappeared into thin air.

CHAPTER 51

THE FOUR PRISONERS BOUNCED around like steers in a cattle trailer heading to the slaughterhouse. They tried sitting at first, but they were so tightly shackled to the wooden bar on the wall that their shoulders ached from holding their arms overhead. The only option was to stand on wobbly legs, feet hip-width apart for balance. No matter their positions, though, when the truck bumped and bounced, the metal bracelets chafed their wrists.

"Why did he use these things?" Celine asked. "All he had to do was lock the door."

"I don't know," Mouse answered. "He's gone to a lot of trouble to get these chains and shackles just right. He's been thinking about this for a long time."

"He must have planned on having Atlanta here, too," Tim said. "There are five sets and five locks."

"Is he going to kill us in these?" Celine asked.

"He could have killed us anytime," Mouse said. "He has that gun. And like he said, he could have shut off the air supply to the bus. But like you said, why these chains—why lock us down? I think he's on some weird timetable that makes sense only to him—like, if he's got something bad in mind, it's got to happen at a certain time. Problem is, we have no way of knowing what or when."

"Then we're not being held for ransom?" Celine asked.

"If we were," Mouse said, "he'd have taken something to prove he had us."

"Like what?" Celine asked. "A finger?"

"No, like a piece of clothing. But he didn't. So it's probably not about money."

"Then why'd he take us? And what's he planning to do with us?" Nobody dared guess again, at least not out loud.

After they had bumped and jostled along for another five minutes, Mouse asked, "Anybody got a hairpin?"

"A hairpin?" Tim asked.

"Yeah. In the movies sometimes they use a bent hairpin to pick a lock."

"Even if I had a hairpin to give you, would you really know how to pick these locks?" Celine asked.

"No, but I'd try. Hey, never give up."

"Well, Mouse, we appreciate the thought," BJ said. "But even if we did, I doubt you'd be able to pick these. This one is like a good bike lock. Only needs a couple of key pins to line up."

"Even if we opened the locks," Celine added, "we'd still have that sliding door to deal with—from the inside."

***

Caroline showed up at the girls' cabin in a bathing suit and flip-flops, a heavy towel around her neck. Maggie was ready to go.

"Just a minute," Juanita said, rummaging through her bag. "Can't find my stupid flip-flops."

Caroline lay down on one of the unused bunks, wadding her towel into a makeshift pillow.

"I like your parents," Maggie said. "They're really nice. Have they been doing camp work a long time?"

"A couple years. Dad worked for a circus."

"He wasn't a midget, was he?" Maggie asked, the words escaping her mouth before she could catch them.

"Not exactly. He did two things. He was an acrobat—like the flying trapeze—he's very athletic. But he was best known for his high-dive act, from a tower into a vat of water."

"Not a bathtub?"

"No, more like a really deep wading pool—three feet deep. The secret was his swan dive—hitting chest first, not head first."

"Chest first? Ouch! That must have hurt!"

"He told me he built up thick chest muscles over time. He started low, worked his way higher, got used to the impact. Obviously you can't dive into three feet of water the way you'd dive into a pond, or you'd break your neck on the bottom. Except for a couple of broken collarbones, he wasn't hurt. He's got great pictures in his scrapbook, plus a reel of video footage."

"Is that how he got his waterfront certification and this job?" Juanita asked, pulling a single flip-flop from the bag. The three of them laughed. "I don't know if this one's the flip or the flop. I'm going down for another look." She stuck her head back in the bag.

Maggie kept up the conversation. "How about your mother?"

"Same circus. That's where she and Dad met."

"Mom worked in the circus, too?" Juanita asked, coming up for air.

"Yeah, she was a bookkeeper and fortuneteller."

"You're kidding," Maggie said. "A fortuneteller?"

"She used the tarot deck, dolphin cards, crystal ball, and intuition. One of my favorite pictures is of her in her gypsy outfit."

"So, were you, like, born in a circus wagon?" Maggie asked.

"No, I was born at Maine Medical Center. Mom and Dad got married and left the circus. They'd been out of show biz for years by the time I came along."

Juanita, appearing with the matching flip-flop, asked, "How does Bando fit into all of this? Was he with the circus, too?"

"Nope. Dad was a kid when they met. Bando was an adult, a neighbor who made wind catchers, sound catchers, and light catchers out of recycled material. Back then Dad called him Uncle Bando, even though he wasn't a relative. He says Bando saved his life when four hoods were bullying him on the New York subway."

"Bando fought off four hoods?" Maggie asked, astonished.

"That's what Dad says. Some writer told the story as 'Uncle Bando's Chimes' in a book called *Oddest Yet*."

"So, does Bando know karate?" Maggie asked. "If he fought off a gang, he must be a martial arts expert."

"Dad said Bando never lifted a finger."

Maggie cocked a questioning eyebrow. "How can that be?"

"I don't know, but Dad wouldn't lie. And you've met Bando. He's—well—different."

"Yeah, but still—" Maggie hemmed.

Caroline shrugged. "Hey, what can I say?"

Juanita put a hand on the screen door. "The waterfront beckons." But before she could open the door, she closed her eyes and placed her fingers on her forehead.

"You okay?" Caroline asked.

"I'm hearing a voice, very faint. It's not that first one, not Atlanta. It's the second one. She's talking to somebody about locks—no, a lock. *Only needs a couple of key pins to line up*, she's saying. *And we'd still have that sliding door to deal with—from the inside.* She's echoing. And if there's a sliding door, they've got to be in a container. A bus doesn't have a sliding door. Sounds more like a storage unit somebody would rent."

"Or a delivery truck," Maggie suggested.

"We've got to tell Dad and Bando—right now."

And they were out the door and racing up the hill toward Bando's office.

CHAPTER **52**

THE KIDS AND TWAIT stood by the boathouse, watching Rose walk down the hill toward them. Charlie's and Twait's bathing suits were still wet from the private swimming lesson.

"A little bit of good news," Rose announced. "They found Mo's cousin Atlanta. She's fine—exhausted and has a concussion, but she'll be out of the hospital in a couple of days."

Mo breathed an audible sigh of relief.

"What about the others?" Charlie asked.

"They haven't found them yet. But Atlanta said they were okay when she escaped."

"Escaped from where?" Mo asked.

"An underground school bus. That guy in the sketch—the police are pretty sure it was this Bronson in a bald wig and sunglasses—he buried them underground at his sand quarry. They dug their way out, but Atlanta was the only one who got out before he came back for them."

"But the others are alive?" Maggie asked.

"We assume they are. When the police got to the bus, they were gone. Looks like Bronson moved them."

"They're chasing him down, though, right?" Mo asked. "They'll catch him, won't they? Those kids will be okay?"

"They're circulating a recent photo of Bronson they found at his home. And the kids' pictures are everywhere. Everybody in Maine is on the lookout."

"So what can we do?" Mo asked.

"We can stay out of the way for now, let the police do their job."

Twait added, "As Bando said, we can enjoy camp this morning, learn to canoe and kayak." Before they could grumble, he added, "Let's haul these boats down to the water and put on our life preservers."

Twenty minutes later, after a little basic instruction, an odd flotilla took to the water—Charlie and Twait in one canoe, Juan and Mo in another, the three girls and Rose each in her own kayak. Everyone wore slim-line life preservers and appeared comfortable on the water—even Charlie, whose confidence had grown immeasurably since his crash swim course with Twait.

"Okay, spread out," Twait instructed. "Let's flip them. The water's deeper here, over your heads. We'll see if you learned your lessons in the shallow water."

The kayaks flipped easily, but the canoes took more rocking. After countless shouts of mock terror, everyone wound up in the lake, laughing and splashing.

Once they righted the six boats, Twait and the boys paddled across the lake while Rose and the girls lined up for a race to the far end.

Caroline challenged Juanita and Maggie. "Mom and I will give you a hundred-yard head start."

The two novices paddled ahead, and once they were set, Caroline turned to Rose and cackled, "This is the day you meet your match, Big Momma! Ready, set, go!" And they were off, putting their backs into it, taking long sweeping strokes as they glided over the glassy surface of the lake.

Bando sat in his office examining the dreams journal Charlie had shown him. One of the latest entries wasn't a dream; it was the mental picture he'd conjured up when Bando suggested the word vortex. The boy had taken great pains to get the details down on paper. Juan's suggestion was paying off: the discipline of writing was broadening Charlie's gifts.

The bright yellow object on the edge of Charlie's funnel cloud made more sense now that the police had found the underground school bus. But the information was too late and hadn't helped them locate either the school bus or the children.

Something else poked out of Charlie's swirling dust and debris tornado, though—a giant orange horseshoe. Had all five kids seen it, or just Charlie? Regardless, Charlie had recorded it here. What did it mean?

Then there was his entry about the car going airborne, crash-landing on the lake, and sinking. Somehow Bando sensed the two were tied together—the orange horseshoe and the sinking car—even though they appeared in separate journal entries. He picked up the phone and dialed.

***

Rose and Caroline shot past the two girls. Sweat broke out on their faces as they stroked hard, their kayaks nose to nose.

Caroline switched from a long stroke to a shorter, rapid-rotation racing stroke, her arms a windmill of motion. "You're going down, woman," she taunted, her face a portrait of determination. "You've met your match!" Her kayak inched ahead of her mother's.

Suddenly Rose, who had been on the left, disappeared from Caroline's peripheral vision. Caroline realized her mother had either given up or something had happened. She couldn't have fallen back from sight that fast. Caroline glanced back to her left.

Her mother was nowhere to be seen. No kayak, no paddle, no Rose. She'd simply disappeared. Juanita and Maggie were far behind.

Caroline dipped the paddle blades in a braking motion, stopped, and back-paddled. She turned the kayak and scanned the waters.

"Mom?" Terror and panic crept into her voice. "Mom! Mom, if you're messing with my head, this is a terrible joke."

Maggie drew closer. "Caroline, did you see that? Your mother's kayak nose-dived. It was like a car going into a tunnel under a river."

"Look!" Juanita exclaimed, pointing.

A kayak paddle shot from the depths, broke the surface, and floated. Maggie grabbed it.

"I'm going down," Caroline shouted. She tossed her own paddle in the water, stripped off her life vest, and gulped some air. Then she flipped her kayak.

Juanita and Maggie saw flashes of skin and bathing suit beneath the kayak as Caroline wriggled out and swam down into the murk.

After half a minute that felt like an hour, with no sign of life below, the girls yelled for help. In the distance Twait and the boys mistook their shouting and hand-waving for a greeting. They waved back. When the girls kept up the frenzied waving and screaming, they started paddling furiously toward them.

But before they could reach the girls, Rose's kayak popped up nose-first like a submarine surfacing. Rose sat exactly as she had when she went down—in the kayak seat—except that now Caroline's arms were wrapped around her waist. The two of them hungrily gulped in fresh air.

Juanita and Maggie began to cry.

"Did you see them?" Rose asked.

"I did," Caroline answered. "Both of them. And I heard them. I saw them and I heard them."

"Who?" Maggie asked.

"The mother and daughter," Rose said. "Karen and Addie Beals, from the waterfall."

"You saw them down there?" Maggie asked. "Under the water?"

"Yes. Maybe it was the only way we could see them—underwater. I think they dragged me down so I could see them and listen to them."

"They waited for me," Caroline added.

"Wait," Maggie said. "You're saying they pulled you two to the bottom of the lake—just to get your attention? They didn't want to hurt you?"

Rose said, "I think they're saying something's going to happen at the waterfall."

"How do you know they weren't telling you that's where they drowned?" Juanita asked.

"We already knew where they drowned," Caroline said. "They wouldn't go to this trouble to show us themselves trapped in the whirlpool, and also speak the word *waterfall*."

"So there are two different things here—whirlpool and waterfall, right?" Maggie asked. "But they said *waterfall*?"

"Mom and I both heard them."

"Underwater?" Maggie asked. "You heard them underwater?"

"Why not?" Juanita said. "Remember Juan and me with that kidnapped woman? He saw and I heard through a goldfish in a bowl? If I could hear voices through water, why couldn't they?"

Twait and Charlie glided closer in their canoe, their faces sweaty. "Everybody okay?" Twait asked.

"We're fine now," Rose answered. "I'll tell you about it on the way back in. That's enough water fun for one day. We girls will skip our canoe time, thanks."

"Then we boys will pass on our kayak session," Twait said.

Charlie breathed a sigh of relief. Thanks to Twait he had become a basic swimmer—dog-paddling and treading water—in a half hour. Even so, just the thought of having to slide into that tight cocoon of a kayak put his stomach in knots.

As they headed for shore, Caroline glanced back at the black waters that had swallowed her mother, nearly becoming her grave. Whatever or whoever had dragged Rose's kayak to the bottom hadn't wanted her life, it had only wanted her attention—and Caroline's. There was a strange bond between the drowned mother and daughter and the living mother and daughter. The reason wasn't yet clear. But after seeing her mother dragged to the bottom of the lake, Caroline knew it was a connection she couldn't afford to ignore.

On the shoreline by the boathouse Bando waited, brooding, unusually worried.

CHAPTER 53

THE FIRST THING ROSE AND CAROLINE DID was tell Bando what they'd heard and seen at the bottom of the lake. He listened, his face unreadable. When the tale was fully told, he said simply, "The waterfall."

As the group walked toward their cabins to change out of their bathing suits, Bando said, "Mo, your mother called. She'll be here to pick you up between two and three, depending on the storm. I guess there's a big one predicted."

Mo looked as if he were in pain, but it wasn't physical. "Aw, come on. I need to see how this turns out," he whined.

His friends' faces offered sympathy—or perhaps it was empathy. They knew how he felt. None of them said, "You'll hear about it on TV" or "We'll call and tell you how it ends." They understood Mo was invested—not just in the hearing and seeing how it turned out, but in being part of it. He hated to leave them now. He belonged, contributed—was part of something bigger than himself. These two days had gripped him like nothing else in his short life. He'd never felt so alive and engaged, so connected to comrades he'd only just met. This whole thing was more than a mystery—it was cosmic—and he had a part to play in it.

"Anything new from the police?" Twait asked Bando.

"Just one thing."

Everyone turned.

"What?" Mo asked eagerly.

"The picture of Karen and Addie Beals that Caroline found in the classifieds—from Bronson. Apparently Mr. and Mrs. Beals noticed it, too. Bronson ran it for three days, Sunday through Tuesday—yesterday. Today's is different. Mrs. Beals called while you were on the lake. The message under the picture this morning says: *All conditions and sacrifices will be met today. I eagerly await the return of my beloved on this perfect anniversary.*"

"The perfect anniversary? What's that mean?" Mo asked.

"In this instance, perfect probably means the exact date and exact time," Bando answered.

"Okay," Caroline said. "This is the date. What's the time?"

"I asked Mrs. Beals. She remembers them getting the phone call at suppertime, which means Karen and Addie drowned mid to late afternoon. I called and asked the police to check."

"So he's going to do something today mid to late afternoon," Charlie said.

"Involving the waterfall," Caroline said. "Which is why Mom and I got that message just now."

Juan disagreed. "I'm not so sure. You and your mother saw and heard something down there, and I believe you. But I also trust Charlie's dreams—like the one about the car sinking into the lake."

"Maybe that dream was about Mom's kayak—not a car."

"There's water in the waterfall," Juanita argued. "Lake, pond, stream, waterfall—whatever—its all water. And that's where they drowned, not in the lake."

"Yes, it is all water, but it's not all the same," Juan continued. "Maybe Charlie's lake is a lake. He dreamed a car sinking into a lake, not a waterfall."

"But Juan," Caroline said, her voice pleading and persuasive, "everything so far is tied to the waterfall."

Mo took Juan's side. "Rose's kayak didn't disappear into the waterfall."

"But Mom and I heard *waterfall*."

"Wait," Maggie interrupted. "There's another way they tie in. The waterfall is really part of the stream that feeds our camp lake. It's all connected."

"Maybe so," Juan shot back, "but my intuition tells me Charlie's onto something."

Bando held up a hand, silencing them. "Ready, Charlie? I think you're on." He kept the hand up so Charlie could see it.

A slow recognition appeared in Charlie's eyes as he stared at Bando's raised hand.

"Ah hah. I recognize the hand now. This is where you pull my notebook from behind your back, isn't it?"

Bando reached back. The notebook appeared. Had it been tucked in his waistband or did Bando pull it from the air?

Charlie smiled. "Go ahead, sir. Tell us the group needs to work together, but that we also need to honor the individual gifts while trusting our separate instincts."

The others slowly caught on to what was going on. Charlie had already dreamed this scene.

"You've said it so well, Charlie. I don't need to repeat it," Bando said, a sly smile curling the corners of his mouth.

Charlie smiled back. "I knew you were going to say that."

"Must be quite a strange feeling."

"Yes, it is."

"And you know what I'm about to say next as well."

Charlie nodded.

The others' eyes shifted from Charlie to Bando as if the conversation were a tennis volley.

"So go ahead and say it," Charlie said. "I may already know, but they haven't heard it before."

Bando's eyes twinkled. He hesitated, playing the crowd like a fisherman reeling in a fish.

"They're getting hungry," Charlie said. "We're all getting hungry." Then he added, "I knew I was going to say that," and giggled.

Bando laughed. "Okay, I'll say it."

They all held their breath, waiting for something profound.

Bando opened his mouth. "Lunch in half an hour."

He and Charlie watched the disappointment register on the others' faces, and then they began laughing heartily, as if only the two of them knew the punch line to an inside joke.

"That's it?" Mo asked.

Charlie took the notebook from Bando. He unclipped the pen from its cover and opened to a fresh page, where he wrote something.

Bando looked at Charlie, eyes asking, "Now?"

Charlie nodded.

"The kitchen ran out of propane gas," Bando said, "so Rose can't cook. Which means we're going to the pizza place for lunch. Meet by the van and the car at 12:00."

Charlie held out the notebook for the others to see. On the fresh page he had written: *We're going to the pizza place for lunch. Meet by the van and the car at 12:00.*

While the others stared at each other in disbelief, Mo said, "How do we know you two didn't work this out ahead of time?"

Charlie turned the page of the notebook and held it out for his friends to see. It read: *Mo said, "How do we know you two didn't work this out ahead of time?"*

Mo's eyes went wide. A moment later he grinned and said, "Pizza sounds good," and they headed for the cabins.

In the distance to the west above New Hampshire's Presidential Range, they could see an ominous cluster of thunderheads. In an hour the huge storm Mo's mother had warned of would invade Maine and overshadow Free Camp, bringing with it darkness and torrential rains. For now, though, the promise of hot pizza dominated the forecast.

CHAPTER 54

THE MORNING SUN BLINKED OUT and the sky darkened as the U-Haul turned onto a narrow dirt driveway pocked with potholes.

"One wicked storm coming in this afternoon," Bronson said to no one in particular. "That stream'll be rushing."

He slowed the truck to a crawl and shifted into low gear. "Hold tight, campers. We're in for a rough patch," he called back, knowing full well they couldn't hear him in their metal prison. He carefully negotiated the driveway through the pines, the truck's sides brushing back branches as it bumped toward his Uncle Dave's hunting and fishing camp.

When the front bumper was six feet from the little cabin's door, he cut a hard left and backed up. The van fitted neatly beside a low lean-to barn that housed a tarp-covered snowmobile, a dented aluminum canoe, and Uncle Dave's rusty Jeep.

He shut off the engine, walked back to the tailgate, and raised the slide-up door. The four prisoners blinked as harsh light flooded the cargo area.

"Lunchtime," a man announced.

The voice they heard was the same, but the person it had come from wasn't the bald militiaman. This man's sunglasses were squarer than the others had been, and he'd sprouted pork-chop sideburns that went with his black cowboy hat. Above a pair of western-cut jeans he wore a black shirt with roses stitched on the pocket flap and collar. This man looked like a country singer headed for Nashville—except he had no guitar or banjo in hand—this country singer had only a .45. Same man, different look.

"Look around. I wanted you to see that we're out in the middle of nowhere. So when I shut this door again, don't waste your voices yelling to me. I'm going to town for a few things. Do you want me to pick up lunch for you, too?"

His voice had softened, catching them off-guard. The absurdity of such a caring, considerate question in this context—a glimpse of kindness—left them momentarily speechless.

"Well? We haven't got all day."

Mouse, without thinking, turned to the others and asked, "Sandwiches? Pizza? Sodas?"

Celine said to the man, "Wait. Is this like a last meal or something?"

His face clouded over like the angry sky behind him. He slammed the pull-down door and latched it. Once again darkness enveloped them.

A minute later they heard the Jeep fire up and drive off. Thirty seconds passed before Mouse asked, "You think he'll still get us something?"

***

Bronson's first stop on his round of errands was about fifteen miles away. He parked the Jeep at Lords & Ladies Bride & Groom Shoppe and went in. Ten minutes later he emerged carrying a cellophane-covered black tuxedo and two white dresses. He carefully placed them on the back seat. A second trip into the shop yielded three shoeboxes, one quite large, the other two smaller. He used the boxes to anchor the rented outfits.

Bunny's Florist wasn't far from the Bride and Groom Shoppe. He left Bunny's with a long narrow box and a small corsage box, both of which he placed on the floor.

Next came Pierce's General Store. He went in, walked up to one of the refrigerated cases, and selected five plastic-wrapped sandwiches. He also bought a six-pack of Diet Coke. He was sure the two girls would complain if it weren't diet. Had Addie been with them in the U-Haul, it's what she'd have wanted.

He kept the sunglasses on when he walked to the counter to pay. He hadn't been in Pierce's in years. The owners and clerks had changed anyway, so there wasn't much chance anyone would recognize him, especially not in his country outfit. He looked nothing like the driver's license photo on the news. He'd worn the same outfit weeks earlier when ordering the wedding clothes, the shoes, and the corsages. He paid for the lunches and left.

The last stop was the stonecutter's barn. He'd phoned earlier to be sure the engraved block of pink granite was ready, with its iron ring attached. It was. He owed these kids something. He'd soon be in their debt. He lugged the heavy block to the Jeep, set his legs and hips so he could lift it in, and with a grunt hoisted it and set it inside the tailgate.

Errands done, he drove back toward Uncle Dave's cabin. He had sandwiches to deliver, and Diet Cokes, and the pink-granite marker he'd dedicated to the kids who would soon help bring Karen and Addie back. This time around, though, he and Karen would do things right and proper.

CHAPTER 55

THE OFFICER-IN-CHARGE was at the camp office when Bando got back.

"Didn't happen to bring along a big cylinder of propane, did you?" Bando asked.

"Nope. Why?"

"The kitchen tanks ran out. Rose can't cook lunch."

"What's that leave—peanut-butter and jelly?"

"No. We'll take the kids out for pizza. It's their last meal together, so it should be special anyway. Mo's mother is driving up for him this afternoon. The other parents will be here tomorrow. This will give them a chance to say their goodbyes."

"Yeah, that's important. Even after a couple of days of camp, kids bond."

"Anything new on Bronson? I mean, anything you can share?"

The Trooper relaxed visibly under Bando's gaze and—whether he meant to share information or not—the words rolled easily out of his mouth.

"We considered what you said about Bronson's connection to the camp and the waterfall. It's unlikely he'll try anything with law enforcement so visible here. So we're shifting some of our resources."

"To where?"

"The Portland Jetport."

"Why would you do that?" Bando's voice was hypnotic.

The officer relaxed deeper into his chair. "We got a hit on our electronic crosschecking. He's flying to Florida tonight."

Bando considered this. "One ticket?"

"Three."

"Who are the other two for?"

"Karen and Adeline Bronson."

"Not Beals?"

"Nope. Bronson."

"Bronson? As if they're married and the little girl finally shares his last name? Does that tell you anything?"

"It tells us he'll be at the airport a little past suppertime for his 8:30 flight. We've already spread a few plainclothes people around inside and outside the Jetport security area."

"But before he goes to the Jetport, what will he do with those four kids?"

"We don't know. If we don't get a break before he hits the Jetport, we'll try to make him tell us or show us where they are." The officer's face grew grim. "We're doing everything in our power—"

"And hoping for the best," Bando finished. "I appreciate everything you're doing."

The man in the chair smiled weakly, his eyes drooping like a dental patient whose anesthesia hadn't yet worn off. Bando shook his hand.

"If you'll excuse me, I've got to get the kids to a pizza party." Bando walked out of the office, leaving the officer to shake the cobwebs out of his brain.

"Bronson bought airline tickets for tonight," Bando told Twait and Rose as they met by the vehicles. "Three—one for himself and one each for Karen and Addie Bronson. Not Beals—Bronson."

"So he's into magical thinking," Rose said. "Whatever he's got planned for those kids, he believes it will somehow change reality and bring Karen and Addie back."

"Yes. I think he plans to sacrifice them, trade them for the two people he lost."

"You think he's following some kind of weird spell?" Twait asked.

"I doubt it. I think he's got more than normal grief eating at him, maybe a physical thing, and it's twisted his thinking. It's taken him over, so he's following some bizarre plan that makes sense only to him."

Caroline rolled down the van window that had been open only a crack. 'So Karen and Addie are hanging around because they want to stop him from making a terrible mistake?"

"I think they want to help the kids get away," Rose answered. "In the process they want to help Bronson escape his personal demons."

Five minutes later Rose's car and FreeK Camp #2 rolled down the driveway and onto the road that led to town. A low roll of thunder rumbled in over the lake and raindrops pocked the surface. Not far off in the western mountains a bolt of lightning shot from the clouds as if the devil's forefinger were touching the earth. A loud crack followed, shattering a mighty, towering pine that had dared to mock its power.

CHAPTER 56

THE FOUR CAPTIVES WERE RELIEVED to hear the patter of rain. Maybe it would cool the U-Haul's roof and bring down the cargo area's temperature. They were sweating profusely now and in serious danger of dehydration.

The sound of the Jeep rattling over the potholes gave them a shot of hope. They heard it rev as Bronson pulled up and then backed the vehicle in under the shed roof again. A minute later the door handle clanked and the door slid up, filling their cell with fresh air.

"Lunch is served!" the country singer announced, and slid a cardboard beer-flat filled with sandwiches and Diet Cokes across the aluminum floor toward them. It came to a rest against Mouse's foot.

"Bet that cool air feels good, doesn't it?" the man said, his broad smile making him appear genuinely friendly. "And I know those deli sandwiches and drinks will hit the spot. Mine sure did. I ate it on the way home."

"Our hands?" BJ said. "We can't eat or drink like this. Could you unlock us for a few minutes so we can stretch?"

The man looked momentarily confused.

"We won't go anywhere," Mouse pleaded.

The urban cowboy stared at Mouse as if he'd uttered the words in some foreign language. Then he reached into his pocket and pulled out a key.

"Oops. That's the ignition key. Wait there a minute. Be right back."

The driver's door opened and quickly slammed shut. Bronson reappeared with the .45 in his waistband. His hands worked a small ring of keys as if they were rosary beads. He climbed onto the step bumper and into the cargo area.

"No fast moves," he said, patting the gun, the militiaman snarl in his voice again.

It took him three tries to match the first key to the right lock. He got the next one in two tries. Once the shackles were off, he ordered, "Sit. Right here. Not on the tailgate. Here. This isn't a picnic."

"Can we have some water, too?" Tim asked. "We're so thirsty. And there's no air circulating when that door's down."

"I didn't bring extra water—just those sodas. Sorry. The tap in the cabin is shut off from this winter. Eat those sandwiches and drink up fast. Once I change out of these duds, we roll again. Then you'll get your water—plenty of it."

He jumped to the ground and stood there staring at them. When they sat facing each other that way, they looked like they were gathered around a campfire. Drops of rain made an odd tap-dancing sound on the crown and brim of the cowboy hat.

Suddenly he winced and clapped a hand to the back of his neck.

"Mister, are you all right?" Tim asked.

The man didn't answer. Instead he reached up and grabbed the handle, barked "Twenty minutes," and pulled the overhead door down.

While the others ate and drank in the dark, BJ went to the shackles and felt around for the key ring. It was hanging there, the last key in the last padlock Bronson had opened. She touched each of the five keys the way a blind girl might read a story in Braille while memorizing it. Then she worked her way along the wall and did the same with each of the five locks.

Fifteen minutes later the door flew up and a new batch of cool, damp air rushed in along with gray daylight. Their eyes had to adjust again, this time not only to the light—but to a different Bronson standing in the pattering rain. No more urban cowboy, no more pork-chop sideburns, no

embroidered shirt, and no broad-brimmed Stetson. Before their astonished eyes stood a groom—a man in a black tuxedo, white vest, and black
top hat. He was a weird mix of Barbie's boyfriend Ken and Batman's
insane arch-villain Penguin. It didn't take long to determine which.

He strained to hoist a granite block into the van and struggled to lug
it across the aluminum floor, where he set it down in their midst.

"Time to hook you up. But don't get up. Finish your lunch."

He grabbed four shackles from the wall, leaving the entire length of
chain, the fifth shackle, and the fifth lock hanging there. With four quick
motions he padlocked each shackled prisoner to the stone's iron ring.
Etched in the granite they could see the words *to those who died so others
might live* and the date. There was barely time to gasp.

A moment later the door rolled slowly down like a theater curtain at
the end of Act Three. Who would be left for an encore?

CHAPTER 57

THE FRONT DOOR OF THE SLICES AND ICES pizza parlor and ice cream emporium opened into a well-lit, high-ceilinged dining room. The booths against the left and right walls offered bench seating for four to six people, while the center of the room was set with freestanding square and rectangular tables.

All the tabletops were covered with sheets of disposable white paper rather than fabric tablecloths. In addition to a napkin dispenser and the usual offering of pizza-parlor condiments, each table had a bowl of crayons that could be used on the paper table covers while waiting for the meal to arrive.

Above the booths on the left side hung Little League team photos. On the walls over the right-hand booths hung various types of Maine maps.

A horde of small children in pointy paper hats jammed the booths on the Little League side. Any crayon masterpieces they had done were splotched with pizza sauce or soaked by spilled drinks. One mother calmed a sobbing child as two others passed out the cake and ice cream that would soon add a fresh coat to the table-cover art.

Bando's gang stood inside the door and waited to be seated. All but one of the freestanding tables were crowded, and it was a small square one. There was also one booth table available on the right side. The waitress let Mo and Twait move the square table next to the booth table. The six kids slid in, leaving the add-on table for the adults.

Menus, ice water, and napkin-wrapped place settings appeared. When the waitress returned, they ordered three pizzas, cold drinks, and a cup of hot water for Bando, who pulled out his own special tea bag.

While they waited for their food, they talked about their all-too-brief camp experience and then the kidnapping, laying out once more the hard data of the case plus their own "soft" data and hunches—in case they'd overlooked something. While they talked, each of the kids picked up crayons and doodled absentmindedly on the sheet of white paper. The time flew by in an instant, and before long the waitress set the pizzas down. The famished kids fell upon them like lions on a downed gazelle.

As Mo was polishing off his third slice, he glanced up at the wall. "Hey, weird map, not like one I've ever seen."

"It shows you the terrain," Twait said from the far end of the table. "Altitudes, depths, feet above sea level. You can also see natural land-marks and a few manmade ones, like towers. That map is local. It shows you this part of Maine."

Bando said, "See if you can locate Free Camp on it—and our lake, and the stream, and the waterfall."

Mo and Charlie sat across from each other and farthest in, so they were close to the map. Charlie scrunched up his nose and squinted through his wire-rims, then used the straw from his soda as a pointer. He tapped it on the map, on a body of water that appeared as a wavy-edged oval. "There's the camp lake."

"Up to the right," Caroline added, "is where Mom's kayak went under. Down at the bottom edge—the south end of the lake—is where the water's shallow. That's our camp waterfront."

"Here's our stream," Mo said, using his own straw to trace an upward line to the north. "It feeds the lake."

"See how the elevation is changing?" Twait asked. "The stream comes down off the high ground, out of the hills to the north. If you look closely, you'll find the surveyors have the name of our waterfall there."

Mo found the falls and pointed with his straw.

"If we trace the stream north of the waterfall," Maggie said, "we'll find its source, right? I'll bet it's in northern Maine or northern New Hampshire, maybe even Canada."

Mo traced the stream with the tip of his straw, but he didn't go far. "Our source is this bigger lake, which is fed by two other streams coming down from the north. So our little stream is just an outlet for that big lake."

"It's all the same water," Juan pointed out. "The big lake, the upper stream, the waterfall, the lower stream, and our little camp lake that must overflow into another little stream that empties somewhere else—like Sebago Lake, and eventually into the Atlantic Ocean. If we threw some dye in way upstream, we'd find it's all the same water."

As Juan finished his sentence, Charlie shut his eyes, a pained look coming over his face.

Caroline was next to him. "Charlie, you okay? Want something to wash it down?"

He shook his head slightly but didn't open his eyes.

"From this far away," Juanita said, pointing to the map, "the lakes look like Connect the Dots."

Charlie's eyes flew open. "That's it! That's it! This exact moment— Mo pointing to the map, us eating pizza, the birthday party with the noisy kids—it's the déjà vu dream I forgot until now! Juan, remember the one you made me write down about crashing the car in the lake? He's taking them to the upper lake." Charlie looked at Bando at the other end of the table. "This is it, isn't it?"

Bando had been sipping his tea. Now he nodded.

"We've got to go," Charlie said. "Right now."

"Mom and I can't go there," Caroline said. "We have to go back to camp in case he brings them to the waterfall. They said *waterfall*."

Rose nodded.

"But don't you see?" Charlie argued. "We've got to go to that other lake. Bronson's taking them there."

Bando raised a hand. "If this is truly your dream, Charlie, and you trust it, you also know who goes where, right?"

Before Charlie could answer, Twait said, "I have to stay with Rose and Caroline."

"Me, too," Juanita said.

"Sorry, Sis," Juan said. "I have to go along with Charlie's dream."

"Time for fresh scenery," Maggie said. "I'm for checking out a new lake."

"Me too," Mo said. "My Mom will be here soon, so why would I go back to camp early?"

"How will you get there?" Bando asked.

In an instant Charlie's tension disappeared. He knew the next words out of his mouth, because Bando had just uttered the words *how will you get there?* This was the script from his dream. Charlie smiled as he placed a hand against his forehead like a fortuneteller guessing cards, and said, "I see you driving us in Rose's car, sir." He tried not to giggle, but the giggle was in the dream, so it was pointless to fight it. The giggle came out.

Bando didn't say anything for several few seconds, and when nothing more came from Charlie, he said in a teasing voice, "Charles, isn't there another word yet to be spoken to fulfill your amazing vision?"

Charlie didn't catch on at first, but then saw where Bando was going with it. "Pleeease?" he asked in a drawn-out, syrupy voice.

The others cringed.

Bando's eyes twinkled. "That was indeed the magic word. It wasn't so hard, was it?"

Charlie shook his head. "Not at all, sir, and thank you."

"Okay," Bando announced. "The lake group goes with me in Rose's car. Twait and Rose, Caroline and Juanita—take the van. Charlie, that disposable cell phone still has minutes on it, right?"

"Yes. I've got it right here."

"Good. Give the phone number to Twait."

Charlie wrote the number down and passed it down the table.

"Twait," Bando continued, "you'll need to stay by the office phone so we can call if we need to. Or, if there's a change, you can call us.

First thing you have to do is let the Officer-in-Charge know we think Bronson's on his way to the upper lake."

Twait nodded.

"Everybody remember, as your camp director, I have to say this—*we avoid dangerous situations. Understood?*"

Nobody nodded.

"Understood?"

They nodded reluctantly, having no way of knowing they'd be unable to keep such a promise.

They slid out of the booth, and everyone except Bando and Rose moved toward the front door. Outside, the rain was coming down in fat drops. Thunder rumbled overhead and flashes of lighting split the sky. The birthday children screeched. Twait and the kids ran for the vehicles.

Back at the booth, as they waited for the check, Rose and Bando examined the kids' tabletop artwork.

Maggie had traced the outline of her hand the way she had in kindergarten. Next to it—but just out of reach—she'd drawn a key.

Charlie had sketched an orange delivery truck with the word Furniture on its side.

Mo had scrawled a villainous figure with a black handlebar mustache. The man's knees were bent as he strained to lift an oversized barbell.

Juan's stick figure was riding a motorcycle and firing a pistol.

Juanita's cadaverous, hollow-eyed bride looked like she had stepped off the cover of a horror comic book.

Caroline's unrecognizable blur of a person was plunging from a high-dive platform toward a barrel marked *Beware: Shallow Water*.

Bando held a hand to his chin as he studied the drawings. "The way the drawings are laid out, Rose, it reminds me of your old Tarot cards at the circus."

"Or your tea leaves, old friend."

Bando sighed. "Trust the Force."

Rose shook her head sadly. "I always do. But this one's really scary."

The waitress arrived with the check. The Free Campers had left the table without noticing what they or their friends had drawn. Weren't the drawings important? Perhaps not, perhaps the kids had simply been clearing the attics of their minds of what they had forgotten was up there—or never knew was there. Maybe it was important to get the images down on paper only so Bando and Rose could see them.

Bando paid the bill, and he and Rose stepped out into a heavy downpour. The storm was what old-timers called a cloudburst; the lakes were swelling fast. In some places the streams and rivers had already overflowed their banks. Both Bando and Rose knew there was never a good time to step into a rushing stream. They also knew that sometimes you had to.

CHAPTER 58

TWAIT SLOWED THE VAN as it approached the bridge. The stream had risen fast and its roaring waters frothed a foot below the metal decking the cars crossed on. The tires hummed on the bridge's cross-hatching and splashed when they hit a puddle on the other side.

A State Trooper sat parked by Free Camp's driveway, the car's parking lights on and its wipers and defroster running.

Twait waved and the Trooper waved back. The camp areas that a day earlier had overflowed with cops and media trucks were deserted now. The background footage had all been shot and the search for the children—and Bronson—had shifted elsewhere.

Twait parked close to the dining hall and the four of them scrambled inside. Rose stopped at the kitchen door, Twait at the office.

"Girls," Rose said to Caroline and Juanita, "Make us a fire. We need something to take the dampness off."

The phone rang. Twait picked it up. "Nope, Bando's isn't here. This is Twait."

Rose stuck her head in. "If that's the Officer-in-Charge, can I speak to him?"

Twait gave her the wait-a-minute signal then passed along Bando's message about Bronson and the upper lake. The Officer-in-Charge promised he'd order two Troopers there.

Rose raised a hand again and, before Twait could wave her off, she said, "Bando said to have them check U-Haul dealers. He thinks Bronson rented a truck. If he did, he'd have given the dealer a driver's license."

Twait relayed the message.

Rose added, "Tell them to be on the lookout for either a U-Haul van or a big orange truck up by the lake. It may say Furniture on the side. Some part of it will likely be U-Haul orange."

Twait passed the second message on. "Rose, he says they'd normally use a helicopter, but with this storm, the visibility's terrible."

Rose shrugged and backed out.

"Any new developments I can tell Bando about?" Twait said into the phone.

The voice on the other end said, "There's one I'd like to tell him, but I can't because of confidentiality—not legal but medical."

Twait knew the Officer-in-Charge wanted to spill it, but he didn't have Bando's hypnotic voice and didn't know how to get the officer to talk.

Then the man asked, "So, is Bando somewhere on the camp grounds?"

"No."

"Is he nearby?"

"No."

"Meaning?"

"He's checking out that lake."

"Oh, great! Is he crazy? What if he's right and Bronson's taking those kids there? We know he's got a gun."

"What can I say? He left from the pizza parlor."

"Has he got a phone?"

Twait gave the man the number for Charlie's disposable cell phone. "A kid will probably answer."

"A kid? You mean he's not alone? He's got a camper with him?"

"Yes."

"Just one?"

"No. Four."

"Four? Oh, for crying out loud! Okay, hang up. I've got to call him. Could the rest of you please stay put there?"

"We're doing our best," Twait said, and hung up.

Rose stuck her head in again. "Nice fire going. Come enjoy it."

Five minutes later Twait, Rose, Caroline, and Juanita sat by the hearth, feeling warm and dry, but worried about the others. They listened for the phone.

From the couch they couldn't know the Trooper at the foot of the hill had just received new orders. They couldn't see his car crossing the bridge and driving north toward the upper lake to help search for an armed-and-dangerous kidnapping suspect who might be driving—of all things to take out in a storm—a U-Haul. For now, what they couldn't see wouldn't hurt them—for now.

CHAPTER 59

AT THE TOP OF THE HILL overlooking the lake, Bronson pulled
over and rested his forearms on the steering wheel. He needed
to release the tension in his shoulders. To avoid detection, he'd taken a
lightly traveled State Road and then an old local road in serious disre-
pair, his route skirting the southwest shore of the lake. For an hour he
felt like he'd been driving through a car wash, the downpour so torrential the wipers couldn't keep up. But poor visibility was only half the
problem. The low spots had become either shallow ponds or fast-moving
streams, their depths impossible to guess. He'd slogged through, trusting the U-Haul's elevated chassis and raised engine would keep it from
stalling out. On the positive side, nothing short of a Hummer or a Land
Rover could pursue him by that route.

The rain had suddenly stopped like a shut-off faucet as he crested
the hill, which he took to be a sign that whoever ruled the heavens didn't
want to spoil his wedding day.

The sky was still dark except for a brightening swirl—perhaps the
eye of the storm—above the lake. He half-expected a rainbow, but maybe
that was too much to ask. Lingering moisture above the waters lent the
lake a ghostlike, prehistoric look, as if a pterodactyl might suddenly flap
skyward out of the mist.

Bronson scanned the near shoreline. At the bottom of the hill sat a
familiar cluster of ruined mill buildings. He put the truck in low and let
it crawl downhill.

This was the perfect setting. How many times had he parked here and launched his fishing skiff from the mill pier? The best day of his life had been here with Addie and Karen, when they fished and had a picnic on the boat. How many years ago had that been? He tried to remember, but the burning coal that was searing his brain stem seemed to have short-circuited his sense of time lately.

The abandoned buildings hunched like gargoyles on the shore. He steered the van into the old parking lot and parked. He opened the glove compartment and withdrew the U-Haul rental contract, which he then clipped to the overhead visor with a note: *Sammy, Sorry I couldn't get it back to you on time. I had a plane to catch. The truck ran fine. Donnie.*

He reached into the tux jacket on the seat beside him, pulled out his wallet, and took from it a laminated newspaper clipping smaller than a credit card. The printed message had come from a cryptic horoscope he'd cut from the newspaper. *Sow perfection upstream that you may reap it downstream.* He had scratched a line through *perfection* and scrawled above it *innocence.* He tucked it into his pants pocket and returned the wallet to the jacket. Then he stepped out and slid into the jacket—a perfect fit.

He banged on the side of the truck. "Have you out in a jiffy." Instead of opening the rear door, though, he strode toward the mill buildings. "Be right back," he called over his shoulder.

In the shadows of a caved-in garage he found his aluminum fishing skiff on its bicycle-wheeled trailer. He wheeled it out of the garage onto the concrete loading pier that stuck into the lake the length of two tractor-trailers. Under normal conditions the driving surface was five or six feet above the lake, but in the last couple of hours millions of gallons of rain funneled into the lake from the surrounding hills, raising the lake level so the gap between the lapping waves and the top of the pier was barely two feet.

Bronson untied the boat from the trailer, slid it into the water, and secured the line to a piling. Then he returned to the truck for his little ship's cargo.

***

Bando's wipers fared no better than the U-Haul's in keeping up with the heavy rain. But because he was driving up the west side of the lake, the road was less prone to flooding than Bronson's route had been. Still, he didn't know where along the lakeshore Bronson might be heading, if he was gong in that direction at all.

The cell phone rang. Charlie answered. "It's the Officer-in-Charge." He handed it to Bando.

"So his driver's license numbers turned up a U-Haul?"

"Ah-hah," Juan whispered to the others. "So, the orange horseshoe in the vortex wasn't a horseshoe at all—it was the letter U. And the color orange goes with U-Haul."

"Medical confidentiality?" Bando said into the phone. Then he switched to his soothing, hypnotic voice. "I know you'd like to help in any way you can. And I'm sure you're thinking at this moment about what it is you can't share." Bando's mouth stopped moving. He listened.

On the other end of the line, the kids could hear the officer's voice, but they couldn't make out his words.

"A patrol car will be coming down from the north end of the lake and another from the camp to the south, looking for a U-Haul," Bando echoed. "And that poor Mr. Bronson—I feel so sorry for him with his medical condition." Bando shut up and listened. Then he said thank you and goodbye, and clicked off.

"Charlie, call Twait. Let him know Bronson has a brain tumor. Tell him, if a U-Haul shows up at camp, it's him."

***

The rear door of the U-Haul rolled up, framing Donnie Bronson's head and shoulders. He slid the loading ramp out from its sheath under the cargo area and set the far end of it on the ground.

"Pick up the block. Haul it right down this ramp."

The four kids shuffled the granite marker to the top of the ramp and crab-walked it down the incline.

"Move it off to the side there," Bronson ordered. "Don't block the ramp."

They moved it out of the way. When they set it down, they were so tightly tethered to it they had no choice but to squat.

Bronson pointed skyward. "Storm's clearing out—at least for now." He walked up the ramp to the dirt bike and untied it.

"What now?" Mouse asked.

"Well, don't run off," Bronson said with an uncharacteristic chuckle. He wheeled the bike down the incline and set it up on its kickstand. "Nice night for a moonlight boat ride, don't you think? Follow me."

"Where are we going?" Celine asked.

"You'll see."

He led them onto the concrete pier that jutted into the dark lake. When they reached the end, he ordered them to put the granite block down. They squatted around it.

The aluminum boat bobbed on the water, bumping and grating against the pier.

"Everybody in. I'll hold the bow. Be careful balancing that weight. You'll want to spread out evenly and face each other, two on the middle seat and two on the rear. Keep the weight as close to center as possible."

"But where are we going?" Celine asked again.

Bronson pointed in the distance. "Think you can make the far shore?"

They looked. The shore looked like it was at least half a mile off.

"Maybe," Celine answered.

With considerable difficulty, while Bronson steadied the boat, they climbed aboard.

"What about you?" BJ asked.

"No can do." He smiled grimly. "I've got a wedding to make and a plane to catch. Besides, you've been itching to get away from me for days. This is your chance."

"There are no oars," Mouse protested.

"Don't need oars where you're going." Bronson untied the bow rope from the pier.

"We have to paddle with our hands?" Celine complained. "How can we do that? We're handcuffed to this stone."

Bronson reached into his pants pocket and drew out the laminated clipping. He stood tall and, as if he were a Catholic Bishop presiding at a Blessing of the Fleet ceremony, said, "Thank you for your sacrifice." Then he read aloud the edited version of the laminated card: *Sow innocence upstream that you may reap it downstream.*

"What's that supposed to mean?" Celine demanded.

Bronson pulled out the .45.

"Watch yourselves. Cover your ears. This'll be loud."

He fired a blast through the bottom of the boat right next to the granite monument. It left a hole the size of a fist. Water spurted in.

Over their cries and screams, Bronson in his tuxedo used his oar to push them away from the pier. The waters, normally ten feet deep, now swollen by the storm's runoff, might as well have been bottomless. A light breeze pushed them farther from the pier, and while they wailed and begged, he ran for his dirt bike.

He'd obeyed the voice emanating from the hot coal that was searing his brain—he had sown innocence upstream. Now it was time to reap downstream. He fired up the bike and roared up the hill, not wanting to be late for the wedding.

CHAPTER 60

THE RAIN STOPPED POUNDING on Bando's windshield as they reached the final rise, and the sky over the lake was brightening.

Suddenly a motorcycle flew by going in the opposite direction.

"Did you see that jerk?" Mo exclaimed. "He almost ran into us. He was using the middle of the road."

"He didn't expect anyone else to be out in a storm like this," Maggie said.

"He must be stupid," Juan said. "Who'd ride a motorcycle in a tuxedo without rain gear to cover it?"

"A crazy man," Bando said, accelerating downhill toward the lake. "I think that was our Mr. Bronson."

"Why aren't we turning around?" Mo asked. "Shouldn't we follow him?"

"He was alone—no kids. We have to get to the lake before it's too late."

Charlie pulled out the cell phone. "I'll call the police and tell them he left the lake on a motorcycle."

"In a tuxedo," Maggie added.

As they neared the old mill, they spotted a colorful orange swatch on the side of a box truck.

"The U-Haul," Mo said.

Juan pointed. "The door's open, and the ramp's pulled out."

"Maybe he left the door open so they could breathe," Mo said.

"I doubt they're in there," Maggie said. "They're probably tied up in one of those buildings."

"But why leave the truck?" Juan asked. "Why take off on the motor-cycle?"

Bando steered the car toward the U-Haul.

***

"Shut up!" Mouse yelled as the lake water inside the boat rose above everyone's ankles. "Stop screaming! It doesn't help."

They quieted down.

"He's gone," Mouse continued. "It's just us."

The water was spurting in like a fountain.

Mouse pulled off his running shoe and sock. He wadded up the sock and stuffed it into the bullet hole, then placed the shoe on top of it and held it there, as if he were applying a pressure bandage to a wound. It slowed the leak only slightly.

"Paddle for land," Celine ordered. "Back where we came from. Use your free hand."

But with each of them having a hand closely padlocked to the gran-ite block in the center of the boat, it was difficult to stretch over the side and paddle with the other. Their palms barely reached the water. The pier was fifty yards away, and they were fighting the breeze.

Tim cried out, "Put the block on the hole," and they substituted the block for the running shoe. The water stopped spurting, but it still bubbled in at a fast rate.

"When the boat goes under, that block is going to drag us all to the bottom!" BJ moaned. "We've got to get loose!"

"No, we don't!" Mouse said sharply. "We don't have to get free of the block. We've got to get back to shore—even if we're still chained to it. For now we've got to stay above water—until we can reach shore. The block's not a problem there. That's logic."

"Logic?" Celine hissed, her eyes narrowing. "Is this really the time, Mouse?"

"This is exactly the time. Everybody, slip over the side into the water."

"What? Are you crazy?" Tim whined.

"Out," Mouse said, and put a leg over the side himself. "Hurry. Just make sure we keep the block on the hole. That means keeping one arm in the boat."

"How will that help?" BJ asked.

"It's not the water that's sinking the boat," Mouse explained. "It's our weight. We've got to get our weight out of the boat so it can float. It'll sink slower without us in it, so we can kick our feet and maybe get to shore. Get out and kick."

The four of them slipped out of the boat, two to a side. Keeping an arm over the edge of the boat was awkward and painful. The skiff was half-full of water now, and although they tried to keep the block on the hole, their abandon-ship efforts and their kicking had pulled it off. The sock washed into the boat and water once more rushed in. Instead of being closer to shore, the breeze had pushed them farther away.

"We're still sinking," Celine said.

"But slower than if our weight was in there," Mouse pointed out.

"Maybe we should get the block out of the boat and try to swim for it," Tim said.

Mouse shook his head. "Way too heavy. And we can't swim with one hand each."

"Sidestroke?" Tim asked.

"Keep kicking," BJ said.

But they were losing ground and tiring fast. Pushing an empty boat would have been hard enough; pushing a swamped one was next to impossible. Meanwhile the inside water level rose. Another three inches and the boat would sink. The granite grave marker would drag them to the muddy bottom.

"We're not getting anywhere," Tim gasped.

"Have faith," Mouse declared. "We're buying time."

"Buying time for what?" Maggie asked. "This boat's about to go under and we're chained to a stone."

"We're buying time until help arrives."

"What help?" Tim asked.

"Whoever those headlights are, coming down the hill," Mouse said. "If they get close, we all yell."

***

Back at the dining hall, in front of the hearth, Juanita cocked her head and said, "Shh! I heard someone."

Rose, Caroline, and Twait sat up, pulling their feet back from the hearth.

"Where?" Twait asked. "Inside or outside?"

"No, in my head. It was a girl, the one who talked about the padlocks."

"What did she say?"

"She said this boat's about to go under and we're chained to a stone."

Twait leaped off the couch and ran for the office phone.

***

Bando and the kids got out next to the U-Haul. The cargo area was empty except for some discarded sandwich wrappings on the floor. A strap and a length of rope hung from the wall where the dirt bike had been tied.

Maggie climbed up the ramp. "What's that?" Something else hung from the wall.

"What is it?" Charlie asked.

Maggie touched the unused fifth shackle. "Something you'd find in a slave ship—like a manacle or a shackle, whatever you call them—irons, I guess—and a padlock. I think he had one of those kids in here."

"From the sandwich wrappers and soda cans," Bando said, "I'd say he had four of them in here. That last one was probably for Atlanta, but she got away. The other kids are still in their shackles."

"My sister overheard a girl talking about locks," Juan reminded them.

"Maggie, feel that padlock closely," Bando said. "Sense it. Imagine the inside of it. Then pass it around. You all need to touch it. It's got something to do with saving those kids."

The phone rang and Charlie answered it. "It's Twait. Juanita heard a girl's voice say this boat's about to go under, and we're chained to a stone."

That's when they heard the cries for help from far out on the lake—and Charlie recognized the start of another forgotten dream. Though he didn't see the outcome yet, he knew what he had to do now.

CHAPTER 61

BANDO RAN TOWARD THE SHOUTING with Maggie, Juan, and Mo close behind. They stopped at the end of the pier, trying to locate the source of the yelling. Then they saw it. Far offshore was a mostly submerged boat—barely a few inches of its aluminum side showing above water—with what might be two heads bobbing next to it.

"Hold on!" Mo yelled. "We're coming! We're coming!"

Juan said, "We need a boat or something that will float."

The five of them ran back along the pier toward the mill, searching. There were no boats, logs, or swimming floats to be found—nothing.

"In here," someone yelled. "Hurry."

They scanned the gray buildings for the source of the voice. Two arms waved by a pair of wide doors—Charlie. They ran toward him.

"I found two barrels in here. But they're wedged tight."

They all stepped into a large storage room with a honeycomb of floor-to-ceiling shelves covering one wall. Some of the shelves still held machine parts. Someone had jammed two metal barrels, one atop the other, under the corner of the shelving to take the place of a rotted support beam.

"Empty oil drums," Charlie said. "They'll float."

"Let's get them out," Mo said, and put a hand on one.

"Wait!" Juan grabbed Mo's arm. "Everything will come down on us."

Mo stepped back. "Then what do we do?"

"Everybody outside," Bando ordered. "Now." His voice was louder than they'd ever heard it.

"But the barrels," Mo protested. "We need—."

Bando froze Mo with a look. "Charlie, is this the way it happens?"

Charlie nodded.

"Then take them outside and tell them what they need to do. Hurry." The others stared open-mouthed at Bando. "Do whatever he tells you. Work together. Trust. But hurry!"

The four of them stepped out, leaving Bando behind.

Charlie gave orders.

"Juan, get that back seat out of the car. It'll lift right out. Lay it on the ground by the front bumper. Maggie, grab the rope and strap from the U-Haul."

"What about me?" Mo asked.

"You and I roll the barrels out and lash them to the ends of the back seat to make the raft. The barrels will float, and the seat cushion can hang down loose between them in the water."

They heard a horrendous crash in the mill building.

"Bando!" Maggie cried, and started for the double doors.

Charlie grabbed her. "Sorry. You heard Bando. Everybody has a job. Go get the strap and rope. Mo and I are the ones who have to go back in for the barrels. Everybody meet by the car. Go!"

Maggie tried to push past him, but Charlie repeated, "No! Go now! Those kids' lives depend on us."

Juan ran to the car, Maggie to the U-Haul. Mo was already at the double doors when Charlie caught up.

It had been difficult to see inside the storage room before, and now a fresh cloud of choking dust made it worse. It was impossible to make out anything clearly. But Charlie knew what the wrecked scene looked like.

"Over here."

Mo and Charlie followed the sound, feeling their way to where the two barrels had been holding up the shelves.

Bando lay pinned under a patchwork of wooden braces and wide-board shelves. The barrels had popped free.

Bando had a smear of blood on his forehead. "I'll be okay. We had to do it this way."

Mo pressed a shoulder under the timber that was pinning Bando's chest and began trying to heave it upward.

"No," Bando said sharply. "The barrels, take them. Don't waste time."

Charlie rolled a barrel toward the big door. "Mo," was all he said.

Mo turned sadly from Bando and began rolling the second one.

"Good luck," Bando called, just loud enough so the boys could hear.

Outside, the four of them lashed the back seat between the barrels, which flopped loosely on the ends. Then they hoisted the makeshift raft onto the car's hood so the barrels rested on the front fenders.

Charlie directed them. "Now it goes up another step, on top." With much effort, they got the contraption onto the roof. The barrels hung over the sides and clunked against the back windows, so Rose's car looked like it had on a weird set of headphones.

"Why didn't we just put it together by the water and drop it in?" Maggie asked.

Charlie ignored the question. "Get up onto the seat. Don't hold too tight. When the impact catapults you off, swim back to it."

Maggie's face screwed into a question mark. "Swim back to what?"

"The raft. I'll get you out there as far as I can."

"What are you saying?" she asked.

"Maggie, just climb on!" Juan ordered from the hood, reaching a hand down to her. "Charlie's driving."

From the lake the screaming started up again. "The water's coming over the sides!"

Mo and Maggie clambered up the bumper onto the hood, then mounted the seat cushion on the car's roof.

Charlie climbed in and started the car. His driving experience was limited to steering his grandmother's car up and down the driveway. Now, nervous and under pressure, he gripped the steering wheel with both hands and pressed his foot down on the gas pedal. The motor revved but the car didn't move.

"Put it in drive!" Maggie yelled from above.

He tried. The shift handle wouldn't budge.

"Foot on the brake while you shift into drive," she yelled.

This time it worked and they rolled ahead slowly. Charlie tapped the gas pedal and the car lurched, then smoothed out. He maneuvered past the U-Haul and away from the lake toward the farthest corner of the parking lot. He removed his wire-rims, folded them, and tucked them inside a button-down shirt pocket. Then, as best he could, he sighted in on the end of the pier, took a deep breath, and gunned it.

The four kids treading water by the boat stopped screaming, partly because the balancing act was over and the weighted skiff was about to go to the bottom, but also because the winding-up engine on shore caught their attention. Barely above the roar of the car they could make out voices—the screeching of other kids. The vehicle's lights were off, so they couldn't see it—but they could hear the car and the other screaming kids racing their way. They stared at the pier, hoping.

Suddenly, from the same spot where Bronson had stood when he shot the hole in the boat, came something huge—flying—a rocket car, and wearing a strange pair of giant earmuffs. It stayed airborne for several car lengths then skimmed the surface for a ways before the front bumper finally plowed the water, its sudden braking action standing the car on its nose, in the process sling-shooting the raft and its three daredevil riders even farther out on the lake. The car briefly balanced upright, then belly-flopped back on its undercarriage with a smack.

The raft riders disappeared beneath the murky waters, but a moment later came up sputtering and disoriented.

Charlie sat in the driver's seat, stunned, ribs bruised, a knot forming on his forehead where it had struck the steering wheel.

"Mo, Juan," Maggie called out. "You okay?"

Two heads bobbed near her.

"I'm okay."

"Me too."

"Charlie?" she called.

"I'll be okay," he yelled out the open window as water began to pour through it. "Juan and Mo, push the raft. Maggie, go to the boat." He tried to climb out, but the crush of water was too strong for him to battle. The car sank fast.

"Hold on! We're coming!" Maggie yelled to the boat. "We've got a raft." The boat was still thirty yards away.

An exhausted voice—Maggie couldn't tell if it was a boy's or a girl's— answered, "We're chained to a block. Boat's going under! Out of time."

Maggie watched the four heads disappear. "I'm going for them. Bring the raft."

Juan yelled, "The car sank. Charlie's still in it."

"Bring the raft," Maggie ordered, and started swimming hard.

Charlie held the steering wheel and tried to get to his knees in the seat. Everything was dark underwater. He had no idea if the car was sinking on its belly or its side. He didn't think it had turned yet, but he didn't know how deep the water was. It could still be a long way to the bottom. If not for his dream, he wouldn't have known enough to open the driver's window before racing down the pier.

He'd thought he could wait until the last second to catch a deep breath, but in the dark he couldn't tell where a final air pocket would be. When the water suddenly hit his chin, he wasn't prepared. He closed his mouth and held whatever shallow breath was already there. He knew he had to squeeze out the window soon, even if the car was still in freefall. Lungs close to bursting, he gripped the top of the doorframe and pulled himself out the window face-up. He planted his feet on the roof and pushed off in the blackness, hoping it was the right direction. With no air in his lungs to buoy him, he lacked flotation and had no sense of up or down. But he was committed now, and he had to trust he was rising. He kicked his feet and stroked with his flipper-like hands the way Twait had taught him. After what felt like an eternity, he burst free at the surface, gulping air and treading water. "Thank you, Twait," he gasped aloud. "Thank you, thank you, thank you, Twait."

Then it was back to the dream. He looked for the raft, spotted it moving away, and began dogpaddling toward it.

Maggie had reached the spot in time to catch a final silvery glimpse of the boat as it disappeared. She had no idea what she could do, but she knew this was her moment, her calling. It involved padlocks, and so it must somehow require her spoonbending skills. She zeroed in on the spot, gulped a deep breath, and went under.

The boat was already on the bottom in fifteen feet of water, five feet deeper than any swimming pool Maggie had ever been in. She opened her eyes, but the blackness was so complete that she shut them again and swam blindly downward, having no idea when she might reach bottom, or if she could locate the boat. If she didn't hit it on this dive, she wouldn't know which way to search. Her lungs ached as her arms fought to take her deeper. Every fiber of her body begged for her to surface for a fresh supply of air.

Her hand touched something, and she had to resist the urge to recoil. Was it the grass from the muddy bottom or something else? She forced herself to touch it and make sense of it. It was hair, long hair—a girl's.

A hand clamped onto Maggie's wrist, pulling her down deeper. Maggie's first impulse was to rip free of what felt like a death grip. But she let the hand draw her to the granite block, where Maggie felt the iron ring, the four sets of shackles—and a padlock. She recalled what Charlie had repeated when Twait called. The locks! But she wasn't a lock picker—she was a spoonbender.

And then the reality struck her—she could manipulate metal without touching it. This girl holding her wrist was the one Juanita had heard speaking about lock tumblers. Now she knew why Bando had made her hold and sense the lock in the U-Haul.

She focused, imagining the inside of the lock. The other girl's grip on her wrist began to loosen. With her lungs screaming and white spots flashing in her eyes, Maggie willed the lock's tumbler mechanism to move.

It did. The lock opened. She felt it and so did the other girl. The shackle dropped off. Before Maggie could let go, though, the girl placed Maggie's hand on a second lock. Maggie opened it, then a third and a fourth.

The five kids fought their way to the surface, bursting through into the late afternoon air, gasping and gulping down sweet oxygen, unable to make any other sounds.

Juan and Mo grabbed them and guided them to the seat cushion of the ragtag raft, where they held on for dear life.

A moment later Charlie dogpaddled up and clutched the cushion too.

A blue flashing light appeared by the U-Haul. A moment later a man's voice yelled, "Somebody out there?"

Mo, the only one with enough strength left to answer, hollered back, "Over here."

"Can you get back to shore?" the Trooper called.

"Yes. But Bando's hurt. He's in the building. Call an ambulance."

It took everything they had to kick for shore together. As they passed the spot where the car had gone down, Mo said, "I can't wait to see Rose's face when you tell her the only thing left of her car is the back seat—and even that is soaking wet."

A second police car, its blue lights flashing too, was coming down the hill. Neither cop had passed a motorcycle on the road.

CHAPTER 62

THE OFFICE PHONE RANG.

"Free Camp. This is Twait."

"This is Mo's mother. I said I'd be there early this afternoon to pick him up, but the storm delayed me. Well, now I'm here—sort of. My car is at the bottom of the camp driveway in the mud. I slid into a gully."

"So you're at the foot of the driveway?"

"Yes. Have you got a camp tractor that can pull me out, or should I phone a tow truck?"

"All I've got is the camp van. It's an old rear-wheel drive, which is useless. Are you real deep in the mud?"

"Pretty deep."

"Just stay put for a minute. I'll come down and walk you back up. We've got a fire going. My wife can call a wrecker."

"That'd be great."

"I'm surprised the cop down there didn't check on you to make sure you're okay. He's on the side of the road near the driveway."

"No cop here. At least, I don't see one. But my windows are fogging up, and I'm probably not looking in the right place."

Twait hung up a second too early to hear her say, "Is it a motorcycle cop?"

The man who knocked on her driver's window wasn't a cop. He was a soaking-wet, mud-covered groom in a tuxedo.

She pressed a button and the window slid down. "I have help on the way, thank you. But I appreciate your stopping."

The man removed his helmet. "Are you the justice of the peace or the photographer?"

"Ph-ph-photographer?" she stammered.

What she'd meant as a question, he took as an answer. "Let's hope the justice of the peace is already at the waterfall."

"Waterfall?"

"For the wedding. Come on. Leave the car there. It's an easy walk."

When she opened her mouth to protest, he wrenched open the door. "Time's a-wasting!" he said loudly, grabbing her arm. "Feet on the ground, ma'am. Out!"

"Leave her alone!" someone barked. A very small but muscular man walked toward them, a mop of red hair protruding from under his raincoat hood.

Bronson pulled the .45 from his waistband and pointed it at Twait. "You the justice of the peace?" he asked gruffly.

Twait stopped in his tracks, saw the woman nod her head ever so slightly.

"Yeah, I'm the JP."

Bronson eyed him suspiciously. "Bring your book with the vows?"

"Know it by heart," Twait said.

Bronson's eyes narrowed. He raised a hand to the back of his neck and massaged it.

"Headache?" Twait asked.

"Wedding day jitters," Bronson snapped. "Is that okay?"

"Happens to the best," Twait said.

"I'm fine. Just keep the chatter down." He pulled Mo's mother out of the car onto her feet. "Just a minute." He unstrapped a small suitcase from behind the motorcycle's seat. "The dresses and high heels, can't forget them." He motioned with the pistol. "Now let's get up to the waterfall. March!"

Rose was on the office phone talking to the tow-truck dispatcher when, out of the corner of her eye, she caught sight of people walking past the porch. Twait and two strangers trudged across the soupy ball field. She was sure the woman was Mo's mother, and the other, with suitcase in one hand and gun in the other, must be Donald Bronson. She hung up and dialed the police.

Neither the police nor Bando had phoned about the missing kids, but it was clear they were no longer with Bronson. She watched Bronson, Twait, and Mo's mother start up the muddy waterfall trail.

"Mom?" Caroline said from the kitchen door, "What's wrong?"

"He's here," Rose said, hanging up the phone. "Bronson. He's got your Dad and Mo's mother. He has a gun."

"Did you call the police?"

"Yes. They're on their way."

Juanita appeared in the doorway behind Caroline. "Where are the police?" she asked.

"The one by the road was sent somewhere else. Who knows how long it will take to get somebody here?"

"So what do we do?" Caroline asked.

"We follow them up the path. But we stay back a ways."

***

The path was a disaster area. The stream had overflowed and the ground was saturated. The hiking surface was gullied and slippery, and tree roots lay exposed in many places. Numerous small trees had fallen over or were left leaning.

The mud sucked at Twait's rubber boots and Mo's mother's shoes as if it wanted to hold them back. Bronson, in his tuxedo, still had his combat boots on.

"Wouldn't a church wedding in town make more sense, Mr. Bronson?" Twait said, trying to engage the man in any conversation that might turn them around. Nothing he'd said so far had worked.

"They'll be here. Don't worry. Just walk."

Fifty yards behind and keeping out of sight, the other threesome slogged uphill, unarmed and without a plan.

Bronson's group heard the waterfall long before they saw it. The little tree-trunk bridge was gone, washed out by the swollen, rushing stream. The pool at the foot of the waterfall had long ago overflowed its banks. The two granite benches so far back from the drowning pool were nearly submerged. Only the seat tops showed above the floodwaters. An incredible volume of water spilled over the cliff above and crashed into the frothing whirlpool.

Bronson waded over and set the suitcase on one of the granite benches. He stared into the roiling pool as if he expected to see something—or someone.

"You okay, Mr. Bronson?" Twait asked.

"You two sit there a minute." He pointed to the second granite bench.

They sat.

Bronson stood by the first bench and opened the suitcase. From it he withdrew two plastic-wrapped white dresses. Without pulling off the plastic, he laid them on the bench. Next he removed two pairs of white high-heeled shoes from the boxes and set them with the dresses. Finally he took out a pair of shiny black dress shoes. He unlaced his combat boots, pulled one off and slipped a dress shoe on that foot, then did the same with the other. His feet, shoes, and the bottoms of his tuxedo trousers were underwater, but he didn't seem to notice.

"I forgot the top hat. It's back at Uncle Dave's camp. We'll have to make do."

"Mr. Bronson?" Twait asked.

The man seemed oblivious to what was going on around him— except when Twait tried to move. Then Bronson waved the gun for him to stay put.

"I'm truly sorry those kids had to die. But it was the only way."

"What kids?" Twait asked, feeling his stomach turn over.

Mo's mother began to sob.

"It's the water from the upper lake." Bronson pointed to the top of the waterfall, then down to its base. "It runs into this godforsaken pool.

It took my Karen and my Addie. Only innocence can purify this water. It's the only way to get them back."

"Karen and Addie died. We can't bring them back."

Bronson waved the idea off with the .45. "No. They'll be here soon."

"Then maybe you should wait for them in private," Twait said. "Hurting this lady or me won't help."

Bronson didn't answer.

Twait pressed further. "If you give me the gun, I can get you some help. We've got a nice fire going back at the camp."

"No." Bronson was agitated now. "They should've come out of that pool by now. They must be stuck up there." He pointed at the top of the waterfall. "Let's go, both of you."

Twait got to his feet. "This poor lady can't climb those rocks. Why don't you and I go? She can stay here."

Bronson looked down on the woman. For a split-second his face softened. Then it hardened again just as quickly. "No. She goes. Move."

The three of them began climbing with Twait in the lead, so he could help Mo's mother. It was a steep, arduous climb. The handhold path alongside the waterfall had always been difficult even under the best conditions. They held onto roots, trees, rock outcroppings, anything they could find. Everything was wet and slippery, and several times Twait lost his grip. It took twenty minutes to reach the top.

Bronson gazed upstream. Although he couldn't see far, he knew the upper lake, the mill, the U-Haul, and his sunken skiff with its four bodies were fifteen miles north. The water should be pure, innocent, but something wasn't right. Karen and Addie hadn't appeared yet. He turned and faced the waterfall.

"See?" he said to Twait. "I knew it. It's blocked." He pointed to a tree trunk wedged in the rocks. It refused to pass over the falls.

"I wouldn't call that a dam," Twait said. "It hardly blocks the flow."

Bronson flashed the .45 again. "Shut up! You two, pick it up and move it." He kneaded the back of his neck with his free hand.

"We can't. She's a woman, and you can see how small I am."

"Move it, Shorty. If you don't, they can't come. Then I'll have to shoot this woman—and you too."

Twait and Mo's mother stepped into the fast-moving stream. Their ankles ached in the icy rainwater.

"Put your backs to it. Don't push it over the waterfall or it'll drop into the pool. Push it aside, over there."

The two of them got the trunk to rock, but they couldn't dislodge it. The running water held it in place.

"Donnie!" called a voice they could barely hear over the waterfall. It had come from below.

"Dad!" pleaded a second voice. "We're here! Let them go!"

Bronson shook his head to clear the confusion. Then he heard them again.

"Donnie! Come down!"

"Dad! We're here!"

He stepped to the edge and peered over. There, by the granite benches, stood Karen and Addie in their wedding dresses, arms upraised, beckoning him, inviting him to join them. Had the stream's blockage been cleared? Was it time to reap downstream?

Bronson's face was masked with confusion. He looked to Twait, whom he'd thought was the justice of the peace, and to Mo's mother, whom he'd mistaken for the photographer, then back to Karen and Addie far below.

The girl cupped her hands to her mouth. "Dad, forget them. Leave them. Come on."

Her mother yelled up at him, "Donnie, we've got a plane to catch."

The man in the tuxedo turned to Twait and Mo's mother. "Sorry I have to do this."

As he raised the .45, Twait pushed Mo's mother aside and sprang at Bronson. The gun went off wide of its mark, and suddenly Bronson and Twait were tumbling off the waterfall.

Those below heard the shot and looked up to see two men fly off the top—one a big man, the other very small. The plunge seemed to unfold in slow motion, and as they fell, the two separated themselves. The mother and daughter couldn't breathe as they watched their husband and father plummet downward toward the water and the rocks.

But halfway down, one of them appeared to regain his balance and almost flew like a swan coming in for a landing. His arms opened gracefully to the side and slightly behind him, and his chest swelled as he drew his chin down into the hollow of his collarbone. The men struck the water simultaneously with a single smack less than twenty feet from the women—one man square on his puffed-out chest, the other flat on his back. Both disappeared in the swollen whirlpool.

The two in wedding dresses ran to the edge of the pool. From the bushes, Juanita stepped out and joined them.

A head popped above the surface—Twait's. Rose, Caroline, and Juanita formed a chain. Rose grabbed him by his red hair and dragged him to shore.

Lying on his side, he tried to mouth, "I'm okay," but with the wind knocked out of him, he could only gasp for breath.

The other head bobbed to the surface. Donnie Bronson's eyes were half open. He had no fight left in him.

With a little breath in his lungs now, Twait cried, "Reach out your hand! We'll pull you out."

Bronson didn't reach out. He couldn't—or wouldn't—move. Instead, he used the last of his breath to say, "Karen, Addie, you look so beautiful," before the whirlpool sucked him down into its swirling waters.

Caroline, Rose, and Juanita pulled Twait farther up onto the bank. Exhausted themselves, they sat beside him, catching their breath.

A while later, three mud-soaked State Police officers emerged from the trail, guns drawn. But once Rose showed them where Donnie Bronson was, they holstered their weapons. The Troopers assured them all the other Free Camp kids were safe—and no, not a single one had drowned at the upper lake.

Caroline yelled the news up to Mo's mother, and two of the cops went up to bring her down.

"What about Bando?" Twait asked the cop who stayed behind.

"He's on the way to the hospital. They say scaffolding or shelving fell on him at the abandoned mill. Sounds like he's got a few broken ribs and a bump on the head, but should be okay. We'll keep you updated."

As had been the case with Karen and Addie Beals five years earlier, a dive team would be called in to retrieve the body of Donnie Bronson, who, oddly enough, had finally been reunited with his loved ones.

CHAPTER 63

THAT NIGHT EVERYONE ENDED UP at the Portland hospital to be checked over, treated, or admitted.

The four kids from the boat were reunited with their parents and received a night of observation. They reconnected briefly with Atlanta, who was already at the hospital.

Because Bronson was dead and the police were sure he had been the lone perpetrator, the five kidnapped kids were able to wait until the next day to make their statements. When they did, no one mentioned exactly how Atlanta got out of the blockhouse, or later out of the hole. They let the police assume she'd hidden behind the door in the blockhouse and had been at the top of the human ladder in the hole. There was no mention of levitation.

Everyone in Charlie's flying-daredevils crew was treated and released. Along with Rose and Caroline, they descended upon a nearby McDonald's before checking into a motel close to the hospital.

Mo's mother, who broke her ankle when Twait pushed her to safety, spent the night in a cast at the hospital.

Twait and Bando had to spend the night—Twait with a broken collarbone that came from the impact of his swan dive, Bando with broken ribs and a head wound that required stitches. They shared a room.

The next day the campers, staff, and families gathered together at a motel. The police took additional statements and shielded everyone from the media hounds.

Later that evening Bando, Twait's family, and the two groups of kids met in the motel's private dining room without their parents. There were plenty of questions and many blanks to be filled in—especially those they hadn't been able to share with the police.

"Donnie Bronson had a fast-growing brain tumor," Bando explained. "He never recovered from the drownings of his live-in girlfriend Karen and their daughter Addie, who drowned saving the former camp director's daughter after she fell into the whirlpool. Mr. and Mrs. Beals disapproved of Bronson, who fathered their granddaughter Addie, but never married their daughter Karen. As the tumor grew, Bronson probably believed he could gain the Beals's respect by marrying Karen and adopting Addie—except they'd already died. But the idea didn't die, and so, with the pressure of his tumor increasing, he developed an elaborate fantasy—imagining he could bring them back through some magical substitution or purification ceremony. He seems to have believed that if he sacrificed the innocent campers upstream, Karen and Addie would materialize downstream where they'd died—in the whirlpool. Once they appeared, he could legitimize the relationship by marrying Karen in a ceremony at the waterfall and adopting Addie. He planned everything with that in mind, including the honeymoon flight to Florida."

"To deal with his guilt feelings about killing the kids," Twait said, "he created a granite memorial that would sink to the bottom with them."

"And who knows?" Rose said. "Maybe there *was* a wedding at the waterfall. Consider his last words. Was he looking at Caroline and me in those dresses we put on to distract him? Or in the end was he actually seeing Karen and Addie in us—or in the whirlpool? If they could show themselves to Caroline and me, why not to him? Love is a powerful force."

Eight pizzas and several pitchers of cold drinks arrived, plus a cup of hot tea. While they ate, the two groups of kids got better acquainted and filled in the blanks around their trials and adventures in the past two and a half days. They were fascinated to learn about one another's gifts, but in the end, fearing others might want to take advantage of them, they swore themselves to secrecy.

The cousins, Mo and Atlanta, hadn't known about each other's abilities—hers to levitate herself, his to lift and move objects—and were thrilled to think it might be genetic. They'd each now carefully approach their parents and other relatives to see if any of them had had similar experiences.

Bando told them about the doodles he and Rose found on the paper tablecloths at the pizza palace. Rose explained that the drawings were a blend of two paranormal phenomena—intuition and automatic writing. Oddly, none of them remembered creating the artwork. Without conscious effort, they had subconsciously gathered impressions from the developing crisis around them—the yellow school bus, the orange horseshoe representing U-Haul, the motorcycle, the wedding dress—and translated them in visual form onto paper.

Juan learned that the "eyes" that had facilitated his remote viewing in Bronson's trailer—and later on the pickup's dashboard—belonged to Atlanta's plush stuffed puppy, the only item Bronson had taken from the van he sank in the quarry pool.

Mouse and Celine seemed to be the only two kids who didn't exhibit distinct paranormal gifts. That didn't mean they wouldn't at another time. But both had proven to be forceful leaders with much courage. And Mouse's logic—getting everyone to shift their weight outside the boat so it wouldn't sink so fast—had bought them the time they needed. Whether it was a paranormal gift or not, everyone agreed that logic was what the situation had called for.

It was BJ's hair that Maggie had felt when she located the sunken skiff at the bottom of the lake. She already knew she could manipulate metal, but she didn't know—until the situation required it—that she could line up the tiny key-pins inside the padlocks without seeing them. Had she "seen" the pins because she'd sensed the makeup from the fifth padlock when she held it in the U-Haul? Or did she "see" inside it by piggybacking on BJ's gift for knowing about the makeup of objects? Neither girl could explain it.

"After Bronson walked past the dining hall window with Dad and Mo's mother," Rose said, "we followed them up the trail. Then when they started to climb the waterfall, we knew it meant trouble."

"We couldn't see what was happening on top," Caroline added. "That's when Karen and Addie appeared in the mist under the falls and told us to put on their dresses."

"So they put them on," Juanita said. "I hid in the bushes so Bronson wouldn't see me."

"We could see him point the gun, but we couldn't see who he was pointing at," Rose continued. "Something made us call out to him. I felt like I was Karen—"

"—and I felt like I was Addie."

"I couldn't help myself," Rose said. "I said *Donnie*."

"And I just had to say *Dad*—but I don't know if I was calling to you or to Bronson. I wasn't fully myself at that moment. Then we heard the shot and the two of you went over the edge. I had heard about Dad's circus diving and saw the old footage, but I was too young to see him actually do it. Now I have. He's awesome!"

The kids were busy eating and talking about whether they might be able to come to Free Camp the following summer when someone knocked. It was Charlie's grandmother.

"Five minutes," she said. "The parents are getting antsy."

Bando nodded and she shut the door.

"Whether you return to Free Camp or not, and whether you continue to work together or not," Bando said, "you need to discover, develop, and use your gifts wisely. While these are *your* gifts, they are entrusted to you for the benefit of *others*. Be very careful. If you tell the world about them, someone—the government, the military, some private party—will undoubtedly try to exploit you for their own benefit."

A second knock at the door brought the Officer-in-Charge. "Those of you who agreed to interviews, it's time. The press is waiting."

"Be right out," Bando said, and the Officer-in-Charge disappeared.

"I propose a toast," Mo said. "To Bando, Twait, and Rose—and to all of us FreeKs."

Everyone stood and raised a water tumbler or soda glass—except Mo himself, who had proposed the toast. All eyes turned his way to see what was the matter. As they did, his glass rose from the table on its own. It floated toward the cluster of raised glasses above the table and clinked hands-free against them.

"To FreeK Camp!" Mo toasted.

They all grinned and clinked again, "To FreeK Camp!"

GLOSSARY OF THE PARANORMAL

Anomaly—an irregular or unusual event that does not fit a standard rule or law. An anomaly is something that cannot be explained by currently accepted scientific theories.

Automatic writing or automatic art—to freely channel your higher self or another soul's words, music, or art without the interruptive interference of the mind.

Clairaudience (from the Latin for clear hearing)—in the past the term referred to hearing voices. Remote hearing (RH) is a variation on this, meaning a person has the ability to overhear distant, this-worldly aural information.

Clairvoyance (from the Latin for clear seeing)—seeing or having mental insights about people and situations. Remote viewing (RV) is a variation on this, meaning a person has the ability to access distant, this-worldly visual information.

Crystalomancy—the art of gazing into a crystal globe, pool of water, mirror, or transparent object in order to discern information about some person or event.

Déjà vu—the sense you are re-experiencing certain events as if they happened at another time, but as familiar as they seem, you cannot recall nor figure out when or where they happened.

Dowsing—sometimes called water witching, generally associated with using the forked rod of a tree branch to locate water. In recent years the concept has been expanded to include several means of connecting with such things as lost pets, lost children, and even lost spirits.

Empathy (the possessor being an empath)—rarely used in modern parapsychology now, the popular usage of this term refers to a low-level form of telepathy wherein the empath appears to be aware of the emotional state of a distant person.

ESP (Extra-Sensory Perception)—knowledge of external objects or events without the aid of the usual five senses.

Inner voice—receiving guidance and assistance from inside oneself.

Intuition—knowing without the use of the usual rational processes. May mean knowing by observation of subconscious patterns or by impressions.

Levitation—lifting and moving of objects (and self-levitation, lifting of self). This is one manifestation of telekinesis/psychokinesis.

Paranormal—beyond or parallel to what is generally considered normal and understood.

Precognition—pre-knowing or acquiring information about an event before it happens.

Precognitive dreams—dreams of events before they happen.

Psychometry—the learning or knowing of information about an object by touching it.

Spoonbending is a slang or street term for a certain form of *telekinesis/psychokinesis*, and refers to the moving or manipulating (often bending) of metal objects. The term and practice came into fashion in the 1970s when Israeli mentalist Uri Geller demonstrated it on late-night TV talk shows.

Subliminal perception—sensory impressions below the threshold of conscious awareness. (Sometimes we know more than we think we know.)

Telekinesis and (newer, broader term) *psychokinesis*—the moving or manipulating of an object without physical means.

Telepathy—to know what others are thinking as if hearing thoughts in your head. Thought transference including the sending and receiving of thoughts.

An Interview with the Author

(Taped February 22, 2010 for the Kids Radio Network)

Q: You say you don't write fiction full-time. In fact, readers are quite surprised when they learn what your day job is.

A: It is kind of funny, I guess. I've been a minister for over 30 years. My church is very small and sits in Lyme, Connecticut. Other than the church, there's the town's original one-room general store and a Grange Hall. We're very rural—only a few hundred people in the middle of State Forest and conservation areas. Nobody around but us and the deer ticks that became famous for carrying Lyme Disease. (Yes, we're the town connected to the discovery and naming of the disease.) I'm the pastor at the Congregational Church, but I spend my spare time writing weird tales and thrillers like FreeK Camp.

Q: One would expect you'd write church books, not weird tales.

A: Yeah, I know. And I have written a handful of church-related books and a zillion articles. But as a writer of fiction I'm basically a young teenager at heart—probably because I grew up watching *The Twilight Zone* and reading comics like *Tales from the Crypt* and *Tales of the Unanticipated*, which I loved. I've always had a fascination with the psychic and the paranormal. So guess what? I write what I enjoy reading—not heavy horror, not blood and gore, but thrillers, adventure, and weird tales. I like making up stories with kids in the starring roles. My passion is literacy, and my goal is to get kids reading and writing for pleasure, to help stretch their minds and imaginations.

Q: Our radio audience is kids around the world, and no doubt some of them haven't heard of you. They may wonder if you're any good at this.

A: Well, I'll read aloud a sample chapter from *FreeK Camp* shortly, and they can make up their own minds.

Q: Hearing your work is one way to judge it, but there are other ways, too, such as critic's reviews and awards. For example, I learned that in 2003 your book, *Even Odder: More Stories to Chill the Heart*, was nominated for the Bram Stoker Award—named after the author Bram Stoker who wrote the original vampire novel *Dracula*. The Bram Stoker is awarded by the membership of the Horror Writers' Association, made up of professional horror writers worldwide. Many consider the Stoker to be the world's top writing prize for Dark Fiction.

A: That's true. But mine was just a little self-published collection of nine bizarre stories. It loosely fell into the Horror category, at least Dark Fiction, but it didn't have the blood, gore, and violence most readers associate with Horror. But kids loved it, and so did many adults, and that's what matters to me. To my surprise, the book became one of the five finalists before eventually losing to JK Rowling's *Harry Potter and the Order of the Phoenix* in the Young Readers category. (By the way, Harry Potter was—to my mind—the clear winner. I was thrilled to even be mentioned in the same breath as J.K. Rowling.)

Q: But then in 2004 the sequel, *Oddest Yet*, earned you another Stoker nomination. There was no Harry Potter that year, but the other three finalists included Dean Koontz and Clive Barker, who along with Stephen King make up the Horror world's Big Three. Yet your book won! It won the Bram Stoker!

A: Yep. Funny story here. I didn't figure a little book like mine had a chance against the big guys. Besides that, I really couldn't afford a plane ticket to the West Coast (the awards ceremony was in Burbank or Hollywood). Plus, it'd be on a Saturday night, so I figured I might as well stay here in Connecticut and preach in my church the next morning (rather than take a vacation Sunday off). Luckily, my agent lives in Hollywood, so she used my ticket to attend. At 11 pm California time—that's 2 a.m. in the middle of the night for me in the East—she called, waking me from a sound sleep. I picked up the phone, mumbled a drowsy and irritated Hello, and heard her say, "It's me, Ellen. Guess what?" Stupidly I said, "What?" And she whispered, "There was an unprecedented tie, first time ever in the Young Reader category. You and Clive Barker each get a Bram Stoker Award." When I announced it to my congregation at church the next morning, they didn't quite know how to respond (Minister wins world's top horror award?), but then they applauded. Later, *Connecticut Magazine* did a feature article on me, titling it "The Sinister Minister." Radio and TV followed. It's been kind of a fun ride.

Q: Someone suggested I ask about the décor of your house. I take it the paintings aren't religious?

A: My writing room is painted midnight blue—like Vincent Van Gogh's "Starry Night"—and has hundreds of stick-on fluorescent stars scattered across the dark blue night sky. When you turn off the light, the stars glow. I find it inspires me. My paintings and knickknacks have more of a Halloween theme, mixed with wizards, black cats, witches, and swashbuckling pirates. I've also got a manual typewriter and an electric typewriter on display (though I write on computer), and on my fireplace mantel (next to the Bram Stoker trophy, which is a haunted house) is a plaster statue of an elf lying down reading a book. My home's theme is reading, writing, creativity, and adventure.

Q: How about school visits? Do you have time, considering you also have a day job as a minister?

A: I do school visits mostly around the Northeast (New York and New England), but I've also done them in other parts of the country. For example, last year I was on vacation visiting my daughter and grandchildren in Colorado Springs, Colorado, I did a program for a middle school in Craig, up in the northwest. I'm planning to return there in May of this year after *FreeK Camp* comes out. I read my work aloud, answer questions, and then work with small groups, where I give them writing assignments that will stimulate their creativity.

Q: Back to the new novel, *FreeK Camp*. It's a paranormal thriller that pits a group of teenagers with psychic powers against a psychotic kidnapper. What can you tell us about the book?

A: Well, although the title is *FreeK Camp* the story is about an old summer camp in the backwoods of Maine called Free Camp. But someone has added a capital K to the camp's name, turning Free Camp into FreeK Camp. That's oddly appropriate, though, because Free Camp's mission is to help kids who are "different"—that is, they're different because they have psychic and paranormal gifts—to discover or refine their "gifts." The kids' mentors at FreeK Camp include an Asian-looking, tea-drinking, yoga-practicing guru named Bando, who has been in my other books. His sidekick is a "little person," a red-haired leprechaun-looking, former circus-performer named Twait, who must attach leg-extenders so he can drive the camp van. And there's Twait's wife Rose, who is the camp cook, but who also sees and hears ghosts on occasion. Twait and Rose's daughter Caroline also lives at Free Camp and will discover a gift of her own in the story.

Q: You said "paranormal powers." Do you mean "supernatural" powers?

A: No, not supernatural. Paranormal and psychic powers. Nobody's got flames shooting out of their fingers; nobody's shooting spider webs out of their wrists; and nobody's lifting a train engine with their bare hands. This story is set in a real world and has the kids employing gifts that we all imagine might be possible. One girl can bend spoons with her mind, the way the mentalist Uri Geller did. A boy whose hands are like lobster claws has the power of precognitive dreaming—he knows about some events before they happen, but only *just* before. A Hispanic brother and sister (twins) have gifts that are individual but also complementary—he has remote vision and she has remote hearing. There are other kids and other gifts, too.

Q: So it's just about kids at summer camp?

A: Not exactly. The first vanload of five kids is on its way to camp on Day One. But a crazy militiaman has in mind a recipe for deadly mischief—the missing ingredient being five campers—so he carjacks them. A second van is two hours behind them and arrives safely at camp. Now you have five kids in peril and five kids wanting to help. Don't forget, though—none of these kids know each other; it's Day One of camp. Some of them know they have unusual gifts, but not all of them have discovered their gifts yet. So both groups of kids must discover and/or develop and refine their powers. They have to quickly jell as teams. The task of Team One is to try and escape; the task of Team Two is to unravel the mystery (at the same time the cops and media are working on it) and to locate the imprisoned kids and free them—with the bad guy still on the loose and eluding everyone.

Q: Kids with their lives in jeopardy? And kids with weird powers trying to solve a mystery and save each others' lives? What more could we ask for?

A: Hopefully, you'll ask for another FreeKs thriller so it becomes a series.

About the Author

STEVE BURT is one of a kind—a Congregational minister by day and a popular author by night. He's been featured on many television and radio stations, and in 2009 *Connecticut Magazine* profiled him in an article titled "The Sinister Minister." He insists that his weird tales and paranormal mysteries are written for Middle and High School Readers—by far his biggest audience, for whom he offers numerous school-author visits—but his books have also garnered legions of adult fans.

Burt's rise started in 2001 when his modest collection of weird and ghostly tales, *Odd Lot: Stories to Chill the Heart,* won the silver **Benjamin Franklin Award for Best Mystery Suspense Book of the Year.** Teachers across the country were using the fun, scary stories for classroom read-aloud and demanded more. So in 2003 Rev. Dr. Burt penned a sequel, *Even Odder,* which was named a finalist for the **Bram Stoker Award for Young Readers,** arguably the world's top prize for writers of dark and weird fiction. (It eventually wound up runner-up to J.K. Rowling's blockbuster, *Harry Potter and the Order of the Phoenix.*) But the following year, his third book, *Oddest Yet,* not only made the Stoker finals—it topped Dean Koontz and tied Clive Barker to win the **Stoker for Young Readers**. A fourth book, *Wicked Odd,* rounded out the series, winning the Honorable Mention **Independent Publisher Award (Ippy)** in 2005 for Best Young Adult Collection in any genre.

FreeK Camp is the first book in Burt's new ***FreeKs*** series of novels about kids and adults with paranormal powers.